W9-CGK-019

DISCARDED
BY
ONEIDA LIBRARY

HAND-BARKER MEM. LIBR.
ONEIDA, N. Y.

THE PROSECUTOR

Also by James Mills

THE PANIC IN NEEDLE PARK
(1966)

the

Farrar, Straus and Giroux
NEW YORK

Prosecutor

James Mills

Copyright © 1968, 1969 by James Mills Inc.
Library of Congress catalog card number: 78–85236
All rights reserved
Printed in the United States of America
Published simultaneously in Canada by
Doubleday Canada Ltd., Toronto
First printing, 1969
Designed by Patricia de Groot

Author's Note

This book tries to show a little of what it is like to be a prosecutor of criminal law in the United States. It concentrates on one particular prosecutor: James C. Mosley, chief of the homicide bureau in New York City's Queens County District Attorney's Office. Mr. Mosley was involved in many cases during the seven months I was with him, and I have included in this book three which appear specially significant. The first two—one relating a confession, the other a denial—are offered as an introduction to Mosley as a prosecutor and to the type of problems he and every other big-city prosecutor may encounter. The main section of the book dissects a particularly involved and crucial case, the Mafia murder of one of its own professional killers. I should point out that all quotes in the book were either actually heard by me or taken from tape recordings or stenographic transcripts. The quotations in the main section from the autopsy report and from the trial testimony were used without indications of omissions.

For their various roles in assisting with this book, I would like to thank Thomas Mackell, Queens County District Attorney, and the members of his staff; the many New York City detectives who lent their cooperation; *Life* magazine, which sponsored the entire project and in whose pages much of this book originally appeared; and, most strongly of all, James Mosley himself, who for all those months and through many trying situations endured the author's constant presence.

J. M.

Contents

To Introduce:
A glance at two killings,
confession and denial

1

The History of an Assassination:
A long look,
the hit and the trial

51

To Introduce:
A glance at two killings,
confession and denial

confession

He speaks for murdered men, represents the dead against the living. He is The People, a mild man, quiet, honest, innocent as the law, and as brutal. "My name is James Mosley," he says to a killer. "I am an assistant district attorney. What is your name?" He has asked the question a hundred times before, and now, in the police chief's office of a small upstate New York town, it comes again—gentle, innocuous, invisibly burdened with the ancient battle between "Thou shalt not kill" and "No man shall be compelled to be a witness against himself." In the interrogation that begins with this question, the solemn weight of constitutional protection for the accused contends against the right of society to be sheltered from crime. All agree the contest is uneven, though with whom the advantage rests is everywhere in bitter, broad dispute.

And nowhere more bitter than in New York City, where crime outraces all efforts to control it, and homicide today has surpassed some major diseases as a leading cause of death.

Jim Mosley, at 39, is one of a score of assistant district attorneys who prosecute New York's killers. Born in the Bronx to a vaudeville booking agent, he was graduated from a high school so demanding that it only considers applicants who are in the top 10 percent of their class. In high school and college he concentrated on math and Latin, liked the logic of law and decided to study for the bar. He is married to a pretty redhead bright enough to belong to Mensa, the super-IQ club. He earns $16,000 a year and lives in a simple house in a less-than-elegant neighborhood.

His special preserve today is Queens County, a 119-square-mile tract of modest homes and businesses sandwiched between Brooklyn and Long Island. This year more than sixty of its residents will be disposed of by bullets, bombs, bludgeons, bare hands, knives, poison, and various other means of rapid dispatch. Mosley's job is to see to it that the killers are prosecuted, locked up, and left locked up.

Today one of those killers is in the little town of Fallsburg, and Mosley is there on the unlikely chance the man might want to confess.

You can make the drive to Fallsburg—a tiny resort town with only one hundred year-around residents—in two hours, but it has taken Mosley two and a half. He is a careful man, with a strong reserve some people could find dull or irritating. Physically he is unimposing—a little too much weight, not quite enough chin—and he lacks the brash, blustering force of his fictional counterparts in films and television. His most apparent characteristic—the one which most highly recommends him for his job—is integrity. His only loyalty is to the law, and he has an uncommon quantity of conscience.

Jim Mosley displays an automatic, involuntary respect for minor virtues that some more sophisticated people have long held obsolete. He smokes 8¢ cigars down to the last inch, and when that inch goes out, he relights it, not with a thought for thrift but simply because there is something wrong with waste. When he objects in court to some attempted violation of The People's rights, his normal reserve withdraws and he speaks with the how-dare-you indignation of a young girl who has just been touched some place she thinks she should not be touched. He is square, in precisely the serious, no-nonsense sort of way you would want your doctor to be square, or a teacher or a judge.

In his eleven years as a homicide specialist—first in Manhattan, then in Queens—Mosley has prosecuted some fifty killers, about thirty of whom saw the light along the way and took pleas to something less than the original charge. Of twenty who went the distance, fifteen were convicted. "I never prosecute someone until I'm convinced of his guilt," he says, "and then I go all the way. This 'innocent until proved guilty' business doesn't hold with a prosecutor. In court it's an adversary system—for me he's guilty and I'm out to make twelve other people agree with me."

The most effective way to make the twelve other people agree has traditionally been with a confession from the accused. But Supreme Court interpretations have made the whole affair of confessions so tricky and dangerous that when police have good physical evidence against the accused, they may prefer that he *not* confess. They thus avoid the risk that because some legal technicality was overlooked in the taking of the confession a murderer provably guilty goes free. And when a confession is thought necessary, they like to have an assistant DA in on the case early, to run the legal labyrinth and reduce the chance of error.

And so it was that when a 22-year-old named Barry Schwartz was arrested in Fallsburg for possession of a stolen car, detectives phoned for Mosley. The stolen car was the least of Schwartz's transgressions. He also had shot a number of people—including a young girl whose apartment he was looting and a detective who tried to arrest him—and had killed the superintendent of a Queens apartment house.

When the call came, Mosley was sitting in his office in the Queens County Criminal Court House, surrounded as always by detectives and thick clouds of cigar smoke (in that office, remarked one visitor, you don't even have to smoke a cigar to smoke a cigar). Four of the detectives filled the available chairs and others stood leaning on the walls and half sitting on a table opposite Mosley's desk. The talk in the office centered exclusively on the detectives' cases. They came regularly to Mosley for discussion, suggestions, information on legal points and, in their failures and frustrations, for commiseration. Six of them were on the same case, and had been for almost three years. Two summers earlier a young housewife named Alice Crimmins had reported her two small children missing. The bodies of the children, a boy and a girl, were found within days, tossed into different fields not far from her home. From the start, it was obvious that Alice Crimmins was lying about certain details of the disappearances. Some detectives thought she had killed the children, others that she merely knew who had done it. Most of the detectives had young children of their own and by now they were obsessed with the case, could think or talk of nothing but finding out what had happened to the Crimmins children.

Another detective sat silent and patient, waiting to get in a few words on his own case, totally different from the Crimmins investigation but no less haunting. For nearly three years Joe Price had been working full time on the case of a hoodlum named Ernie "The Hawk" Rupolo, who washed up like a dead fish onto a Queens beach, bringing with him six bullets in his head, twenty-five knife wounds on his body, and two cement blocks chained to his ankles. Five gangsters were now awaiting trial for the murder—the first time in twenty years that anyone had been brought to trial for a Mafia murder—and Price had some details he wanted to discuss with Mosley.

As Mosley and the detectives sat talking that afternoon, the most wanted criminal in New York was young Barry Schwartz, then only a few minutes away from arrest in a motel in Fallsburg. Early that morning a boy had telephoned Seymour Farber, the police chief of Fallsburg, and said someone was flashing a lot of $100 bills at the Hillside Motel. Farber and another man went over and checked the plate number of the big spender's car. The car was stolen. They peeked through his motel-room window and saw piles of clothes, radios, and other items that had the suspicious look of loot. They called for more men and firepower, and then Farber knocked on Schwartz's door.

Schwartz answered and surrendered quickly.

In the police station, Schwartz casually volunteered that he was wanted in New York. Farber called New York and discovered with some surprise exactly what it was that Schwartz was wanted for.

When Mosley pulled up at the Fallsburg police station it was already 6 P.M., and a sudden burst of rain was tamping down the heavy June heat. He and his secretary, who had come to take down in shorthand the hoped-for confession, rushed through the torrent into the station. As Mosley brushed the rain from his coat, two Queens detectives came out of the chief's office where Schwartz was being questioned and quickly filled him in.

"He's right on the edge, Jimmy. He goes for the burglaries and it's like he wants to go for the homicide but he just can't."

The detective is Charles Prestia, an intense, slender man with a reputation for steadiness and brains. He has white, scarlike patches of discolored skin on his face and wears dark glasses.

"A couple of other shootings we asked him about and he said flatly, 'No, I didn't do that,' so we didn't push it. But he doesn't say he didn't kill the guy, he just says he won't talk about it."

"What about the cop?" Mosley asks. The detective Schwartz shot had been staked out at a service station where Schwartz once bought gas.

"That he goes for. Shooting the detective. He admits that. Jimmy, I think he'll go for the homicide, too. It just takes some more time. He doesn't say he didn't do it, he just says he can't talk about it. You know, it's as if he really wants to, but he just can't get it out. I think it'll just take some more time."

"Take your time," Mosley says. "Take all the time you need. I'll be right here."

Prestia briefs him on the finer details of what Schwartz has told them and then goes back into the chief's office. Mosley takes off his coat and lays it over the back of a chair. He is in a large, simple classroom type of room with a conference table, folding metal chairs, and walls hung with architect's drawings of nearby golf courses. He sits down at the table with the secretary, a red-haired young woman named Audrey Mantay, and starts going through some 61s (reports of crimes, in this case Queens burglaries) that Prestia has brought with him.

In thirty minutes Prestia comes out again and shakes his head. The story is the same. Schwartz readily admits the burglaries and shooting the detective but shies away from discussing the murder of the superintendent. Prestia seems less optimistic but wants to keep trying.

Mosley finishes studying the 61s and walks slowly around the room, studying the drawings of the golf courses. Every few minutes a detective emerges from Farber's office to report no change in Schwartz's willingness to take the plunge.

The rain stops and Mosley puts on his coat and walks to a drugstore on the corner and buys cigars. He spots a bar across the muddy, puddled street from the police station, and after a few minutes back from the drugstore he tells a detective that if and when Schwartz gets talkative, he'll be waiting for the news over a beer.

Across the entrance of the bar sprawls an enormous, shaggy, muddy, red-eyed St. Bernard. Mosley steps over the dog and orders a beer. He says something to the barmaid about the size of a stuffed sailfish hanging on the wall. Another customer, an aging, beer-drinking man in a T-shirt, not totally sober, sizes Mosley up for a city slicker and remarks with a playful glance at the barmaid, "We caught it in the lake here."

Mosley smiles. "That's right," he says, "and after that you drained the lake."

The man laughs. "Something happening over there? They catch someone?"

Mosley shrugs, and another local customer offers the T-shirted man several theories, none correct, on what the commotion is about across the street.

In half an hour Prestia comes over. There has been no change. "He'll go for everything but the homicide. He practically tells us he did it. He doesn't deny it. He just won't take the leap."

"Well, then," Mosley says, "we'll have to bury him on the burglaries. Will he identify the property in the burglaries, the stuff in his motel room?"

Prestia says he will.

"Good. Then we'll get him on that. He says he shot at the cop when the cop was down, or running from him?"

"Yes."

"That's attempted murder, twelve and a half to twenty-five. With that and the burglaries we should have him."

They talk some more and Prestia goes back to ask Schwartz more questions about the burglaries.

"The ultimate objective," Mosley explained later, "is to keep the guy off the street so he can't kill anyone else. If you can't do it with a homicide, you do it with something else. If you can get him doing time for two burglaries consecutively, it could amount to fifteen to thirty years. He can't go to trial on the burglaries because he'd be convicted for sure. He'll have to plead. And if I can get him to tell me all about the burglaries and shooting the cop, then maybe after all that he'll figure what the hell and tell me about the homicide, too. Sometimes that happens. The crucial thing is just to make sure he stays off the street."

Mosley goes back to the police station and waits. A detective comes out. He looks tired, and in answer to the obvious unspoken question, he shakes his head. He sits down wearily next to Mosley. "You know," he says, "it's a funny thing. He says that he knows he's a dangerous guy because he doesn't look like he's vicious. He says people trust him and that makes him especially dangerous. He's a good-looking guy, clean-cut. If you found him standing on your fire escape you'd ask him in for a cup of coffee. He said if he'd had a minute's warning he'd of shot it out with the cops at the motel. He said he was thinking about writing a book. He said, 'Oh, if I told you everything I've done, the things I've done. . . .'"

It is ten o'clock now and cooler. Mosley steps outside and looks up at the sky, dark and overcast. A soft fuzzy slice of moon shines through the clouds. Prestia comes out and stands next to him. "We're at an impasse," he says. "He just won't budge. Do you want to go in and see what happens?"

"What do you think?"

"It's up to you," Prestia says.

"No. It's up to you. It's your investigation. Do you want to try some more? I'm happy to wait if you think you can do any more."

Prestia thinks and then says again that they are at an impasse. Mosley agrees to have a try.

Schwartz is indeed clean-cut. He is wearing a crisply pressed green sport shirt, dark, well-creased trousers, and new shoes. He looks like a college football star dressed for a date. He is handcuffed and his left ankle is manacled to a steampipe. He is biting his lip, looking very serious and respectful. A detective removes the leg iron and Schwartz sits in front of Farber's desk, leaning on it with his cuffed hands.

Mosley is introduced, and tells Schwartz that he is an assistant district attorney. He warns Schwartz that he does not have to talk, that anything he says can be used against him, that he may have a lawyer if he wants one, and that if he does not have money for a lawyer, a lawyer will be secured for him. Schwartz nods. He has heard it all before.

"Now," Mosley says in a quiet, getting-down-to-business tone, "I've seen a lot of guys go on trial in New York for felony murder and the verdict is usually murder one [first-degree murder] or not guilty. Murder one in New York is life, and that means twenty-seven and two-thirds years before you're even eligible for parole. So you have a decision to make now, and think about it carefully because you'll never get another chance. If you want to tell me about it, the homicide, I can tell you you'll get less than murder one. You'll get manslaughter. Or you can take your chances with the jury.

"We've got you in the place before the homicide, we've got you with the gun before the homicide, we've got you with the gun after the homicide. I can try you with that and maybe it'll be not guilty and maybe it'll be twenty-seven and two-thirds years. So think about it. I'll be outside."

Mosley goes back to the room with the table and the golf courses.

"I gave him the two-dollar speech," he says to Farber. "I said I'd let him plead to manslaughter. With his sheet, that's ten to forty."

Prestia opens the door and motions to Mosley to come back in. Audrey, the stenographer, walks in with him, sits down, and puts her notebook on the edge of Farber's desk. Prestia and the other detectives are standing up, taking their own notes.

Mosley again introduces himself, for the sake of Audrey's stenographic record.

"My name is James Mosley and I am an assistant district attorney. What is your name?"

"Barry J. Schwartz."

"And how old are you?"

"Twenty-two."

"Where do you live?"

"You mean right now?"

"What is your home?"

"Right now, I would call home the Hillside Motel."

Mosley's opening questions are innocuous, ordinary, designed as much to relax Schwartz as to establish his background. He asks about his school, his employment, his family. Then he gets to his whereabouts the past March 15, the day he stole the credit card used to buy gas at the station where he shot the detective. Schwartz replies that on that date he was living alone.

Finally Mosley puts the big question: "How were you supporting yourself?"

Schwartz balks. "This is it," he says.

"Well, look," Mosley says, "as you have already been told, you have the right to answer my questions or not. If you do answer them, what you say can be used against you. If you don't have money for a lawyer, we will get you a lawyer. Now, on March 15 of this year, specifically, did you burglarize an apartment at 147–25 Northern Boulevard, in Queens County, and take a credit card, Kessler's credit card?"

Schwartz looks at his feet. "I won't answer that."

The detectives, Farber, Mosley—all are silent. Then Mosley says, "You don't want to answer that for me?"

"No. Of course not."

"You have already told the police. I mean I would just like to get down in your words exactly just what you told the police before. I know and you know that you have used that credit card quite a few times, and I know that you left that credit card in the gas station in the Bronx where you had the shooting with the detective, isn't that right?"

"Sorry, I don't remember."

"I would rather you would say you don't want to answer this rather than to tell a lie that you don't remember," Mosley says. "If you don't want to answer, say so."

"I would rather say I don't remember."

"Well, that's not true."

"That's a matter of opinion. I'd rather say I don't remember."

"Do you remember having the shoot-out with the detective?"

"No, sir, I don't remember."

"The detective remembers. You know that?"

"Excuse me?"

"The detective remembers. You know that?"

"I'm sorry, sir, I don't remember."

Mosley hands him a many-paged, single-spaced list and asks if that is an inventory of the property found in his motel room. Again he adds, "You don't have to answer me if you don't want to."

"I have to say I just don't remember."

"You don't remember that either? There was also a .25-caliber pistol. You recall that?"

"No."

"You don't remember that?"

Mosley lifts from the desk a small, nickel-plated pistol. "I show you a Colt automatic, caliber .25 . . ." He turns it in his hand, looking for the serial number ". . . number 29274. Have you ever seen that pistol before?"

"I don't remember."

"You remember telling the detectives when you had gotten that pistol?"

"I don't remember."

"You remember telling them that it had been in your possession, and never left your possession, from the time you got it until the time they recovered it today?"

"I don't remember."

"Well, I have some other questions I wanted to ask you. Would your answers be the same?"

Schwartz indicates that they would. Mosley gets up and leaves the room.

Soon Prestia comes out and says Schwartz wants to see a lawyer. That puts the lid on it. Only one lawyer in a thousand would advise a client to do anything but keep his mouth shut.

Farber goes to the phone, and fifteen minutes later a local attorney arrives, a fiftyish man in a gray cardigan. He is willing to advise Schwartz, and Mosley explains the case to him.

"We've got him with the gun before the homicide," Mosley says. "He admitted to the detectives when he bought it and where, some place on the Lower East Side in Manhattan. We've got him with the gun after the homicide. He had it in the motel. We've got an admission from him that it was never out of his possession during that time, and the detectives have found one of his girl friends who says she saw him with a gun that matches the appearance of this one. We've got him at the premises before the homicide, committing another burglary. I can indict him with this. I've explained to him that if he wants to he can take his chances with a jury, or he can talk and I'll give him man one [first-degree manslaughter]."

The attorney listens closely. "But," he says, "these admissions to the police don't have any weight because. . . ."

"Oh, yes!" Mosley interrupts. "They do. He was warned of his rights as soon as they picked him up."

"That's right," Farber says. "He was warned right in the motel room. I told him even before we brought him in that he was under arrest for possession of a stolen motor vehicle, and then I informed him of his rights."

The attorney thinks for a moment. "I'll talk to him," he says. A detective shows him into the chief's office.

Mosley and the other detectives wait outside.

"This is a strikeout," Mosley says with disappointment. "We're going to strike out. We have a weak homicide. I can indict him, but it's weak. It's a weak homicide."

They wait.

After several minutes the lawyer comes out, nods, and says to Mosley, "He wants to talk to you."

All of them—the lawyer, Mosley, detectives, Farber—go back in. Schwartz is very nervous, biting his lip, rubbing his eyes.

Mosley moves behind Farber's desk and sits down.

"You've been in jail," he says to Schwartz. "And you've heard all the jailhouse lawyers talking. But for everyone who ever beat a case, there are ten doing more time than they might have, because they wanted to gamble. You know that's true?"

Schwartz nods, squirms, bites his lip. "Yes, sir, I do."

Mosley explains that a guilty plea to man one could, with Schwartz's record, mean ten to forty years. Then he mentions the burglaries. "I know how it is," he says. "You told the detectives what you knew they knew. But when we go back and start checking the property in your motel room against all the 61s, then we're going to get some more Queens burglaries on you, right?"

Schwartz nods. "Yes, sir."

Schwartz has been through this before and is far from stupid. He asks if sentences he might receive for non-Queens crimes, like burglaries in the Bronx and a shooting in the Bronx, can run concurrently with whatever sentence he gets for the homicide.

Mosley levels with him. "They can," he says, "but I can't promise that they will." He is an assistant DA for Queens and cannot speak for the Bronx authorities.

Schwartz looks at the attorney and rubs his face and tries to think.

"Ten to forty . . ." he says slowly, shaking his head, "ten to forty . . . ten to forty . . . ten to forty."

He looks again at the attorney. "Well," he says smiling, "I can always swallow some glass."

Mosley leaves and Schwartz is left alone again with the attorney.

In a few minutes the attorney beckons Mosley back into the room. Mosley takes the seat behind Farber's desk and Audrey again readies her notebook. Detectives stand silently around the edges of the small office.

"All right, now, Mr. Schwartz," Mosley says, "I started speaking with you a little earlier, with the stenographer here, and I told you that you don't have to talk unless you want to and that everything you say could be used against you later on in court, and that you have a right to an attorney, and if you don't have money for an attorney, an attorney will be provided for you. And I asked you questions about your age, where you had lived, who you were living with, and I reached the point where I asked about a specific date, March 15, and a specific burglary. And at that point you told me you didn't wish to answer my questions, and I asked you some more questions and you told me you didn't remember. Then you indicated that you wanted to see an attorney, is that right?"

Schwartz is leaning forward, listening intently. "Yes, sir."

"The chief of police here was good enough to get an attorney to come down to see you, and you and he conferred privately. Is that right?"

"Right."

Mosley continues, for the sake of the stenographic record, to run over the off-the-record conversations they have just completed. Then he asks, "Are you now prepared to tell me the truth, to answer my questions truthfully?"

Schwartz hesitates. Everyone is looking at him—crisp, clean, handcuffed in front of the desk.

"Yes, sir," he says.

"On March 15, 1967, did you burglarize the apartment at 147–25 Northern Boulevard in Queens County, where you got a Shell credit card in the name of Kessler?"

"Yes, sir."

"Tell me about that."

"Well, I burglarized his apartment on the ground floor."

"About what time?"

"Seven o'clock."

"This is in the evening?"

"Right."

"How did you get in?"

"Through a window."

"How? Did you open the window?"

"I had broken the glass with a screw driver, unlatched it, and gotten in."

"Where did you break the glass? Any specific spot?"

"Any place convenient to the latches, so that I could open more if there is more than one."

"You mean latches?"

"Yeah."

"I assume no one was home?"

"No."

"What did you take from there?"

"I took the credit card and $90 and possibly—did I take anything else? Well, I grabbed the whole pocketbook and there was $90 in there."

"Grabbed?"

"It's very hard to remember what else I took. That's what stands out."

"Did you use that credit card?"

"Yes."

"Where did you use it?"

"Any place in the city I needed gas."

"Did you use it in a gas station up in the Bronx?"

"Yes."

"On about how many occasions?"

"Ten, twelve."

"Did you use it at the gas station where you had that incident with the cop? With the detective in the Bronx?"

"Yes."

"Tell me what happened."

"I had driven into the gas station to get gas in the car, and a car pulled in front of mine and two men got out. One identified himself as a police officer, asked me for my license and registration. And I started to back off. I took out the gun. Both men jumped at me and we started to wrestle. I was on the seat of the car and the gun went off and I shot myself. Then they backed away and I fell down to the ground and I got up, and the policeman was running, sort of like crouched, trying to open his coat to get to his gun, trying to get behind one of these gas pumps. And while he was running, I was shooting at him, and I had shot about five times, not knowing—I didn't know if I hit him or not as I was shooting. He was running further away. I put the gun in my pocket and jumped in the car and I pulled out of the station and he continued to fire at me. I got away."

Schwartz is speaking fast now, and the detectives strain over their notes. Mosley moves into the critical questions.

"Did there come a time when you were burglarizing an apartment at 3324 Parsons Boulevard in Queens, around March 7, 1967, about ten o'clock at night?"

"Yes."

"Tell me about that. What happened?"

"I had entered an apartment on the ground floor and it was a vacant apartment. I pulled open a window. I think I jimmied it. I was walking around in the apartment for a few minutes. Then all of a sudden, you know, somebody came into the room, and I believe the man was taller than I was and a little stockier and he came up on me very suddenly, and my heart started to pound—the adrenalin in my system, when, you know, somebody says boo to you—and I jumped. I almost automatically, without any thought, I just grabbed the gun. I fired."

"What happened then?" Mosley asks.

"I dove out the window."

"Do you know how many times you fired?"

"I believe twice."

"Now, why did you go into the apartment?" The killing might not be considered first-degree murder unless Schwartz fired the shots during the commission of a burglary or other felony.

"To burglarize it."

"You dove out the window?"

"Yeah."

"What did you do then?"

"Well, I went back up to the Bronx. Just went home. And shook for a long time."

"You talk about a gun," Mosley says. "This gun that I have shown you, is this the gun that you shot that man with?"

"Yes."

"On the eighteenth of February of this year, somewhere around Thornton Place in Queens County, did you somehow have occasion to shoot a girl?"

"Yes."

"You want to tell me about that?"

"I had entered an apartment and I think the window was open and I thought it was uninhabited and I was going to commit a burglary, and the girl came in while I was in the closet and I grabbed her and was trying to point the gun at her to quiet her when she broke away, and as she was running I fired at her and then I ran out of the apartment."

"And you went to that apartment to do what?"

"Burglarize it."

"When you shot at her, was this the gun, the .25-caliber Colt?"

"Right."

"Now, you're making this statement voluntarily here of your own free will?"

"Yeah."

"And you have been advised by counsel?"

"Yeah."

That is it, except for one final detail. As Mosley is leaving Farber's office, a detective from the Bronx whispers to him, "Mr. Mosley, would you ask him about shooting that guy in the Bronx?" The shooting happened on the street, to a man evidently unknown to Schwartz. The case is out of Mosley's jurisdiction, but he puts the question anyway.

"Did you shoot a man in the Bronx on . . . ?" He gives the date and circumstances.

"Yes," Schwartz answers quickly.

"Why?" Mosley asks.

"I don't know," Schwartz says. "I just felt bad. I felt like hurting someone. So I shot him."

The detectives and Mosley shake hands with Farber and thank him for getting Schwartz and for helping with the questioning and finding a lawyer.

"This was one in a million," Mosley says. "Most lawyers just tell the guy what to do. 'Keep your mouth shut.' At least this one explained to the kid what the situation was and let him make up his own mind."

Prestia and another detective put Schwartz in their car for the ride back to Queens, and two other detectives prepare to drive back with the loot in the stolen car Schwartz had at the motel. It is past midnight.

"Take it easy," Farber says to the driver. "Some of the troopers may still have this as a stolen car. You don't want to get shot."

denial

Mosley's success in winning a confession from Schwartz did not reduce the weight or urgency of his other investigations. He feels a great, almost warlike hostility for criminals—a hatred that is an outgrowth of, and never overshadows, his love for the law. For the law, he has let murderers go free. On one occasion he was preparing a case against a confessed killer when a detective remarked that the confession came after a slap in the face. Only Mosley heard the remark, and he could easily have ignored it. But he went to his superior, repeated what the detective had said, pointed out that the confession was technically illegal, and announced that although he had no doubt of the man's guilt, he would not prosecute him. His boss agreed and the case was dismissed.

Mosley's reverence for the law is indeed fortunate, for the law lends him enormous power. Before a man is tried in the formal hoopla of open court, he has already been tested and convicted in at least three hidden trials, each with the full power to free him. When he is first picked up, the suspect is carefully scrutinized by detectives. They hold their own court, considering the facts of the case and the likelihood of his guilt. Found innocent by them, he is released. Found guilty, he proceeds to an assistant district attorney, who must then hold his court with the detectives, perhaps the suspect, perhaps the suspect's attorney, and with his own experience and knowledge of the law. If he finds the suspect guilty, the case proceeds to a grand jury where twenty-three lay citizens hear testimony, consider evidence, and themselves vote to indict or not to indict. If the accused is indicted and pleads not guilty, he then goes finally to the court we all know from movies, mystery stories, and television: the visible, judge-on-the-bench, jury-in-the-box court.

This filtering process has advantages. All suspects cascade into the large end of the judicial funnel and only those who appear to be most clearly guilty trickle from the spout to stand final trial. But the sheer luck involved distresses Mosley.

"I'm disturbed," he says, "by the haphazard nature of criminal justice. One guy sticks up a store, and the detective on the case is sharp and a good talker and he gets the complainant to go to court and tell the story convincingly, and it comes out fifteen to thirty years. Another detective happens to be a boob, and the complainant either says forget it, or he botches up his testimony, and the guy walks.

Or maybe one ADA is alert and cares about his job and pushes the case, and another one just lets it go down the drain. There ought to be a way where it always comes out the same. I guess that's not possible. Maybe there isn't any way. But when you think that fifteen to thirty years of a man's life depend on pure chance, on who catches the case, how it's handled. . . ."

A prosecutor's handling of a case can involve forbidding, godlike decisions that leave him tossing in his bed, questioning his beliefs, ferreting his brain for bias. In his head the hot facts of a man's misstep encounter the cold, indifferent realities of law. Dismiss the case—or put it to a grand jury? Ask for murder one—or manslaughter? Accept a guilty plea—or push for trial? At these times the prosecutor is alone with the law, and it is an awesome loneliness.

One lonely decision—whether or not to put a certain case before the grand jury—had been gradually descending on Mosley in the weeks since he came from Manhattan to Queens, lured by a chance to head the homicide bureau there. On July 14, 1965, two years before his arrival, a pretty 24-year-old mother, estranged from her husband, had called police to report the disappearance of her two young children. Her name was Alice Crimmins and her case was to become one of the most sensational in New York history. She told detectives she fed her 5-year-old boy Eddie and 4-year-old daughter Alice (everyone called her "Missy") at 7:30 P.M., took them with her to get gas in her car at about nine, then put them in their cribs, securing their bedroom door with a hook-and-eye latch. (She locked them in, she said, because the boy had a tendency to get out of bed and raid the icebox. Detectives later discovered a more likely reason for the lock: the boy on at least one occasion had discovered her with a boy friend.) She said she took her dog, a spitz named Brandy, for a walk, looked in on the children at midnight (she took the boy to the bathroom, the girl rolled over and went back to sleep), and went to bed. She was awakened at 3 A.M. by a phone call from her husband Eddie, who worked nights as an airline mechanic at Kennedy Airport. She said they discussed financial problems and a pending suit over custody of the children. At nine in the morning she unlatched the door of the children's bedroom, looked in, and found them missing. The right side of a casement window had been cranked open ten inches and the outside screen was on the ground three feet below. The children had climbed out the window before, she told police, and she immediately ran outside to look for them. They were not there. She called her husband and accused him of taking the children. He said he did not have them and made counteraccusations. Finally, he called police.

Later that day the little girl was found dead in a field less than half a mile from the apartment. Her pajama top was looped loosely around her neck. Five days later the boy's body, skeletonized from the waist up, was found covered with a white mound of maggots in thick, tangled weeds on a highway embankment.

While uniformed police and helicopters were searching for the children, detectives had been questioning the parents. And right off the mark, there was something wrong about Alice Crimmins. She said she bought gas with the children at nine, but the gas station attendant put the time at five-thirty. He remembered the time well, he said, because he had been annoyed at the lateness of his relief who was due at five. Alice said she locked the children in their bedroom and that they must have gone out the window. But the first detective who walked into the room found undisturbed dust on a table in front of the window. A lamp was on the table—blocking the window—and when he lifted it, it left a ring of dust, indicating it had not been moved for some time. Alice said she fed the children at seven-thirty and saw them alive at midnight. But the medical examiner said food in the girl's stomach indicated positively that she was dead two or three hours after feeding.

Despite these inconsistencies, Alice stuck to her story. As questioning continued, she grew hostile and unresponsive, claiming with stubborn anger that each detail was correct. She did not give the appearance of a woman anxious to discover who had murdered her children.

A week after the disappearance, the Queens medical examiner announced that in his opinion the girl was "strangled manually . . . while she was still in her bedroom." He said that "bruises [found] on either side of her windpipe are fingerprints, muffled by the pajama material." The body of the boy was so decomposed that the cause of death could not be determined.

The following December, Alice and Eddie Crimmins appeared before a grand jury investigating the case—and took the fifth amendment. The Queens DA commented at the time that he was astounded by their refusal to testify "inasmuch as the purpose of this investigation is to determine who is the killer of their children."

By the time Mosley inherited the Crimmins case from his predecessor, Mrs. Crimmins and her husband had become totally unapproachable. They refused to talk with detectives or an ADA, referring all inquiries to their attorney, a catch-as-catch-can negligence lawyer named Harold Harrison. Harrison, in addition to representing Mrs. Crimmins and her husband, also represented one of her many boy friends, a married man with seven children.

When Mosley arrived in Queens, the number of detectives on the case had dwindled to six, and some solid conclusions had been reached. Alice's husband, though not entirely free of suspicion, was not thought to be the crime's central figure. He was again living with his wife, despite her frequent dates with other men, and had become something of an enigma to detectives. "He is either a saint," said one, "or the dumbest man alive."

Every possible theory concerning the deaths had been discussed, dissected, and rediscussed a hundred times. No one, no matter how wildly the facts were stretched, could shape any theory that did not eventually point to Alice Crimmins. If she had not killed her children, then the nicest thing that could be said about her was that she knew who did and wasn't talking.

Because of the possibility—a very strong one—that another person was involved in the murders, the investigation had expanded to include Alice's almost numberless lovers. A large closet in the squad commander's office of the 107th precinct, where the children were first reported missing, was jammed with reports, photographs, charts, and tape recordings. After two years of probing, the detectives had learned enough about Alice and her friends to make Peyton Place look tamer than a nursery at nap time. But they had found no hard proof that she killed her children. She still refused to talk to detectives or to an ADA. Mosley had told her lawyer that if she would testify before a grand jury he would grant her immunity to prosecution for all crimes except the actual homicide. If she had committed any other crime—moved the bodies, for example—she would not be prosecuted. Mosley received no response to the offer, and uncertain if it had even been passed on to Mrs. Crimmins, he finally called her on the phone. She claimed never to have heard of it.

Now, virtually at an impasse, the detectives wanted Mosley to put the available evidence before a grand jury and seek an indictment. Mosley was against the idea.

"You've got to understand," he said, "that I don't want just an indictment. I want to be reasonably sure I've got a good case that I can get a conviction on. Look, there are six guys in this room as familiar with the case as a grand jury could ever be, and even we aren't in *complete* agreement. We're all agreed she's lying and we can prove she's lying, but we *can't* prove she killed her kids. Maybe she only knows who did it. I've got to be convinced beyond a reasonable doubt that she killed her kids, and I'm not. None of us is. So how could a jury be?"

The youngest detective is a small, lean, crew-cut man named Jerry Piering. He caught the case originally—was on duty when the first report came in—and technically it is his property. He will be on it until it's over, and if and when an arrest is made, he will make it. Piering has three young children himself, and the case has obsessed him. He collects tropical fish and remarks to Mosley that he has named each one after an individual in the investigation.

"Except one," he says. "I named one Herman. He's an angelfish."

"And he's probably the one who did it," Mosley says.

During the two-year investigation, detectives had put a tap on Alice's phone and had bugged her kitchen and bedroom. They spent hundreds of hours listening to her conversations, but she spoke with such caution that they rarely yielded more than a timetable of her trysts with lovers. One detective, however, did report having heard a conversation that sent him leaping for the phone. He had been listening for several minutes to the sounds of Alice moving around the apartment, and then suddenly he heard an outburst: "All right! You know I did it, so I'll tell you! I did do it! I did it! I did it!"

The words were followed by three fast pistol shots.

The detective was dialing the precinct when he heard a man's calm resonant voice say, "We will continue with our story after this commercial."

When the phone tap and bugs proved useless, the detectives followed her—or tried to. She quickly learned all the tail-discovery techniques normally employed by Mafia gangsters: she raced over the crest of a hill and stopped suddenly on the other side to see if any familiar faces drove by. Or she turned into a one-way street the wrong way and looked back to see if someone else made the same "mistake." Detectives were forced to resort to "sight tails," placing cars along routes to the two or three places they thought she might be going, or to tailing her loosely, far back in traffic, sometimes breaking off the tail when she appeared suspicious.

When questioning witnesses, as he must often do, a prosecutor frequently finds himself forced into the role of bad guy. A preceding police investigation may have uncovered extremely embarrassing facts known only to the suspect. If the witness is a friend or relative of the suspect, the prosecutor is then forced to ask questions that imply outrageous accusations. He may have to invade areas even the family doctor would think too delicate for approach. A homosexual is murdered by a male partner, and his wife, unable to accept the accusation implicit in the questions, reacts with rage against the prosecutor. A 16-year-old girl is murdered by a secret lover, and her mother leaves the DA's office vowing to destroy the prosecutor who could challenge her daughter's purity. Or a pretty young housewife murders her children, and friends and relatives aim wrath and vengeance at the investigator.

Alice Crimmins repeatedly displayed an extraordinary facility for winning over witnesses, for silencing them completely—and, when they wavered, for reinjecting them with an almost hypnotic allegiance. In almost every instance she managed to convince the people near her that the entire investigation into the death of her children was a vicious, senseless plot to harass her. One young man closely associated with her had been questioned several times by one of the detectives, a bright, spectacled man named Bill Corbett. (Corbett himself was particularly peeved by an inconsistent, inexplicable element in Alice's personality: she never swore. "Can you imagine a woman like that, the things she does, and she won't even say damn?") Corbett had told the man of Alice's involvement with boy friends, and of the probability of her involvement in the murders too, but the man had refused to accept this. Corbett knew the man was not actually involved in the crime himself, but he thought Alice might have told him something. He also thought it would be a good idea for the man to meet Mosley and hear from him the truths that he had been unwilling to believe.

"I am not convinced she killed the children," Mosley starts when the man is in his office. "But I am completely convinced she has the key. She knows things she hasn't told us. She's lied to us. Now, a lot of cops figure—and it's surprising how often they turn out to be right—that if someone's lying, they're either guilty or they know who is. And when they find Alice lying right from the beginning, they naturally want to know why. I don't have the answers. I don't say she did it. But I do say she's lying. Why?"

The young man is nervous. He sits forward in his chair with his hands in his lap and speaks quietly.

"Her lawyer says maybe you want to put her in front of a grand jury and make a fuss over it for the election." (Mosley's boss, Queens County DA Thomas Mackell, is running for reelection.)

Mosley reddens.

"That's ridiculous! I don't work that way and my boss doesn't work that way. I was an ADA in Manhattan for ten years before I came here, and if you want to check on me over there you can. I am frankly not concerned with grand juries. I'm concerned with finding out who killed the kids. And we're not going to stop. These people are going to be bothered and bothered and bothered, ad infinitum, until we find out who killed those kids. We don't want to bother people. Frankly, we're looking for help."

"But all it does is just hurt people." The man's voice is very low. "And it won't bring the children back."

"Well," Mosley says, "it's easy to say let everyone just go on their merry way. But that's not the way the ball game's played. Don't *you* want to know who killed her children? Doesn't she? Well, *we* do—and we're going to find out. And you should think of something else. If she didn't do it—and, as I say, I'm not sure she did—then there's someone walking around out there who could do it again."

The man nods weakly. "What do you suggest she do?"

"I *suggest* she tell us the truth."

"You keep saying she lied. Where did she lie?"

Mosley tells him one statement she had made and stubbornly stuck to that was demonstrably false.

"Well, what does that prove?"

"It proves she's lying."

"But why would she lie?"

"Exactly!"

The man thinks a moment. "But just because she lied doesn't mean she killed her children."

"That's true. But she has some reason for lying. Maybe fear. Maybe reluctance to admit she lied earlier. But when someone makes an honest mistake, you can sit down with them and point out where other facts indicate the error, and you can get to the bottom of it. She won't do that."

The man grows firm. "I know she didn't kill them, and I don't think she's lying."

"That's the ostrich approach," Mosley says. "I think maybe you know she's lying, but you're afraid of the truth. You want the answer, but you're afraid of it. I can understand that."

The man thinks a long time, moves nervously in his chair. Mosley and Corbett say nothing.

"I just . . ." he says slowly, ". . . I just don't like to think that she's shacking up with people."

"Why won't she come in?" Mosley asks. "Why won't she talk to me? I've offered her immunity to everything but the homicide. Moving bodies, disposing of bodies, failure to report a death—forget it. Just the homicide. If she didn't do it herself, she has nothing to worry about. I want to know who killed those kids."

"Well," the man says, "I wish she was here now."

"So do I," Mosley says.

"I'll talk to her and ask her if she'll come and talk to you."

"Do that."

She never came.

Mosley spoke, too, to Alice's mother, and again found himself having to convince someone that all he wanted was to find out who killed the children.

She was a slender, elderly person, and when she walked into his office, Mosley stood up, put out his hand, and smiled. "How do you do," he said. "I'm Mr. Mosley, the villain of the piece."

When she sat down, he explained about his offer of immunity to Alice and said, "All I'm interested in is who killed the children. If she's guilty of anything else, I don't care. Who killed the children. That's all."

She was unhelpful.

A girl who had known Alice for some time came in and refused to tell Mosley anything. After the interview Mosley said to a detective, "I don't like her at all. Do you know what she said? She said she doesn't want to get involved. We've got two dead kids, and she doesn't want to get involved. She said she had heard one of Alice's boy friends has underworld connections, and she's afraid about her own three-year-old."

One of Alice's boy friends, a dapper, well-dressed young salesman with a wife and children, sat down in Mosley's office and, though professing to know nothing about the murders, spoke readily of his adventures with Alice and her friends. Mosley listened silently. When the man was finished, Mosley thought the words over for a moment, and then suddenly, forgetting the case, asked a personal question for himself.

"Do you love your wife?"

"Yes."

Mosley looked bewildered and shook his head. "That's all," he said and and the man left.

Sometimes prosecutors and detectives can exert a little pressure on reluctant witnesses. One of Alice's lovers was scheduled to appear before the grand jury, and it was thought a way might be found to encourage candor. He was friendly with a number of underworld characters, particularly one connected with a rather lucrative bookmaking operation. Detectives began an unusually strict surveillance of the bookie, severely cutting down his activities. Word was dropped that if a certain person did not cooperate with the grand jury, the pressure might increase. The bookie put the screws to the witness to cooperate, and the witness grew more and more upset. But not upset enough. He appeared before the grand jury, and though he did answer questions, the answers provided no new information.

One witness in the Crimmins case, a boy friend strongly suspected of having more information than he was giving, had been under close scrutiny for many months. His wife had long suspected there were other women, but the witness, who boasted he was "the best con man in the world," had succeeded in convincing her of his faithfulness. His name was Joseph Rorech and he owned a home-improvement contracting business on Long Island. When his attention to other women cut into his finances, Rorech claimed bad business conditions, and his wife went to work selling encyclopedias door to door. To avoid unpleasantness to Rorech's wife and children, detectives had taken pains to conceal from them knowledge of his varied amorous adventures. But eventually they became so frustrated by his refusal to cooperate in uncovering the murderer that they considered threatening him with exposure. When Mosley decided to put Rorech before a grand jury for questioning under oath (with a promise of immunity from prosecution for any crime but homicide), the detectives vowed that if he took the fifth they would remove their kid gloves and call his wife.

Rorech appeared before the grand jury—and took the fifth. The detectives sat in Mosley's office, and one of them wrote Rorech's phone number on a piece of paper and tossed it on the desk. They all looked at it sitting there, but no one picked it up.

Mosley went to a judge and obtained an order requiring Rorech to show cause in court why he should not be held in $100,000 bail for contempt of the grand jury in refusing to answer its questions. Confronted with the order, Rorech showed up in Mosley's office and agreed to talk. For five hours he sat while Mosley and four detectives questioned him. He was nervous, but composed. His answers were evasive.

After almost five hours, Mosley said, "Well, you've got five people here who are all in agreement that you're lying. Frankly, I don't think you're going to do any better convincing those twenty-three people on the grand jury."

"But I told you everything," Rorech pleaded. "I told you everything I know."

"But that's what you say every time anyone talks to you," Mosley said. "And then you always end up giving us a little more, a little something you didn't come up with earlier. This sparring has got to stop. This is the end of the line."

"But I told you *everything*," he said. "I swear on my wife and children, that's all I know."

The next day Rorech went again before the grand jury. This time he did answer questions, but so evasively they added nothing to the investigation.

One thing had been gained. The grand jury appearances had put the main targets of the investigation—Alice and two of her lovers—under increasing pressure. Remarks overheard on tapped phones indicated considerable anxiety, particularly on the part of the boy friends. "But if we don't break it within the next two months," Mosley told the detectives, "we'll be shot down. After the grand jury ap-

pearances, the publicity, she'll figure she's invincible. She'll
be a rock."

A rock she was, impenetrable. Until another woman
found courage to tell a story she had been hiding in fear for
more than two years. Some months after the murders, the
Queens DA received an anonymous letter from someone
who claimed to have seen a man and woman put the children into a car near the Crimmins apartment. Laboratory
tests made on the letter and analysis of the handwriting
revealed only that the writer was probably a woman. Detectives questioned and requestioned every tenant in the build-
ings surrounding Alice's apartment house. None admitted
seeing anything. Then, a few weeks after Mosley's predic-
tion that the case would have to be broken soon or not at
all, detectives found a woman who admitted that she had
written the letter.

She was a heavy, blond, 43-year-old housewife and
mother named Sophie Earomirski, an unexceptional
woman, simple, honest, hardly different from the thousands
of others who live with their families in inexpensive apartment-house developments across Long Island. She had
been questioned before with Alice's other neighbors, but
said she had been too afraid then to admit what she had
seen. She told her story to Mosley and detectives, but not
until they pleaded with her and showed her pictures of the
murdered children would she agree to go before a grand
jury.

To avoid possible prejudice on the part of a grand jury
that already had heard testimony about Alice's free-for-all
sex life, Mosley convened a new panel ignorant of all facets
of the case. Sophie Earomirski went before the jurors and in
quiet but thoroughly determined tones told what she had
seen.

The night had been hot and muggy, she said, and she was having trouble getting to sleep. She got out of bed and sat by her curtained casement window looking down at the street. As she looked, she saw a man walking up the street from the direction of Alice's apartment house. Behind him came Alice, carrying a bundle. Alice was leading a young boy by the hand, and a small dog was following them. The man was talking to Alice, trying to hurry her. Alice, referring to the dog, said to him, "I can't go any faster, she's pregnant."

They arrived at a car parked under a street light just opposite Sophie's window, and the man, taller than Alice and good-looking, took the bundle from her arms and tossed it roughly into the back seat.

Alice said, "Don't treat her like that."

"What difference does it make now?" the man said. "Are you sorry now?"

Sophie Earomirski, watching from behind her curtains, became frightened and began to crank the window closed. As she did so, the window squeaked. Alice and the man looked up. One of them said, "Someone saw us."

Then they got into the car and drove off.

Sophie said she recognized Alice from having seen her several times in the neighborhood. She identified a picture of Alice. She said she did not recognize the man.

Detective Jerry Piering appeared before the grand jurors to fill them in on details of the investigation. Then Mosley spoke to them, explaining the law and pointing out their various alternatives. Because the strongest case against Alice involved the death of her daughter, she was charged with that murder only. Finally, the jurors were ready to vote—to indict or not to indict.

Jerry Piering, Bill Corbett, Jerry Byrnes, John Kelly—

detectives who had been on the case since the start—were understandably anxious for an indictment. Piering stood outside the grand-jury room, pacing like an expectant father and complaining of a headache. He had been awake most of the night.

The jury finished its vote, and Mosley walked out of the jury room. Piering looked at him.

"Well?" Piering said. "What do we have?"

Mosley put a legal-looking document on a table and pushed it toward Piering. Piering looked down at it.

"Grand Jury Findings," it said. And below that: "Murder, first degree, as charged."

Americans can display an almost vicious hatred for the criminal—as long as he is a fugitive and unknown. But once he is arrested, identified, acquires a name and face, the underdog syndrome takes effect and pity replaces hatred. Assistants of an elected district attorney may therefore find it prudent to avoid actions that cast their boss as a victorious giant straddle-legged above a vanquished prey. And their resulting kid-glove treatment of suspects may be encouraged by appeals courts' sympathy toward defendants thought to be unduly detained or inconvenienced during arrest.

And so even before Alice Crimmins's indictment, hours had been spent in planning her arrest. She would not be arrested at work (she was a secretary) lest her lawyer argue that she was unnecessarily humiliated in front of her fellow employees. She would not be arrested after work, lest the procedure—fingerprinting, photographing—extend beyond court hours and she be forced to spend a night in jail. She would not be arrested at her apartment in the morning, lest she slam the door and force detectives to break in after her. She would be arrested, it was finally decided, outside her apartment house as she entered her car to drive to work. The arrest would be made by Piering and Jerry Byrnes, accompanied by a policewoman. And it would have to be done neatly—Alice's lawyer reportedly had advised her that were she ever arrested she should lie down, in the street if necessary, and refuse to move.

After the arrest, all paperwork would be expedited and she would be arraigned as quickly as possible. Normally in murder cases the district attorney asks that no bail be granted. In this case Mosley's superiors decided to recommend an unprecedented low bail of $75,000.

At seven o'clock the morning after Alice's indictment, Byrnes parked his car in a driveway across the street from Alice's apartment house. By driving out of the driveway and across the street he could, in a very few seconds, enter Alice's driveway and draw abreast of her car, which was parked near the apartment-house entrance. Piering sat beside him and in the back seat was a mild-looking, thirtyish policewoman. At 8:05 Alice walked out of the apartment house and Byrnes stepped on the gas. His car shot across the street and stopped next to Alice's just as she slid behind the wheel. Piering got out and opened the door of her car and told her she was under arrest for murder in the first degree. He told her she had been indicted.

"I don't believe it," she said angrily, and clutched the steering wheel.

"Look," Piering said, "why don't you come with us? Your neighbors are watching. Don't make a scene." Her fingers gripped the steering wheel and she would not move.

The policewoman spoke to her, explaining that she had to come and that it would be better not to make a fuss. Alice then released the steering wheel and got into the back of Byrnes's car.

On the way to the station house Piering remarked, "You know, you could have done it easier. You could have told us from the start."

"Drop dead," she said.

"Well, I guess I will, sooner or later," Piering said.

"Better sooner," said Alice, and finished the drive in furious silence.

At the station house, she was led into the detectives' squad room and her lawyer and husband were called. She was fingerprinted, but refused to sign the fingerprint cards. She said nothing. Her lawyer arrived and told her to sign the print cards. They waited for her husband. Mobs of newsmen had arrived, and TV crews were setting up cameras on the station-house steps.

Her husband did not arrive. Alice and her lawyer decided not to wait, and she was led out of the squad room and up to the lieutenant's desk for booking. Cameras flashed. She covered her face with her hat.

She was led into a paddy wagon and driven the fifteen miles to Manhattan police headquarters for photographing. She refused to raise her head or open her eyes. The police photographer told her he could wait as long as she could. After a few minutes she relented, the pictures were made, and she was taken back to Queens for arraignment.

The courtroom was filled. Alice's mother, brother, and husband sat in a back row. Newsmen crowded into the seats in the jury box. Mosley stood, hands behind his back, while Alice's lawyer asked the judge for bail "between $5,000 and $7,500." The lawyer pointed out that Alice had a job, had never shown any indication to flee, had always been "available." He pleaded that she should be granted modest bail so that "she can continue to do the same things she's been doing." At this Mosley raised his eyebrows and pursed his lips into a silent whistle. He asked $75,000 bail, arguing that imprisonment was necessary "for her protection" since another person involved in the crime was being sought.

The judge set bail at $25,000, and it was posted immediately by Alice's family. At 1:05 P.M. Alice walked out of the court house with her husband. She had been arrested, fingerprinted, advised by her lawyer, booked, driven to Manhattan, photographed, returned to Queens, arraigned, and bailed in exactly five hours—less time than it can take to pay a parking fine.

The detectives were depressed. A few of them retired with Mosley to a local bar called the Happy Time and sat morosely drinking beer from pitchers and eating sausage-and-pepper sandwiches. The detectives thought that high bail might have kept Alice in jail a few days and that during that time she might have broken down and confessed.

Mosley shared their unhappiness. "She's out in time to go back to work this afternoon," he said to the detectives. "That's a hell of a thing, isn't it? You arraign someone for first-degree murder, and they miss half a day's work. In this day and age, you can't hold them at all. She'll probably go over to the Part I [a bar across from the court house] and have a couple of whiskey sours."

Someone asked Mosley if he did not at least feel good that finally, after more than two years, evidence had been uncovered sufficient to indict Alice.

"No," he said. "Because we're only on first base. A prosecutor never feels good until he sees the jury foreman stand up in the box and say, 'We find the defendant guilty of murder in the first degree.' *Then* he feels good."

"I'd like her behind bars a few days," a detective said, "just so she'd know what it's like. Then when it comes to trial, she'll know a little what it'll be like if she loses, and maybe she decides to cop out."

Mosley grinned. "And if you put her in the can," he added, half joking, "she'd have her natural hair by the time the trial came up." Then he added more seriously, "We'll never know. There's no way to get her back in, and we'll just never know if she would have broken. But sometimes you have to think about public opinion. Can you imagine the noise her lawyer would have made if we'd timed things so she'd spend a night in jail? Or if we'd succeeded in getting her held without bail? He'd be yelling to the papers about how this fine, upstanding, bereaved young mother was imprisoned without bail."

Mosley would like to be able to ignore public opinion and politics. His interest is the law, and he abhors the tendency of politics to tamper with it. His greatest ambition is to be a judge, but he despairs of his chances. "You know," he said at the end of one particularly wearisome day, "I rolled over in bed last night and I thought to myself, 'You'll never be a judge. You know more about a detective squad than a political club. So you're stuck with the cops and robbers.'"

Mosley prefers cops and robbers to the other alternative —becoming a defense lawyer. Many young attorneys take jobs as ADAs to gain experience and prestige, and after a few years go on to a lucrative private practice. Mosley says, "I could only be a prosecutor or a judge. I could never change sides. I couldn't defend a man I knew was guilty. And trying to discredit a witness you know is telling the truth—can you imagine going to work on a detective like John Kelly and trying to make him look like a liar, when you know he's telling the truth?"

A prosecutor is bound by law and professional ethics to

be reasonably certain of a defendant's guilt before bringing him to trial. If he has information even tending to cast doubt on the man's guilt, he must—by law—give it to the defense. His oath commands him, "not to prosecute, but to see that justice is done." His obligation is as much to the accused as to the state. Defense lawyers, on the other hand, are obligated only to their client. They are fully justified in defending guilty men. They are required to bring nothing to the attention of the prosecution. Even when a murderer confesses privately to his lawyer that he is guilty, the lawyer may still—without violating law or ethics—plead him not guilty and fight to have him freed.

With the indictment of Alice Crimmins, Mosley and the detectives set out to locate the man who had been seen with her, tossing the "bundle" into the car. Leads were numerous, but generally unproductive. Then a stool pigeon came forward with information that had the ring of truth. As the informant's story was checked and pursued by detectives, it began to sound better and better. One problem, however, was that part of the information had come from a hoodlum with a widespread reputation as a braggart and liar, a man sometimes inclined to make wild statements, even admissions, merely to impress hoods.

"Now," Mosley explained, "you see one of the problems with the Supreme Court ruling that detectives must make suspects aware of all their rights to silence and legal representation. We are now forced to rely too heavily on informants. An informant can say, 'So and so told me he killed this guy,' but he can't offer any corroborating details because at the time he understandably did not want to get nosy and start asking questions. Or maybe he just wasn't interested at the time, couldn't have cared less. Now even if you believe the informant completely, you still have no way of knowing if the suspect's admission to him was the truth or just a boast. It used to be that if a detective got an admission, he could go further with it, talk to the suspect, question him casually, probe a little, find out if he had really done what he said he had done. So what's happened now in effect is that we're forced to substitute the reliability of a stool for the reliability of a trained, professional detective. And this is what it leads to. Our informant on this case has an admission, but what can you do with it? Is it all on the level, or is it nonsense? All you can do is pursue the lead as far as possible and hope you get lucky and find evidence confirming the admission."

For the several months preceding the trial, the case would normally have dropped from the papers. But Mosley's remark in court that another person was involved in the crime provided Alice's lawyer with a chance to keep the publicity alive. He let it be known to the press that because of Mosley's statement he had demanded police protection for his client. The protection was immediately granted, but the next day detectives discovered that Alice herself wanted a police guard about as much as she wanted a chaperone, and it was withdrawn.

A criminal lawyer short on clients and forbidden from advertising may stay awake nights yearning for a sensational case to spread his name across the papers, and when he gets one he is likely to try to get as much mileage out of it as possible. After Alice's arraignment, Mosley talked to a defense lawyer who admitted that if he had the chance he would take the Crimmins case for nothing, just for the publicity.

Mosley asked him what he would do if she admitted to

him that she was guilty. "Would you tell her to settle for one to three years with a guilty plea to second-degree manslaughter?"

The lawyer thought a minute and said he wasn't sure, that he might like to plead her not guilty anyway. "I just might like to go to bat with it," he said. "Of course, I'd leave the decision up to her, but I wouldn't urge her too strongly to cop out."

"So you see," Mosley said, "how sensational ones go. There's no cop-out. You've got a trial."

When the trial started, the prosecution had three strong points on its side—Alice's lies to police, the medical examiner's report that the girl could not have been alive at midnight if she was fed at seven-thirty, as Alice claimed, and Sophie's testimony of what she saw from her window. But still the case was weak. A good defense lawyer could knock it around enough to give a jury doubt. Mosley needed something else, an extra bit of evidence that would lock it up. Two days after the trial started, he got what he was after.

For several days an assistant DA named Tony Lombardino had been trying his hand with the reluctant Joe Rorech. He saw him frequently, and each time he hounded him about the dead children, and about his responsibility now, for once, to do the right thing and tell what he knew. Rorech had heard the routine before, and he wasn't buying it. Then one night Rorech, Lombardino, some detectives, and a DA investigator named Walter Anderson were in a restaurant having dinner. Again Lombardino was bending Rorech's ear about his responsibilities. After a while Lombardino turned from Rorech to speak to a detective. Unaware that he had lost Lombardino's attention, Rorech said, "You know, Tony, you're a good salesman. I'm a salesman, too, and one thing I learned is that you can be too good a salesman. You had me sold but then you oversold yourself."

Lombardino didn't hear it. Anderson did. He raised his hand. "Everyone be quiet. Joe, say that again, what you just said now. Say it again."

Rorech repeated what he had said.

"I think we ought to leave and go some place else," Anderson said. He, Lombardino, Rorech, and a detective went to a private room, and into the small hours of the morning Rorech told them of a conversation he had had with Alice.

Two months after the children died, the two had been drinking at a Long Island motel. "Alice started crying," Rorech said, "and she just kept crying. I said to her, 'Missy and Eddie are dead. No one can speak for them, no one can help them. Only you and I can help them.' And she repeated over and over again, 'They will understand. They knew it was for the best.' She kept crying and she kept saying this over and over. And then she was still crying and she said to me, 'Joseph, please forgive me. I killed her.'"

Two days later Rorech told his story from the witness chair. Then he went to Mosley's office. He was in shock. Now the newspapers had the story—all of it—and his wife knew, and his children knew. He was destroyed. He sat down, surrounded by detectives, but did not seem to see them. Someone standing next to him asked him why he had finally decided to come across. "Missy," he said softly, almost in a trance, "little Missy. Everyone was always worried about Alice, but no one said anything about Missy.

Last Saturday my little girl made her first Holy Com-
munion. She's the same age as Missy would have been. I
looked at her and I thought, 'No one's been thinking of
Missy.' "

Mosley, Rorech, and the detectives went to dinner. There
was a lot of talk around the table, but Rorech was in
another world. He looked at the man across from him.

"I'll never be closer to anyone than I was to Alice," he
said. "If she hadn't been there in court, I couldn't have said
it. I had to be looking at her in the eye. It doesn't matter
who believes it. She knows and I know that it's true. It's
been eating my insides out and I had to tell it. No matter
what happens, if she's convicted or not, for better or worse,
I just had to get it out and over with and say it."

Rorech had finally found the courage to reveal Alice's
admission, but the detectives and Mosley were still not
convinced he had gone all the way. He had an annoying
habit of giving up information bit by bit, never really
coming across with everything he knew. It seemed very
likely that Alice had told him even more than he was letting
on, that perhaps she had told him everything, what exactly
had happened to the children, who the man had been who
was with her under Sophie's window. The detectives and
Mosley were hoping that after the smoke of the trial had
blown away, he would come through with all the answers.
Already he had hinted strongly that he had more to tell.
The day after his testimony, he was in a motel cocktail
lounge with detectives and excused himself to go to the
men's room. A detective went with him. While Rorech was
washing his hands, the detective took out a photograph.
Ever since Sophie's letter first arrived at the DA's office,

detectives had been working day and night to locate the man Sophie said she saw with Alice. Finally they had come up with a good suspect. Now the detective held a picture of the suspect in front of Rorech.

"Ever see him?" he asked.

"Yeah," Rorech answered readily, and mentioned the man's name. Then he smiled. "But Alice has a better picture of him than that."

The night before she was due to take the stand, Sophie stayed with a policewoman named Margie Powers. Ever since the night of the murders she had been living in great anxiety, and now she was terrified. Defense lawyers had finally discovered her identity and address, and their investigator—a beefy muscleman nicknamed Sam Spade—was banging on doors trying to get to her.

Sophie repeated her story from the stand. Her voice wavered, but she did not break. When it was over, she made it to the door leading out of the courtroom, and then collapsed. A detective at her side threw his arms around her, and he and Margie Powers got her into a nearby empty office. Sophie sat there in a wooden chair with her head back. There were tears in her eyes but she was too exhausted to sob. Margie clutched her hand. A detective tried to say something, but all he could think of was, "It will be all right, it will be all right." John Kelly came in and stooped down by the chair and took Sophie's hand and smiled and said, "It's all over now, Sophie. You were a winner. You were wonderful. You were a real winner, Sophie."

Sophie was helped back to Mosley's office. Rorech came in. His testimony was finished and he was leaving. He went around the room saying goodbye. He had never met Sophie. When he got to her, she said, "I want to shake your hand. I know how hard it was for you to do what you did." He looked embarrassed, and shook her hand and left.

"I read in one of the newspapers," she said, "that I was the one who could be responsible for sending her away to prison for life. . . ."

"No, Sophie," Margie said quickly. "Don't think like that. You just told what you saw. It isn't you who's responsible, it's the jury and the judge."

"No, it's not," someone else corrected. "It's Alice."

At 2 A.M. the verdict came in: guilty. Mosley sat in his office with some friends, trying to relax, trying to come down from the tension of the trial. People had been drinking beer in the office while they were waiting for the verdict, and now Mosley picked up a half-empty can. The DA's press relations man came in. He tried to get Mosley to go down and pose for the newspaper photographers. "They want you down there, Jimmy. You've got to go down."

Mosley leaned back wearily and smiled. "Tell them if they want my picture they'll have to come up here."

"Why, Jimmy? What's up here that's so important?"

Mosley looked at his friends. "A chair, a cigarette, and half a can of beer."

The History of an Assassination:
A long look,
the hit and the trial

Characters

the hit

Ernie (The Hawk) Rupolo
Willie Rupoli
Eleanor Cordero (Rupolo)
Detective Harold Fox

the trial

THE DEFENDANTS:	THEIR ATTORNEYS:
John "Sonny" Franzese	Maurice Edelbaum
Joseph "Whitey" Florio	Philip Vitello
William "Red" Crabbe	Herb Lyon, Philip Santoro
Thomas Matteo	William Kleinman,
	Mark Landsman
John Matera	Louis Vernell

THE PROSECUTION:	THEIR WITNESSES:
James Mosley	Charles Zaher, John Cordero
Detective Joseph Price	Richie Parks, Jimmy Smith
	John Rapacki

the hit

The body is that of a middle-aged white man, 5′ 9″ tall, scale weight not yet determined. There is a heavy rope ligature looped around the neck. The wrists are tied together with an intricate series of turns of a yellow woven plastic cord which also encircles the abdomen. [*In the New York City morgue, the medical examiner stands over the body of a man found floating in shallow water at a Queens County beach in August 1964. As he examines the body, he dictates his findings to a stenographer.*] There is also a rope around the abdomen tied with several knots, and this yellow cord passes through it. The rope projecting from the abdominal ligature is a heavy triple-stranded one, and to one end of this was tied two concrete blocks, which are also tied together with similar heavy rope and yellow cord and chain. . . .

I identified him in the morgue. Identified him! I couldn't *even* identify him. It was just—like a skeleton with some stuff on it. [*Willie Rupoli, a bookie, talks about his brother Ernie, who had been a Mafia gunman and professional killer before his body was found on the beach.*] I told them, "To tell you it's my brother, I can't. Not the way he looks. Not what you're showing me. When I saw him he had the cinder blocks on him. And the rope around. I can't understand it. That's an awful thing. That's what I can't see, why they had to do it like that. It's not even a clean knockoff. It's, I don't know, savages. Shot him, stabbed him, I can't understand it. To kill him, that's one thing. But not like that. Not only me, but even the others in the underworld, his own friends, they can't figure it. If you live by the gun, you die by the gun. But do it right. Wait outside his home or something and hit him when he comes out, but not like they did it. If you want to get rid of him, hit him clean. Like get him in a car, hit him, and throw him out of the car. What's all this here rigamajig? I don't know if they saw television, or what."

. . . The iron chain, fairly heavy, is at present rusted and covered with sand, as is the body. This chain is also attached to the ankles. There is a considerable amount of mud and sand, still moist, on the body and in the clothes, and also some broken mollusk shells. . . .

He was brought up by his mother to be another Al Capone. He'd come home and give his mother money, and she knew it had to be from something bad, and that pleased her. Because she was always after him to be another Al Capone. [*Harold Fox, a retired New York City detective, knew the dead man and calls him by his underworld nickname, The Hawk.*] I said to him, Hawk, you come from good people, how'd you ever get mixed up in this? And he said, his mother, she told him he could be another Al Capone. The Capones had lots of money. He'd come here from Chicago, and he had lots of money. The mother knew people he gave money to, and he'd say how he left Brooklyn and became a bigshot in Chicago. She figured if Al Capone could do it, why couldn't her son do it?

Ernie had dreams, you know, that someday he was gonna be the head of the Mafia. And I says, "You couldn't! You can't tell *me* what to do. How're you going to tell anyone else what to do?" That was my answer. [*Eleanor Cordero, the dead man's common-law wife for the six and a half years before his murder, talks to friends.*] And he'd say to me, "You don't know what you're talking about. If it wasn't for me, they'd kill you." Because like I hated his friends. They were ready to shoot me on sight any time they ever saw me because I couldn't stand any one of them. He'd bring them up to dinner, you know, parties and dinners and this and that. I didn't want them in my house.

I told Ernie, "The only reason they hang around is because you're a good-time Charlie, and if you weren't buying them drinks and dinner and everything else, you wouldn't even see them. They haven't got two dimes to rub together so they're kissing your ass. Roy Roy and Butch and all those other bastards."

Ernie used to tell me, "But they're my friends. They'd lay down their lives for me."

And I said, "The only thing they'd do for you is kill you."

. . . The yellow cord is tied around the right shoe and ankle. There are also several loops of heavy chain. . . .

So I couldn't even identify my brother. I explained to them that for me to make a positive identification would be hard, that there was a doubt, because what I really saw was—well, you couldn't tell if it was a human being or what. So I gave them information about a mesh in his stomach, that he had an operation for a hernia and there was a mesh screen in his stomach. And I told them, you'll find a bullet in him because he's been walking around with a bullet in him for years and years, and they could never take a chance of trying to take that bullet out.

And I identified the shoes he wore, and the pants. I can't miss them, those were my pants. That day he was wearing my clothes. The zipper was broken on his pants. He was in my store, a real hot muggy day. He went to the bathroom and he must have pulled the zipper and he came out and he says, "I broke the zipper, now how can I walk around?"

And I says, "Sit down, my wife'll be here in a minute. She'll fix it. Or take a pair of my pants, a pair of my slacks." And I says, "Don't worry about it." Because every time he had a fight with his wife Eleanor and he needed to sleep some place he used to ring my bell, three and four in the morning, and he'd say, "I want to sleep here."

And I'd say, "Go ahead, brother." Because he wouldn't go to no other brother, but he'd come to me. Then when he made up he'd go back. So a lot of times, he'd be wearing my socks or my shoes.

That day he's there in my store and he's got Roy Roy with him and he says to Roy Roy, "I gotta go to my brother's house and change my pants." And Roy Roy drove him to my house with me following in the Caddy. They come upstairs and I gave him a pair of my slacks and a sport shirt. He was broke so I gave him $20. I'll never forget it. I took $20 out of the register in the store. I says, "Here, put this in your pocket." And then when he got found in the river, he had $50 on him.

So when they were leaving, Roy Roy invited me to come with them for a drink at the Coco Poodle, and I says no I was too tired and that I'd have to make it some other night.

And that was the last I saw of him, when he left with Roy Roy. I never saw him again. That's the last I saw my brother. The next day I waited for my brother. I don't see him. I don't see the kid no more.

. . . There is evidence of an old hernia operation with the presence of a small fragment of recognizable tantalum mesh and some black sutures. There is a pair of trousers, extensively torn, with a leather belt now pulled down to the left knee and leg. The fabric is ripped. The zipper is partly open. On removing the shoes and socks, the epidermis of the feet, which is macerated, comes away with the socks. . . .

When I was about 10, in school in Brooklyn, I liked the teacher, I was her pet, and I schemed up something that I could annoy her, to make her pay attention more to me. [*Some years before his murder, The Hawk sat with Detective Fox and talked into a tape recorder about his past crimes.*] And what I did scheme was I looked up her name in the phone book and I started to call her up at night. I called her up night after night, and every time a different story about what had happened to a pupil in school, where he got run over or he's sick. And she would get grief over it and say, "Who is this calling?" Well, I never told her who was calling, but one day the call was traced and I was caught in the phone booth by two detectives, and they took me to the station house where they made me face the teacher. And she was shocked to know it was me. And I couldn't face her. I was ashamed. I was brought to court, she had signed a complaint, and I was given six weeks in the New York Catholic Protectory in the Bronx.

And then I went back to school, and the teacher told me that she was sorry she had to sign the complaint, that she didn't know then it was gonna be me. And I said I was sorry for what I did, I was punished for it, and that's all.

And I stood in school awhile and then when I was 12 I had in mind to get out of school. I schemed for my birth certificate to be forged. I erased my date of birth, I made myself 15 years old, and I brought it to the school, brought it to the board of health, and the school fell for it, and the board of health fell for it, and I got my working papers and got out of school. I got out of school and I started what I always wanted to do, a career of crime.

I started by burglarizing. We called it the bucket racket, myself and one other boy about 18. What we used to do is ring a bell, and if a woman came out we'd have a car outside and we'd say, "Can we have a bucket of water, the car's steaming." And if nobody answered the bell, we'd break in. We'd ransack the house, go for the bedrooms, jewelry, money. The jewelry, we'd get rid of it, take it to a pawnshop or sell it to people out on the street that we knew. I was 12. We did about seventy-five or a hundred burglaries. Then I was arrested, me and this other fella. Then I was 13, but I told them I was 16 and they believed me. I got a suspended sentence of three years.

So I kept on burglarizing. There were three of us now. I was arrested again, coming out of a house. We were all shot at by detectives, caught red-handed. I was sentenced to one day to three years in the New York City reformatory. I was still 13. I did ten months. Then I went out, and this time I went on with crime, but no burglaries. I did robberies with three other fellas, older than me. I bought a gun off another hoodlum. I was 14.

One day we were given chase by two cops in a radio car. While they were chasing us, we threw the guns out of the car. They got up to us, stopped us, searched us, and took us in. I was held for violation of parole and went back for another eight months.

Then I went back to the neighborhood. I was out a couple of weeks, and I got a letter from my brother, that he was in trouble, to go and see him at Raymond Street jail. He was in trouble for robbery. He asked me to help him out, to go to New York [*Manhattan*] and get in touch with these fellas that he associated with, to join them, to join their outfit, to help my brother, join them in what they were doing, committing robberies. I went to New York, I joined them, and any robbery we did I put my share on the side for my brother, to help him with his lawyer. So what happened was that my brother received five to ten years in state prison, and I was shot, which I almost died.

When I used to go out with these fellas, one of the fellas was taking a share out for a girl he was living with at this apartment. There were four of us. He wanted to put the girl in for a share. And he did put her in a few times. So I had an argument with him. I told him I wouldn't take it from him. I called him names. So I was going on and on and he told me to shut up, "Or I'll shoot you right in the head." And I told him, foolishly, that he hadn't got the guts enough to shoot me in the head.

Well, the first thing you knew, I was shot. As I'm falling down, the girl started screaming, the other two fellas scrambled out, and this fella told the girl, "Let's throw him out the window." So she hollered, "No," and that's all I could remember.

So I hated Ernie's friends, but he always said, "No, Eleanor, you're wrong, you're wrong." I told him all they'd do was hurt him. Like when his eye was shot out. His version to me about how he lost his eye, they were in a hotel, and he was with some people, and somebody was bothering somebody else's girl, and he told the guy not to bother her. And the guy says to him, "Shut up. Mind your own business or I'll let you have it." And Ernie says, "You punk, I wouldn't care what you did." And the guy turned around and he opened a drawer and he took a .45 out and shot him. And he falls over the table, and the last thing he remembered the radio was playing "My Blue Heaven" and they said, "Let's throw him out the window." Ernie told me,

"I wasn't even dead and I hear these guys saying, 'Let's throw him out the window.' They didn't kill me by shooting me so they're gonna throw me out the window."

After my brother lost his eye, and his face was disfigured, he didn't care for his life anymore. That's what really turned the kid. When he looked at himself in the mirror—and before he was a real good-looking kid—he just went berserk. He went berserk. And the smart guys who was coming up, they knew that this kid is going to be a good kid for us to use, in other words that's what I call it, to use him, so we'll put him on the payroll, and give him this, and make him stop this here stealing or anything like that, and he became under their wing. Because when he had both his eyes he was doing a lot of robberies, and that's how he got the name "The Hawk." He never missed anything. He had eyes like a hawk. So they made him stop the stealing and they gave him contracts. And that's all he did after that. He was just a hit man, since he was 16.

. . . Examination of the head discloses considerable maceration and separation and loss of the skin of the nose, with fracture of the nasal bones. The right eyeball is absent, and the socket is scarred. . . .

Ernie used to call me, "My Heaven." He'd call me on the phone, "What are you doing, My Heaven?"

"Nothing."

"All right," he'd say, and he'd call and call and call. He was always calling up. He'd leave to go to Brooklyn and he'd call up from the station, he'd call up when he got to Brooklyn, he'd call up when he reached the bar he was at, he'd call up at least ten times a day.

On Sundays he'd be home and he'd baby-sit and I'd go antique-hunting all day with my niece. You know, we'd go driving around. He would give me the world if he had it. If he went to the *moon*, he'd come back and say, "What are you doing?" I would throw him out and say, "This is it, this is the end!" I would move away from him, right? And two days later, there he'd be. I would move, I would disgrace him, embarrass him. He'd be having dinner with people and I'd walk in, "Give me money and get out of my life." You know—insult him, degrade him. And he would always be there.

. . . When the scalp is examined there are two entrance bullet wounds found on the right posterior parietal region. More posteriorly there is a third bullet perforation, an exit wound. The brain tissue, which is liquefied and pultaceous and green in color, oozes through this large exit wound, and during the manipulation of the head a tarnished, 380 metal-jacketed bullet emerged from this hole with liquefied brain. . . .

I was shot right in the eye. When I gain consciousness in the hospital I seen this fella that shot me and a girl brought in front of me with a squad of detectives, and they told me, 'Here's the fella that shot you. We know he did it, now tell us yourself."

I said, "I don't know him and I don't know the girl.

Leave me alone." I didn't want to get revenge on him that way. I figured if I recuperate, I'll take care of him myself.

So when I got out I looked for him, but I couldn't catch up with him, and later every time I was out of jail, he was in jail. Every time I was in jail, he was out.

Then after a while I had an opportunity to meet one of the two fellas that was in the room and ran out and left me when I was shot. And they was supposed to be friends of mine. I never forgot that. I met him in a hangout, playing dice. I got alongside of him, and I started gambling against him. He told me, he says, "Don't bet the way you're betting. It's foolish. I'm going to take your money."

I says, "There's no friendship in gambling. If you take my money, you take it." Which he did.

So when I lost my money, I went downstairs from the hangout and I went down in the cellar where I used to have guns hid down there. I took one gun, went back to the hangout where the dice game was, and I stuck up the game. I told the fellas in there that it's not meant for them, that it's meant for the fella in the corner. Well, they were satisfied to hear that. So I asked him, I said, "I want all your money and make sure you produce it." Well, at first he didn't give it to me, he says no. I says, "I'll count three. If you don't give it to me by three I'm going to shoot you in the leg, and the second shot, you ain't gonna feel it."

So I count three, and he didn't produce the money, so I shot him between the legs. But I didn't hit his legs, I grazed them. When I did that, he took his money out of his pockets, put it with the money he had in his hands, and he give it to me and he pleaded with me, "Don't shoot me, don't shoot me no more." And that was that. I went downstairs, put the gun away, and went across the street in the poolroom and stood around.

The Hawk was a fella you couldn't help like. He had a helluva personality. You'd never have known that he was the bastard he was. Even though I was a detective, he used to talk to me a lot, and he was very sincere. But he wanted to be a bigshot. When he did something he'd go to his mother to give her some of the money to show he amounted to something. And then he'd go to his wife—that was his first wife, not Eleanor—and she'd say, "What's wrong? What happened?" And he'd say, "I just put a slug in someone." And she'd put cold towels on his head and settle him down and put him to bed.

People used to tell me, "Eleanor, I don't know how you get away with it. I've seen that guy *kill* people for less than that, the way you talk to him."

And I'd say, why that son of a bitch couldn't fight his way out of a paper bag. Because this was the way he treated *me,* but he could *terrify* anyone else. And I could never believe that he could terrify anybody else, because I'd walk in and give him a smack and that would be the end of it.

Like I'm sitting in this bar once, and I'm sitting there, and I'm drinking. I'm drinking with one of *his* girl friends, I want you to know. But she's not supposed to be his girl friend. She's *my* friend now. I've got the money on the bar, so she's my friend now. And I say, "That son of a bitch, he'll never leave me alone. I can't stand it anymore." And now it's getting late—two, three in the morning.

And so all of a sudden she says to me, "He's here!"

And I says, "So what, he'll never kill me because when he

kills me then he hasn't got me anymore, right? Don't worry about it."

So that bar emptied out like in two seconds flat, and he comes in. And he puts a gun right in my back, and he says, "Are you coming home?"

And I says, "No," and I was drunk. "I'm not coming," I says. "And if you don't take that gun out of my back I'm gonna take this glass and I'm gonna smash your *other* eye out."

And he says, "You're very brave, aren't you?"

And I says, "You're damned right. A punk like you, I could wipe the floor up with you any time."

And he says, "Oh, please, baby, come home."

"Leave me alone!" I says. "Get out!"

And he says, "I'll get you when you come home."

I says, "And I'm coming home with a whole frigging army." I says, "I'm calling Mr. Nits."

Now at this time Mr. Nits, this cop, was out to get Ernie for bookmaking. So Ernie says, "Yeah. That's something you would do."

I says, "So you know I'm gonna do it, so shut up and get out of here."

And he left. And the whole bar left, and I was there alone. All these good people, these stand-up guys. Let there be a little trouble, they all disappear.

And now I go parading home, and I walk in the house and he's there. I says, "So? What do you want now?"

He says, "You think you can get away with all this?"

I says, "Look, kill me. After I'm dead go aggravate somebody else. Because my life isn't worth living anyway."

I mean these scenes were like commonplace. We'd fight, I'd kick him out, and then he'd call with stories, you know, and I used to feel sorry for him and I'd say, "All right, come on home," and I'd go and I'd get him wherever he was and bring him back home.

After I stuck up the guy in the dice game, I joined this outlaw outfit, fellas that were against the racketeers, that knew that the bigshots and racketeers had everything sewed up, that would take money off different people. So we figured we'd take it off them, off the racketeers. We'd stick them up.

And there was a funny thing happened one time. This one guy was known as a top hoodlum, a very tough guy, very respected and all that. I and another fella cornered him in a hallway one day. We got $800, $900 from him. It took us exactly two or three seconds at the most. And during that time we had a laugh because he lost control of himself. What I mean is self-control.

We got called on the carpet many a time. We were warned, by the top men. They'd tell us to lay off what we were doing. But we'd deny it, and we always told them, "You don't know what you're talking about." Because we all—five of us—used masks, and they weren't so sure it was us. We felt very bitter toward them, because anything you tried to do, they would come over and say, "That's *my* spot. This is *my* store. Don't touch *that* fella. Don't touch *this* bookmaker." You couldn't do nothin'.

My brother was a hit man for them. And they were afraid of him. They figured if they were gonna hit *him,* they'd better do a good job. You know, that's the reputation the kid had. That's why the kid kept walking around. And then the kid was good. I mean the only time he went bad was goin' to people he shouldn't of gone to, grabbin' people by the throat, takin' money off them.

Like he walked in behind a bar, Dino's Bar, and he asked for money and got refused. He went behind the bar, he took the money out of the register, gave everybody drinks. That's the type of guy he was. "If you don't wanna give me no money, I'll take it."

In the later years he was not a thief, he'd just grab you for your money. In other words, he didn't go out on stickups, he didn't go out on burglaries, he just, "I'll get my money, I'll walk into this guy and I'll get my money." He'd go to a bookmaker, put a pistol to his head, "I want a thousand." He'd go into a shy, he knew the guy was shying, that he had money, and "I want $5,000." That's the type of kid he was, "I want $5,000 or you don't operate." So he'd bring a couple of hoods with him, and he'd make sure he got the $5,000. So he always got the money.

But he knew it couldn't go on like that forever. He knew he was gonna get hit sooner or later. He used to tell me when he got drunk. He'd say, "You know, Willie, I'm living on borrowed time. How much more do you think I can go around takin' people, takin' people, takin' people?"

. . . The entrance of the bullet which popped out of the scalp is the mouth. The bullet, in penetrating the mouth, grazes the tongue and produces a rather deep furrow. The track then continues backward and upward through the base of the skull. . . .

It sounds ridiculous, but it really was like this, back and forth, six, seven times a year he'd move in and out. One time I put all his clothes down the incinerator. I said, "I quit, I don't care if you walk around with your ass hanging out. Don't come back."

And he would come back. His brother Willie said one time, "Eleanor, if he knew that you were going to hit him over the head with an ax when he walked through that door, he'd walk through the door anyway, as long as it was *you* hit him over the head with the ax."

One time he's not living with me again and he runs into some guy who says he had a couple of drinks with me. And now he comes home, he's going to *murder* me! This is it. He's killing me now. And a friend came home with him. So his friend told me later they had gone into the kitchen, he got a big kitchen knife, and he was gonna cut me up to ribbons.

So anyway I went to bed. You know, like he's telling me he's going to kill me, he's going to murder me, and I says, "Oh, yeah? Go frig you, too." And I'm getting undressed and I'm going to bed because he's telling me this all the time. So I'm lying in bed and I'm going to sleep. I'm *tired,* right?

I hear something going on outside, but I don't know what's going on out there. I don't even care. I'm just going to sleep. But he comes in and says he's gonna give me a beating. For some reason he forgot about the knife. He picks up the coffee table and he comes *charging* into the bedroom and—CRASH!

I says, "*Now* you've had it." I says, "I've been waiting five years for you to put a finger on me. That's *it.*"

I pick up the phone next to the bed, dial operator. "*I'm getting murdered!*" I scream at the operator. So I get connected with the police, the 66th precinct. I say, "*This son of a bitch is killing me!"* I says, *"Hurry up!"* I says, *"I'll be dead before you get here!"*

Now they come charging over, up the fire escape and everything else, and now they've got him, right?

And I says, "I don't care *what* you do." I says, *"Look* at this, look what he did to my leg, look at this." I says, "He's gonna *die* for this. That did it. Get him out. I don't care *where* he goes, just get him out of here."

They took him down in the elevator and off he went. They let him go. So Ernie took it on the lam for a couple of days. And now I have him. He hit me, right? And, oh, how the presents start coming, and, oh, I really had it made then. He came with hundred-dollar bills, "Honey, buy yourself something." *Nothing* was too good for me.

. . . There is also a bullet perforation with macerated edges on the anterior surface of the neck below the chin on the left side. This bullet also is a 380 deformed missile, and drops out of a segment of the spinal canal. . . .

So we were very bitter about the bigshots and we kept on taking money from them, and this went on several months. And then one day I'm in a poolroom and a squad of detectives come down and arrest me for a robbery. I didn't really know what they were talking about until I got in the station house. And the tipster of that robbery was there and he says, "That's the man."

So really the tipster didn't know that I really didn't take part in that robbery. I was supposed to go, and he always thought I went on the robbery, but I didn't go. But I was given a share of the loot, for friendship's sake. I wasn't worried about anything because I wasn't identified by the people who were stuck up, but I laid in Raymond Street jail almost nine months.

One of the fellas that had done a little talking himself but admitted that I was not on the stickup, but that I was supposed to go, that I was given an even share of the money, came down to me when we were in jail and told me that the tipster was the one that did all the talking, and that he'll take care of him.

I said, "I don't care what you do, you're just as bad as him." So they took care of the tipster. They cut him up in jail. He got twenty-seven stitches on his face. He's still disfigured to this day.

Then I got a contract by an organization to put two fellas on the spot, two hoodlums [*Willie Gallo and Ferdinand "The Shadow" Boccia*]. But I refused the job. I told them, I says, "I wouldn't put no one on the spot for you people. If there's any killing to do, I'll take the contract myself. I will kill them myself."

You see, puttin' a fella on the spot, a hoodlum, it isn't something that you'll be well-liked by the underworld. It's somethin' really low, when you put somebody on the spot. And any men that would put their own kind on the spot—I'm talking about hoodlums—not many of them are living today who put the finger on them, because they themselves are destroyed, because you did a thing like that.

So I got the contract to kill them. And there was another fella with me in on the contract. The contract went on for a few months. It was well planned. Nothing could go wrong. There was plenty of time and plenty of money involved. I had one of the fellas that was going to die most of the time, sometimes I had the two of them. And lots of times they were lucky, that they missed by inches. Something would go wrong. You know how that is.

Well, the time finally came that everything was clear. I had one of the fellas [*Willie Gallo*] that was gonna die with me, and the other fella that was gonna do the killing with me. We gave this fella a dinner, we drank, a woman— in other words we gave him a good time. When the party was all over we knew what we were gonna do. We walked out, we drove to a certain block, I took a gun out of my pocket, I put it to this fella's head, and I keep firing and it don't go off.

So the fella told me, "What are you doin'?"

I says, "Well, I'm only kidding you."

"Kidding!" he says.

"That's all I was doin'," I told him.

Well, he was a little drunk, he thought that probably I *was* kidding.

He says, "The way you're marked? You carrying a gun with you? Put it away."

Well, I was going to ask to go and put the gun away anyway, and I'd be right back, but not really to put it away, to put some oil on the gun. Which I did. And I tried out the gun, and it went off. And I went back to where my partner and him were waiting for me, and I says, "Okay, I put the gun away." I told him, "Let's go a few blocks. We're going to meet a certain party." He okayed it. He says all right. He was wobbling a little bit from the liquor.

So when we got to this certain spot, I let it go off. So between I and my partner, we gave him seven shots. We thought he was dead. The only thing he said was, "Oh, Mom," and that's all. We figured we left him for dead.

Well, we went to sleep for a couple of hours and the next day we went down to see this organization where they were at. Well, they didn't like the idea, that the fella had lived. They knew the other thing was taken care of, the other fella was killed, a few hours before this one was shot. Well, they did a little yelling because it was done wrong, but we just listened.

Then they sent us to some of their people in another state. We were there for a while, and my friend that was with me was afraid. He figured that we didn't do it right, that we were gonna get killed in that state. I told him, "No, they wouldn't kill us. What do you think that for?" Well, the next day I was taken to a doctor, to be operated on for my eye, to get a glass eye put in. And after the operation, which didn't work anyway, I went back to where we were hiding, and that night my friend told me, "I'm sorry, I have to leave you alone." He says, "I'm going home, back to the neighborhood." He says, "I don't trust these people."

I says, "Wait till I get better. I'll come with you. Don't leave me this way."

What really had got him scared is when we were alone in the hideout he happened to open up a closet and he seen machine guns, shotguns, and pistols layin' around there like nothin', and that made him scared.

So he really did what I didn't expect him to do. He really left me alone. So if there was anybody to be killed there, I would have been killed alone. So I was there after that two weeks. All I did was ate, drank, and had a good time up in the hideout.

And then I was sent back to New York. I was given information that the fella I shot talked on me and my partner, told everything he knew, that we shot him. And that he's living yet, that he's still in the Kings County Hospital, still in serious condition. They told me that they'll take care of it, to come back, that they'll take care of things.

But before I went to New York, I went to Brooklyn. And when I got there I met a fella, the same fella I caught in a dice game. The same fella that was in the room when I got shot. The same fella that I shot in the dice game.

He came over to me, he shook hands with me, and he says, "I'm sorry for what happened, let's be friends."

I said, "It's all right with me."

He says, "Where are you going now?"

I says, "I'm going to New York."

He was the only person that knew I was going to New York, beside the organization. Well, I took the train and I went to New York. I got off at Canal Street. When I got upstairs, it was no coincidence, there was a squad of detectives waiting for me, just turning the corner. And they grabbed me and threw me right in the car.

I was brought in front of the man I shot in Kings County Hospital. He identified me. The detectives told me he had made a death-bed statement, and "You're just lucky he's living yet. We don't know if he'll still live."

He wanted to talk to me.

He asked me, "Why did you shoot me?"

I told him, I said, "Why did you talk on me?"

He said, "But that ain't the question I'm asking."

I says, "What's the difference what I shot you for? You could of got revenge later on, instead of talking, saying that I shot you."

Now the reason for that was this, that he was no lily himself. He was a gunman himself. He held a gun in his hand many a time.

Ernie would get up in the morning—I never got up one day in six and a half years before twelve o'clock—Ernie would get up in the morning, shut the bedroom door, change the baby, wash the baby, get Ellen's lunch, then he'd get Ellen's breakfast ready, do everything, wash the floors, clean the house, make my coffee, and knock on the door.

"It' twelve o'clock, honey. Do you want to get up?" He'd come in, stroke my hair, and say, "Do you want to get up?"

And I'd get up and I'd drag myself to the kitchen table, and I'd say, "Ohhhh, I'm so tired." Because I would of been up all night waiting for him to come home. He never really told me too much about what he was doing. I mean he wouldn't tell me anything to make me nervous or worried or anything like that. He'd come home, he'd say, "There was trouble tonight," or this happened or that happened, and I'd listen with one ear. I knew he was bookmaking, and he shylocked for a while. And this son of a bitch ran off with the money. That was another episode. This Fat Nick. I used to tell Ernie, "This bastard's gonna run away with your money."

And he says, "Oh, he wouldn't dare do that. He's afraid of me."

And I said, "You wait and see. This is the man who's gonna run away with your money." And he did. He really did. He ran away with the money. He *loved* wine, women, and song. His nickname was King Farouk, because he liked to live like King Farouk. He was a big fat thing. And I didn't trust him as far as you could see. And I used to tell Ernie, "He's gonna run away with your money." And sure enough he did.

This guy that was a gunman himself, that was supposed to be a tough guy—well, he says that he's not going to identify me in court. But he lied. He did identify me in magistrate court, and I was held for the grand jury.

While I was waiting trial in Raymond Street jail, I had a lawyer hired by the organization. He came over to see me in jail, and he told me not to worry about nothin', that everything would be fixed up, just to take it easy. Well, I was there about two months. And then I was brought to trial, and before my trial started the judge talked to me in his chambers with my lawyer and with my partner, and he told me, "If I was you, I wouldn't gamble on this case. If you take a plea of assault in the second unarmed I will give you two and a half to five years."

Well, I just listened and then my lawyer grabbed me on the side, and he says, "Don't take no plea. Everything is fixed up. You're going out this afternoon."

So I told the judge, "No, your honor. I want to stand trial. I'm innocent."

"Well," he says to me, he says, "once that trial starts there's nobody gonna stop it. Remember that."

Well, he kept his word. The trial started, the man I shot got on the stand, and he *buried* me. He told the truth, how I shot him, and everything. So I was found guilty of assault in the first degree. I was found guilty in five minutes by the jury. The judge gave me and my partner ten to twenty years in state prison.

So we went back to Raymond Street jail, waiting to get transferred to state prison. While we were waiting, we were called again to go back to court for resentencing. Well, during that time we were told that they're gonna try and fix up that we get a light sentence. So we believed it. And when they took us back to court, the judge told us, "The reason I got you back for resentencing was that your counsel was not present when I sentenced you the other day, and that's illegal according to law, so for that I'm gonna take one year off. I'm giving you nine to twenty years."

So I was sent to state prison, and the same baloney used to go on. We used to get word not to worry, that when a different governor comes in we'll be out. All that, you know. Years go by and by and you still live on hope. And live on their baloney stories that they give you.

And many a night I would stay up, and think what really went on, and how foolish I was. Sometimes I would look in the mirror and look at myself, and that was part of my crime career, by looking in the mirror and seeing the way I was. I seen that I was a different person. And plenty of times I used to spit at the mirror. I used to hate myself.

My brother was arrested when he shot that there Gallo, Willie Gallo, and he did nine to twenty he did on that. He did twelve years on that. That's the job he muffed. Him and that there, what's his name. They got the contract to kill Willie Gallo, and they muffed it, the guy lived. He was in most of them contracts at his young age. On the Gallo one I don't think he was 17. The guy lived and put the finger on him and he went away for nine to twenty. They shot him. They used about twelve bullets. They put gasoline on him and his clothes caught on fire and then a milkman went by, and it was in the snow, and turned him around in the snow and saved him. [*Willie's version of this murder differs slightly from The Hawk's account.*] And then he went to the hospital and while he's laying in the hospital they got told to lam and they went to Baltimore, and when he comes back three or four weeks later the detectives are waiting for him at the station.

Ernie knew, he knew. I'd say he knew it for about six months, that he was gonna get killed. I didn't believe him. Would you believe it if somebody just came out and told you, "Honey, they're gonna kill me"?

He wouldn't get in the car with me for six months before he got killed. He was always with these bums, Jerry and Roy Roy, and he'd always get some jerk to drive him around. And I'd say, "Hey, what's the matter with this guy? I've been driving him around for years and now all of a sudden he'll never get in the car with me anymore."

And Willie, my brother-in-law, said to me, "He never gets in the car with you because he's afraid they're going to kill him and they're going to kill you, too, if you're with him. So he won't drive with you."

And here's another funny thing. Ernie had a lot of papers that this woman was holding, and he always told me about these papers. He says, "They'll never do anything because I've got these papers that this woman is holding in her safe." He goes there about, I'd say, two weeks before he gets killed to get this stuff from her.

Now all these years this woman is holding this stuff for him, these papers and whatever the hell it was, that Ernie always felt secure that he had all this stuff. He used to tell me, "She's holding this in the safe." He used to tell me, "Don't worry."

Now, he goes there that day—I'll never forget it—he calls her up, he calls her daughter up, and he makes the appointment to go there.

And there was nothing there.

So she says to him, maybe they're in the safe, in the place like, you know, where all the records are and stuff. They go over there, but they're not there, and now all of a sudden all this stuff she's holding for Ernie like for about seven or eight years is gone. And two weeks later, so was Ernie.

. . . An old bullet is found just to the left of the midline, encapsulated in fibrous tissues. There are six bullet tracks in all. . . .

I did eight years and six months of the sentence, and I went home. Everything was strange. I hung around a while, felt around a while. They contacted me and they told me things had been tough, that they had been double-crossed. Well, I couldn't get so fresh with them. I was alone, and just out. A lot of things happen while you're away so long. I just yessed them, and they told me things are tough, and I've got to be careful now that I'm on parole.

Well, one day I got myself into another swindle. This fella here, he was double-crossing everybody, double-crossing his own organization. He would give tips to certain card games and dice games, and get in with these people, and then would turn on them, and rob them.

And he was trying to set me up, and a couple of other fellas, and I turned around and I went to certain people and I told them about it, and they said the next time he comes in just hit him right in the head. If he comes in with another proposition.

Well, it just happens that one night he pulls his brand-new car in front of my place, gets out of the car, comes in my store, sits me down, and tells me he's got a good thing. Well, I was waiting for him to come. I says, "All right, what's the good thing?"

And he explained it to me. He says, "We'll make a good buck on it."

Well, I turned around, I says excuse me a minute. And I went in back of my store, put a gun in my pocket, and came out and just kept talking to him. And I says, "Well, okay. We do it."

And in the meantime there was a fella come in I knew, drunk like a pig. Well, I had an idea to get in the guy's car with the drunken fella. I told the guy, I says, "Look, let's get this drunken fella out of here. We'll take him home. We'll talk in the car." He says, all right.

Well, when we get inside the car, the drunken fella gets in the center. And I get by the door. So I'm directing him where to go. "Go up this block, turn right, turn left." Well, when we get to a certain spot, the car is going slow, and I says, "Take it easy here."

So I take out the gun, and I told him in Italian, I says, "I'm sorry this is gonna happen. It was gonna be either you or me."

Well, he started hollerin', and sayin', "Please, what are you doin' to me?"

I says, "Well, I'm gonna shoot you right in the head."

So the car was going slow. He couldn't even step on the motor, his legs were shakin'. Instead he turns the wheel on the sidewalk a little. And I shot him twice, right in the face.

And the drunken fella is what saved the guy's life. When I fired the two shots, this drunken fella opened the door and run like a rabbit. He's hollerin', "Don't shoot at me! Don't shoot at me!" So that threw me off. And I had to go back and shoot the guy two more times.

And then I took a handkerchief out of my pocket, took all the fingerprints I could off, closed the door, and went back to my business.

Well, it wasn't long. The next day I was arrested. The man was dying. He identified me in the hospital, told them everything what I did. And here's another fella that's supposed to be a tough guy, a big racketeer, a man that was known as a killer in the mob. He couldn't meet his maker either.

So I did seven years more. It was another one of them cases where everything is "fixed up." And it was all a lot of hooey.

You know how other people, they lie in bed and tell each other how much they love each other? Well, Ernie used to lie there and tell me all these murder stories. This guy he shot. And it was his *friend*, he told me. And he said the guy was *good*-looking. He said, "Honey," he said, "he was the best-looking guy. He was *really* a good-looking guy." And he says, "He was my best friend."

So they call Ernie down—Vito, I guess—and they say he's gotta hit this guy.

"But he's my best friend."

"Hey, it's you or him. Get rid of him."

So now they're out, and they're wining. And he tells me, "We're out having a good time, big dinner, drinking and everything else, and who comes along but this guy Kip."

He couldn't get rid of this fellow Kip. And Kip is drunk out of his mind. So Ernie tells me, "I can't get rid of Kip. I gotta get rid of this guy. I gotta get rid of him, and I don't know what I'm gonna do." He says, "I can't go home. I gotta kill this guy."

I said, "How could you *do* such a thing?"

So he said, well, what happened, they're in a car, they're all drunk out of their minds, right? Kip is in the front seat, but he had passed out, he was so drunk. And Ernie tells me, he says, "We drive up this block, and I take out the piece, and I empty the gun at the guy."

He says Kip wakes up—he sobered up in a minute—and says to Ernie, "Ernie, what did you do?"

"Shut up!" Ernie says. "Don't say a word."

And they take the guy and they threw the guy out of the car. And Kip is petrified, so Ernie drove him home, and he went in, and Ernie went home.

He tells me the guy didn't die. I say, "Didn't die! With all those bullets in him?"

"Yeah," he says. "He crawled all the way to 60th Street, to the bar," he says. "And he *lasted* till seven in the morning. And I don't know if it was the milkman, or the guy came to open the bar, but he sees him laying right in the door. The guy *crawled* all the way there."

Now they pick up Ernie, and the guy says Ernie did it. They take Ernie to the hospital. Ernie tells me, "I run to the bed, I get down on my knees," and he tells the guy, "Who did this to you? I'll get him if it's the last thing I do."

And the guy says, "*You* did it!"

Ernie told me, "I almost came down with a heart attack." Ernie says to the guy, "What's the matter with you? I'm your *friend*. I wouldn't do such a thing."

And Ernie's telling me the whole scene, how he raced into the hospital room, he's kneeling next to the bed, and he's telling the guy, "Who *did* this to you?" And he's the one who did it, right?

And then there was the other one my brother muffed. Where he shot the guy, that there bigshot, what's-his-name. That's when my brother blew his top against the organization, because the bigshot's brother opened up on him after he had promised him no murder rap. My brother muffed it and then he went home, and this guy went to the hospital and he opened up right away. So they picked my brother up at home and went to the hospital and the bigshot fingered him from his bed, his death bed, and the kid says to him, "I'm your friend. I didn't hurt you." And they locked the kid up.

So then what happened, the bigshot's brother went to see him, and he says, "Look, what are you going to do? You gonna rat?" And the bigshot says, "What, are you crazy? No, I'm gonna change my story."

So all the bigshots sit down. They went to my mother's house, and they told my mother, "Look, don't worry. He will be saved. He'll walk out of the courtroom. The guy's taking the stand and just gonna say he had it in for the kid, that's why he said he did it."

So now my brother's wife, my mother, my father, they went up to the court. So this guy takes the stand. Now, the night before they had all met at my mother's house, all the bigshots, Genovese's men, and all of them says, "Don't worry about it. The kid'll walk out."

So now this is a big boss, and he takes the stand, and the first thing he says, "That's the hired killer."

So that's why my brother blew his top on the organization.

THE HAWK POINTS
CLAW AT GENOVESE

The Hawk, a one-eyed per-
petually sneering trigger man,
leaned from the witness box
in Kings County Court today,
pointed his finger at Vito
Genovese, Manhattan racketeer, and identified him as one
of the men who hired him to
help murder (The Shadow)
Boccia in September, 1934.

Genovese shifted slightly in
his chair and stared at The
Hawk. Perspiration glistened
on the face of both men and
The Hawk, who wears a
patch of adhesive tape over
his right eye socket, yanked at
the knot in his tie and unbut-
toned the collar of his shirt.

"What was your occupation
at that time?" Judge Samuel
S. Leibowitz asked The
Hawk.

"I was a gambler," he re-
plied.

"And a killer?" queried the
judge.

"Oh, sure," The Hawk de-
clared.

The Hawk, questioned by
Julius A. Helfand, Assistant
District Attorney, revealed
that he met Genovese in a

Brooklyn restaurant in March,
1934.

There he was introduced to
Genovese by Michael Mi-
randi, who described Genovese as the *"don vin done,"*
which in the Italian underworld lingo means "the big
man—the great man."
—*New York World-Telegram*
June 7, 1946

. . . In addition to the bullet tracks, there are multiple
stab wounds, seven on the left anterior surface of the chest
and four on the right. Two of the four wounds on the right
penetrate the chest. . . .

That Friday, the last time I ever saw him, he was in the
kitchen, leaning up against the refrigerator, and he tells me,
"Honey, they're gonna kill your daddy."

He wasn't living home then, but he was coming home
every day. You know, all that same garbage, back and forth.
And I says, "Oh, another crazy story to get back in the
house." I says, "Don't worry." I says, "If they kill you, I'll
make sure that whoever did it goes to jail."

He says, "Yeah. Don't say that," and on and on.

Now, the next day, Saturday, he's supposed to bring me
money. So he calls up Saturday morning, and he's in a bar
on Fort Hamilton Parkway somewhere and he tells me
about a fire. He says, "I almost died last night in a fire. Two
guys came to the door and I wouldn't let them in and they
were screaming and I was cursing." He says, "Your daddy

was out in the street in his underwear." He was telling me all that was going on.

I says, "Ernie, why do you think up these fantastic tales? Anything to get back in the house." Then he says, "I'm meeting the guys. I'm gonna have the money for you." And I says, "All right."

So he kept calling all day. You couldn't go to the bathroom without him calling, "Where were you, what are you doing?" So he's calling. He didn't get the money, he didn't get the money.

Now it's Sunday and he's calling, and the last time he calls is Sunday night because I'm moving and they shut the phone off Sunday night. He calls Sunday night and, "I'll be there, I'll be there with the money," and on and on.

Now I don't hear from him Monday, right? Because I have no phone, and he obviously didn't get the money because he didn't come. Tuesday I don't hear from him. Wednesday morning I move. Now I figured, "Oh, this dope is gonna show up." By Thursday when he doesn't show up, I call my sister.

"Did you hear from Ernie?"

She says, "No."

I says, "Gee, that's funny. I was so sure he was coming with the money."

So Thursday passes by. Now Friday comes and I says, "Something happened. This has never happened in six and a half years, because this man *never* stayed away a week no matter *what* happened."

All right. Now it's Friday, I don't see him. What's going on? I haven't heard from him since Sunday. By this time he would have had my sister on the cross, "Where is she, what's going on?"

So now I start calling. And calling. And calling. Calling

Roy Roy's mother. She says, "He went away, he went away for a few days."

"He went away for a few days? What do you mean he went away for a few days? Where did he go?"

Roy Roy's mother says, "I don't know. He's coming home, he's coming home, he's coming home."

I called everybody. Everybody Ernie ever knew, I have on the phone. Nobody saw him. Now I call Frances back, Roy Roy's mother. I says, "Look, I'm telling you now," I says, "you better get Roy Roy to the phone. I'm telling you Ernie is *dead*."

. . . Of the seven wounds on the left anterior surface of the chest, four penetrate backwards at various points, cutting through the costal cartilages and also through the interspaces. Of these four, three perforate the left lung. . . .

SINGING "HAWK" NEAR LIBERTY

Ernest (The Hawk) Rupolo, killer-for-hire of the gangster decade '30s, was on his way to liberty from Dannemora Prison yesterday in proceedings before Judge Samuel Leibowitz. This was in accordance with a 1946 promise made by the Brooklyn District Attorney's Office in return for evidence against his alleged underworld paymaster, Vito Genovese, of Murder, Inc. fame.

All concerned in the re-
lease, including "The Hawk"
himself, agreed he is now
marked for murder himself
and cannot expect to survive
long. He had been serving a
nine-to-twenty-year sentence.

With the promised aid of
Brooklyn authorities and the
expected collaboration of
State Parole Board members,
Rupolo will make a desperate
effort to disappear com-
pletely.

—*New York Daily Mirror*
September 24, 1949

So my brother blew his top on the organization. He ex-
posed the big bosses. "I was hired killer for Genovese. I was
hired killer for Mike Miranda. I was hired killer for this
here." So he's supposed to get killed by this mob, because
there is no forgiving. According to the code of the grease-
balls he was supposed to be killed.

But the kid *made* some of the bosses. Because they used
him a lot when he was young, and they always depended
on him to do the jobs that he was told to do. So they sat
down on this here—should he walk the streets or not? And
they forgave him. They said, "Well, this kid did twelve
years, solid years, for us." So for that he got a reprieve. In
fact, Mike Miranda says to him, "Take care of yourself, kid.
Don't worry about nothin'. If you need anything come to
me."

That's why he ran wild the way he did. A guy like him,
what he did, if he wasn't so well liked by them—and if it

wasn't for the work he done for them so some became top bosses today—he wouldn't of lived two minutes.

They never tried to hit the kid. They were scared because, believe me, if someone went after him and he had an idea where it come from, he'd go right up to their doorstep, right to the boss. He didn't care who it was, he'd go right to the boss and wait on his doorstep to kill him. He wouldn't give them a second chance. That's the way the kid was. Let's face it. He didn't care for nothin'.

He used to come to my place every day and eat with my father, myself, and my wife, every day. That's how I knew that when he didn't come in for lunch that day, I knew something was wrong. I knew foul play some place.

And because of the fire. Ten days or a week before, the kid came down to my place and I said, "Where you going?"

"To church to light a candle."

"Why?"

"Because I'm not supposed to be here today."

And I says, "Well, what happened?"

"I don't know," he says. "My whole sofa caught on fire. A good thing the landlord come in and I got out of there. I could have burned to death."

And I says, "What happened?"

And he says, "There was a couple of guys knockin' for me to open the door. And I says, the hell with them, and I was high, and I just laid down and tried to go to sleep." And he says, "Those guys must have thrown a match or a cigarette on my sofa, and it was lucky I wasn't burned alive."

All that time he didn't think nothin'. He just thought it was a couple of drunks looking to get laid upstairs. There were some sporting girls, you know, some whores living upstairs, and that's what he thought at the time. If he had of ever thought like that was, you know, to do something to him, he never would have gone back to the place. Not him.

And then later, after they found the body, I thought back and I figured, well, it *was* something, that they had been looking to get him out of there at that time, and try to do away with him. And when they failed to get him out of there, to walk him out of there or something, I figure they looked to burn him, that's what I figure.

I don't think Genovese had a thing to do with killing my brother. You see, Ernie knew Sonny [*John "Sonny" Franzese, a Long Island mobster*] from when they were kids. And he hated him. Because he said, "While I was away doing sixteen years that bastard was out making money." Sonny never did a day, so Ernie figured Sonny was reaping the harvest while he was away doing time. They hated each other. They really, really did.

Now I think Ernie was stepping on Sonny's feet. Ernie couldn't make money in Brooklyn anymore and he needed money and he figured he'd go out to Queens and start in in Queens in whatever Sonny was doing—bookmaking, muscling in on bars, whatever. And Sonny didn't want that.

What I think happened, I think Ernie was drinking all day, right? And now he's pretty—he's not with it anymore. He's like in a fog. They go to Willie's house, Ernie and Willie and Roy Roy. My personal feeling is that Roy Roy had an appointment to meet somebody and that he stalled at Willie's house. And then Roy Roy told Ernie he'd drop him off somewhere, or something like that. And then he was killed on the way. Roy Roy met some people and they told

Ernie they would drive him home, and they killed him in the car.

. . . On the left lateral surface of the chest there are seven more stab wounds. These are up to six inches in depth. . . .

When they finally did hit my brother, Roy Roy had to be the one to set him up. He drove for him. He was the only one he'd of gone with. That's what they do. They take your best friend and he has to do what they say, even if he *is* your best friend. And they make him walk you into something, take you out, wine you and dine you, and then walk you into it. Roy Roy had to be the one.

But the stab wounds. I don't know. That's what I'm sick over. I seen this here before. Like a lot of bodies, they were never brought up. Like Joe Jelly. They say, "Oh, they threw him in the river. They ripped his stomach and threw him in the river so he won't come up."

It's only a miracle that my brother did come up. Because there's a lot of people—like they say Tony Bender's body's never been found, and they say, "Well, sure, they must have threw him in the river."

That's the only way I can see it. Like that's why they slit a guy's belly. They figure the water won't bring him up. This is just one chance in a million that my brother did come up. Because people who've been hit in the last ten or twelve years, their bodies were never found. Nobody knew, just rumors, talking, "He must be in the river somewhere." Because if a body is either buried or in the river, they figure it won't come up and you won't see it no more.

. . . On the anterior abdominal wall there are six large incised stab wounds, all above the navel and from four to six inches in length. . . .

"I'm telling you Ernie is *dead!*" I says to Frances.

"What makes you say that?" she yells.

"I *know* he's dead. I know he's dead, because if he wasn't dead he would have been breaking my door down by now."

"Don't say that!" she yells at me. "I'm lighting candles for you. He'll be all right," and this and that.

I says, "All right." So she gives me a time to call to get Roy Roy on the phone. And sure enough, I call and I get Roy Roy on the phone. So I says, "Roy Roy, where's Ernie?"

He says, "He's on the lam in New Jersey."

I says, "Don't give me that garbage. You're talking to me!" I says, "You *know* if he was on the lam in New Jersey, he's not going to New Jersey without me, if he had to take me there in chains." I says, "Just tell me where he is."

"What are you worried about?" he says. "You're always throwing him out anyway."

And I says, "That's none of your damned business. I live my life. I want to do what I want to do. But don't tell *me* this guy isn't going to call *me* for a week," I says, "because you *know* better than that."

So he says, "I don't know where he is."

I says, "Roy Roy, you're the last one that saw him alive."

"*Don't say that!*" He got hysterical when I said that.

So I says, "I *am* saying it. And where is he?"

He says, "I don't know, I don't know where he is."

I says, "I'm going to call you up tomorrow morning and

if you don't come up with Ernie by then I'm coming to Brooklyn. And that's it. That's gonna be *it*."

So I called back the next day, and Roy Roy's not around. And I went right to Willie's store, you know, the luncheonette.

"Where's Ernie?"

Nobody saw him.

So I says, "Willie, don't give me any of that garbage." I says, "Where is he?"

He says, "I don't know. He moved out of his room. Roy Roy moved him out."

And I says, "I don't want to hear that garbage! Who saw him and where did he go?"

"All I know is he left the house that night. My wife told him, don't leave, it's raining. He says, no, he had to go, he had to go."

I says, "All right."

So then I see Ernie's jacket hanging in the store. "What's his jacket doing here?"

So he says, "Oh," he says, "it was hot. He left his jacket here."

I says, "Was he drunk?"

He says, "No."

Now Ernie had reached the point where he couldn't drink anymore. He'd have four drinks and he was stoned. I said, "Did he have his teeth in his mouth?"

He says, "No."

I says, "He was drunk. Where did he go?"

He says, "I don't know. They dropped me off. Roy Roy said he was going to take him to the train." He says, "That's all I know."

I says, "Okay. That's all you know?"

"Right."

"Willie, you don't know *anything* else?"

"No."

So I says I'm going right to the police station. Now by this time I'm crying. I says, "He's *dead,* I'm telling you he's *dead.*"

All right. I walked into the 66th. I'm crying like a maniac by now, and I said, "Ernie's dead."

And the cops laughed at me. They said, "You're just looking for him because you want some money, right, Eleanor?"

I says, "No, I'm telling you now, he's dead." Because I had called them a million times before—"Get that bum out of my house!" So now they figure I'm just looking for him. I says, "No, I'm serious." So they said they had to report it to Missing Persons. So I says, "But look for him. Look for him all over. Because I know he's *dead.* If he's not dead, they've got him tied up somewhere. I didn't hear from him for a *week.*"

So they said all right. And I said, "I'll call you later."

From there, now, I go to his apartment on Berkely Place. Now Willie told me he had moved out of Berkely Place, that he's not there. But I look through the window and see his jewelry box on the dresser.

Now I'm wild. I says, "Oh, my God," and I'm banging on doors and I'm kicking. I go up and I start ringing all the doorbells in the building. Who saw him? One guy was telling me about the fire, and I says, "Well, it was *true,* about the fire."

But nobody saw him after that day. "We didn't see him. We didn't see him. We didn't see him."

I says, "Well, now I *know* he's really dead."

I get back home and I say, "He's gone. He's finished. But where? That's the question." He didn't come back because he didn't have the money, right? But I know that would have lasted two or three days, then he would have said, the hell with the money, I'm going to see her anyway.

And I'm calling. I call everybody and anybody. Nobody saw Ernie. I'm calling two or three times a day to the 66th, to Missing Persons. I don't hear anything, and I'm bothering everybody.

Until the day that detective rang the doorbell. I opened the door, and his first words to me, he says, "You're right."

I said, "Where is he?" I figured they found him in some empty lot somewhere.

He says, "We have him in the 100th precinct."

I says, "I don't know where that is."

He says, "Rockaway. Come with me."

And that was it.

. . . Cause of death: bullet wounds of head, brain, neck, and spine. Multiple stab wounds of the chest, lungs, heart, and abdomen. Homicidal.

the trial

The day the newspapers carried the story about Alice Crimmins receiving a police guard, Mosley's office door flew open and a large woman in her thirties, hair up in curlers, charged into the room, shouting. Mosley looked up from his desk and winced. He knew her well. Her name was Eleanor Cordero.

"How come," she screamed, "that some *bitch* who killed her two kids gets police protection, and *I* can't even get a lousy detective to take me to *Brooklyn?* I'm going to get dynamited out of my car someday, and a lot any of you people will care!"

"She didn't get protection," Mosley said wearily. "Only for a few hours. It's been withdrawn. Leave me alone."

It was hard to be too stern with Eleanor Cordero. Her loud mouth and fearless, hair-trigger temper had in a single moment of imprudent fury wedged open the door to evidence that Mosley hoped would bring a first-degree murder conviction to John "Sonny" Franzese, one of New York's most notorious Mafia gangsters.

Some months after The Hawk's murder, his widow Eleanor had been drinking with John Cordero (her fiancé at the time, a gunman for Franzese) in a Mafia motel and bar in Queens. A hoodlum named Joseph "Whitey" Florio walked by the table, and Eleanor started throwing loud remarks about his having murdered The Hawk. John became nervous and tried to silence her. Other customers listened with growing interest. Finally, John hustled her out to the parking lot.

They had walked across the lot when John turned and saw Florio coming toward them. Thinking Florio about to respond violently to Eleanor's accusation, John pulled a gun. He fired three shots at Florio, missing him. Charlie Zaher, another hoodlum, drove into the lot. Florio disappeared, and John and Eleanor got in their car with Zaher and drove off.

The next night Sonny Franzese called a "sit-down," a Mafia "court" to find out what the shooting had been about. Summoned together at a Mafia hangout called the Aqueduct Motel, John, Florio, and Zaher testified to what had happened in the bar and parking lot. When they were finished, Sonny, to his enduring regret, made several admissions, some about bank robberies and one about having ordered The Hawk murdered. Some months after the sit-down, Cordero, Zaher, and two other Franzese underlings were arrested for bank robbery. Cordero decided to save himself years in prison by cooperating with the government and testifying against Franzese. Zaher, a drug addict who had been "wheel man" (getaway-car driver) in two Franzese-bossed robberies, also agreed to cooperate with the government, and before long the other two came over too: Jimmy Smith, a "vault man" who leaps bank counters and scoops up the bills, and Richard Parks, a gunman as wily as he is vicious. First, in a federal trial, all four told how Franzese had planned the bank robberies, and for that crime Sonny drew a fifty-year sentence (but remained free pending his appeal).

Now, three years after the body floated up on the beach, they are ready to tell a jury what they know about The Hawk's murder. In every other murder case Mosley has tried, the problem has always been the same: to convince twelve jurors of what he himself is already certain, that the defendant on trial is guilty. But in this case the issue is far more fundamental. The defendants are all Mafia men, with the wealth and power of the Mafia behind them. With money, treachery, and deception they will try to cajole and muscle their way past the law. If they succeed, their very subversion of the law will be to Mosley a greater crime than murder.

Mosley's chief target in the trial will be the number-one defendant, Sonny Franzese, 48, a bull-necked, stocky, curly-haired man with an engaging smile and a mind the United States Army described (in tossing him out) as "psychoneurotic with pronounced homicidal tendencies." Born in Naples, he was brought to New York by his parents, grew up in Brooklyn, and fought and murdered his way into the Mafia's front rank. He married a slim blonde, bought a colonial-style house on a suburban street named Shrub Hollow Road, and is as dedicated to violence and treachery as Mosley is to law. He has never been in prison.

Once it had become known in the underworld that Cordero, Parks, Zaher, and Smith were going to testify against Sonny Franzese and some of his lieutenants, their safety became a problem. Witnesses in Mafia cases had been murdered before, even while locked in jail. Franzese got his message through: "You don't have to be on the street to be hit."

For more than a year before the robbery trial these four witnesses had been shunted about from one prison to another, always amidst great secrecy, always locked in high-security, solitary-confinement areas, away from other prisoners who might murder them on contract from the Mafia or simply to win a reputation as "having done Sonny a favor." To prevent poisoning, their meals were specially prepared and delivered. If food was brought by a stranger, they threw it into the toilet and went hungry.

Despite precautions they never lost their fear, and they soon decided that testifying against Franzese was too high a price to pay for the years it might cut off their sentences. Zaher tried to avoid the witness chair by getting Cordero to slash his arm for him (it didn't work—he was sewed up and back in the cell within hours). Parks resorted to a more subtle and less painful device. He knew that every word he wrote to any prosecutor's office must, by law, be handed over to defense attorneys during the trial. So he wrote letters containing lies and conflicting statements that would discredit himself and other witnesses, hoping the prosecutor might feel he would do his case more harm than good, and not call him to the stand. Parks's letters—as well as some from Cordero and Smith—eventually wound up with Mosley, who knew that someday he would have to cut his own throat and hand them over to the defense.

During Franzese's trial for bank robbery, these four

witnesses begged to be taken to court in a helicopter or armored car. Guards who drove them to the trial each day said they cringed on the floor of the back seat. By the time that trial ended they had been in virtual solitary confinement for a year and a half, and the "hard time" had begun to show. "Through this whole thing," Parks said with more truth than he knew, "I think I've lost about half my mind."

Some weeks before the trial starts, Mosley and a detective named Joe Price go to talk to the witnesses at the Nassau County jail. Price, bright and painstaking, has been on the case full time for the three years since the body was discovered. He knows the witnesses well.

A guard checks Price's badge, takes his gun, checks Mosley's credentials, and lets them through a locked steel door. On the third floor, another door with a small square window is unlocked and Price and Mosley step into a small, brightly lighted area containing three open cells. One of the cells has a toilet and a sink, and T-shirts hang drying on the bars. The cells are antiseptically clean. Cordero and Smith stand up from bunks and step forward to shake hands. They are in blue uniforms. Cordero is a short, very thin, meek-looking man of 33. He has been a heroin addict and a homosexual, and his handshake is weak and damp. "A big man behind a piece," his friends say, but he doesn't look it here. Smith is taller and older and has been in prison so much of his life that he has never really learned to live on the outside. There are jokes that he doesn't even know how to work a modern car door or select songs on a jukebox. His hair is slicked back straight over white, bulging golf-ball eyes. Cordero does most of the talking.

Franzese is out of jail on $230,000 bail, and Mosley asks

Cordero and Smith what they think about trying to get him remanded when the trial starts. Cordero says he would rather have him on the street.

"Like that way he won't want to do nothing. You know what I mean? Like if he's out he'll figure if he does something the judge will lock him up. But if he's in he might get mad and figure what the hell he's already in, he's got nothing to lose, and have someone do something." Cordero stands with his weight on his heels, his chin tucked in, gesturing with his hands and long thin fingers.

"Well, let's see what the others think," Mosley says, and knocks on the door. A guard opens it and leads Price and Mosley to another group of cells, slightly larger than the first. Zaher and Parks are sitting at a table bolted to the floor. They stand up when Mosley and Price enter. Parks has a heavy three-day beard. His black hair is cut close, almost shaved, and his face, narrow, small-eyed, and nearly chinless, resembles the face of a rodent. Zaher is liveliest of the four, younger and less oppressed by the months of hard confinement. His normally dark complexion long ago gave him the nickname Blackie, but now, after nineteen months in sunless cells, he is pale.

Parks is the one Mosley has really come to see. He is the strongest, the leader. He is sharp and clever, and he has had nothing to do day and night for months on end but think up schemes against his two great enemies: the government and Sonny Franzese.

Mosley has a complicated problem, and how he solves it will depend on the reaction of Richie Parks. The witnesses have already testified at three federal trials. Before testifying, all four pleaded guilty to their part in a number of bank robberies, with the understanding that after cooperating with the government they would be sentenced to terms considerably lighter than they might otherwise have received. If Mosley can delay their sentencing until after their testimony at his trial, he will have a club over their heads: if they sabotage his trial he can go to their sentencing judge, point out the double-cross, and ask that they be given stiffer sentences. But he also knows that if he has this club hanging over them, the defense lawyers will argue that the four are lying to insure light sentences.

There is no question that a club is needed. Men like Parks, Cordero, Smith, and Zaher do nothing for nothing. If they see that they will not gain by helping Mosley, they will not help. To be sure, they already have testified about the murder under oath to a grand jury and told part of their stories at the robbery trials. To recant that testimony now could bring perjury charges against them. But there are ways they can sabotage Mosley's case without risking perjury, and they know them well. The law, for example, requires that a jury hear the entire case without knowing that the defendants have been charged with other crimes. One hint from a witness that a defendant has committed a crime other than the one before the court, one suggestion that he has a reputation as a criminal, and the judge will declare a mistrial. That would mean starting the trial all over, with delays that could be fatal to the prosecution. So Mosley needs to be sure Parks and the others will behave.

The witnesses have been difficult from the start, making clearly unacceptable demands on the authorities. Parks has been the worst. He alone can actually say he saw one of Sonny's men stab The Hawk, and he knows the value of that. He is willing to get on the stand and give an eyewitness, blow-by-blow account of the stabbing, but he wants something in return. At first he said he wanted $5,000 for his testimony. Convinced of the absurdity of that request, he quickly came up with others. Police eventually uncovered evidence of his part in a motel robbery, and with that held over him he agreed to cooperate.

But Parks has been talking to the government for nineteen months, and he has had about enough. He is tired of the fear, and tired of the hard confinement. He wants to collect the reward for his cooperation, and he is convinced that that reward should be not merely a light sentence but a suspended sentence, an SS. He wants to do no more time at all.

Mosley, Price, and Zaher are sitting at the table bolted to the floor. Parks stands nearby, leaning on the wall. Mosley chats with Parks and Zaher for a few seconds, and then starts to feel Parks out.

"What would happen," he asks Parks, "if you were sentenced and got a little time, say a couple of years? What would happen?"

Parks sneers. "I've done nineteen months of real hard time, Mr. Mosley. I don't know if you know what it's like. I haven't been in population for nineteen months. I've testified in three trials. I've done my part. What's anyone done for me? Sonny's on bail, he's on the street, and I'm here. I don't want no time. I want an SS. And I don't want to be here. I want to be in a hotel."

"What if your sentence were adjourned for a while?"

"No good, Mr. Mosley. I've done everything I was supposed to do, and I want to be sentenced now." The words are respectful, but the tone is contemptuous. He leans against the wall and watches Mosley. Then he says, "You know, I have to sell myself to the jury."

Mosley has seen Parks testify in one of the federal trials, and he was a good witness. He did indeed sell himself to the jury. When he told what he knew, there was something about the way he said it that made you believe him. Now he is telling Mosley that it doesn't have to be that way. He can use the same words, but speak them flatly, as if memorized, with a tone and manner no one will believe.

"I don't have to perjure myself," Parks says. "All I have to say is, 'Sonny, the bank robber,' and it's a mistrial. I can talk to Edelbaum [Sonny's lawyer] and there are ways without perjury where I can cut Sonny loose. And I'll do it."

Mosley knows he can. And he knows what Sonny will pay for it.

"I want to be sentenced now," Parks goes on. "And I'd better get an SS. I'm not like them." He nods contemptuously toward the cells that hold Smith and Cordero. "You got a couple of fall guys there. They'll testify for you. They're not even looking for an SS."

They will testify all right, but they did not see The Hawk killed. Only Parks can testify to that.

Mosley stands up and walks to the door. "In other words," he says back to Parks, who has not moved from his position against the wall, "if you don't get an SS right now, you're not going to testify. You're going to tell me to go to hell."

"That's right," Parks says.

Mosley's face tightens. He knocks on the door for the guard. "Richie," he says, "you're making me very angry."

Mosley and Price go back to Cordero and Smith. Mosley tells them that Parks is insisting on an SS, and that he is threatening to dump the case unless he gets one.

Cordero laughs. "He's a bluffer," he says. "You've got to bluff him back. He thinks he has all the cards, and he shoots for the moon. He'll say anything, just to try to get as much as he can. But he'll testify, Mr. Mosley. Sure he will. He's a big bluffer."

On the way back in the car Mosley tells Price he is going to try to get the sentencing of the witnesses adjourned. "He says he'll sandbag me if he doesn't get sentenced now to an SS," Mosley says. "But if he does get an SS, he can sandbag me anyway. What a bastard."

Later Mosley talks to the federal prosecutor who handled the last trial, and discovers that the witnesses were promised that they would be sentenced immediately. There is no going back on it. But there is an ace in the hole. If the judge wants to he can give the four witnesses an "A" type of federal sentence, which allows for resentencing at a later date. He can give them a few years with the tacit understanding that if they continue to cooperate they will later be sentenced to a lighter term, possibly even an SS. That way, if they sabotage Mosley, they also sabotage any chance of getting another, lighter sentence.

The day before the witnesses are to be sentenced, Mosley sits in his office with Price. They have just come back from lunch. Mosley has his feet on the desk and is clipping his fingernails.

"Joe," he says, "what do you think Parks will do if he gets a jolt tomorrow? If he gets time."

"Myself? Knowing him for a year and a half? He'll blow. I really think he will. He'll yell about so-and-so who robbed this and that bank and got three years, and here he's testified for the governmnet in three cases, gave them three convictions, did nineteen months hard time, and so why should he get time. He'll make all kinds of phony accusations about promises that were made, promises that weren't kept. This is a war of nerves, Jimmy, with this guy. It's the best bluffer who wins. He's very obstinate, this guy. And you've got to remember, too, that we're dealing here with half a nut."

"But if he gets an 'A' type sentence," Mosley says, "and then blows up in court, he's going to do the time."

"He doesn't think that way, Jimmy. He figures all he got so far was promises, promises. And now he wants his SS, and if he doesn't get it, he'll blow."

The next day in court Mosley and Price hear the witnesses' attorneys argue for leniency. Then the federal prosecutor gets up and delivers the most impassioned plea of all. He urges the judge to give the witnesses light terms, or suspended sentences, pointing out that they already have virtually condemned themselves to death by testifying against their Mafia bosses. No prison in the country, he says, can hold them in complete security.

The judge listens. When the pleas are over, he gives Parks, Smith, and Cordero an "A" type sentence of five years. Zaher, because he has only driven the getaway car and has a cleaner record, gets an SS and five years' probation.

Parks does not blow up. Mosley talks to the judge and the witnesses and then, outside the court house, walking to his car, he says to Price, "This judge is going to be our club over Parks. If he or the others sandbag me, they'll get shot down by the judge. I told them that, and they understood. Parks is all right."

Smith, Cordero, and Parks had had little to say about drawing five years, but Eleanor Cordero reacted with characteristic intensity.

"Five years!" she screamed to Price. "Why do they give John five years? Red Crabbe only got five years for bank robbery, and he killed my husband. And right after he did that he came into the bar I was working in and bought a drink from me. The bastard. If I had known *then* what he had just done. A rye and ginger—a lousy cheap drink. And he didn't even leave a tip!"

Men like Cordero, Parks, Smith, and Zaher could provide at best a rather feeble foundation for a murder trial. They had committed so many crimes themselves that defense attorneys, in challenging their believability, could easily shift the focus of the trial onto them and away from the defendants. Mosley felt his chances of winning were only 50-50.

"You see," he said, "you've got these four variables, these four witnesses, and you don't know how they'll come out. *You* know they're telling the truth, but limited to the evidence admissible in court, can you convince the jury?

"In a murder case like this, the actual criminal law is nothing. That's easy. The difficult, important part—the real ball game—is preparation and trial tactics. How do you handle these witnesses? How do you keep Richie Parks from sandbagging you?"

Mosley was at lunch one afternoon when a lawyer sat down at his table and asked about the case. "I hear your witnesses are the worst in the world," he said.

"Well," Mosley answered, "you can say what you want about these witnesses—bank robbers, everything else—but I was at the bank-robbery trial, and when you listen to them on the stand anyone would be damned hard put to say they're lying. They're good witnesses."

The lawyer was a short, balding, middle-aged man with horn-rimmed glasses.

"You think it's a good case, a winner?" he asked.

"I've got admissions," Mosley said. "I've got an eyewitness. At the bank-robbery trial, the jury believed the witnesses. Here? What can I tell you? Who knows? The amazing thing is that I really can't do that much for them. It's the vengeance they feel against Sonny. They convicted him once, and now they want to sink him again."

The lawyer shook his head. "They're dead men. It's a strange world they live in, isn't it?"

In the coming weeks the witnesses were brought from jail (Zaher, despite his SS, was held in the civil jail on $10,000 bail as a material witness) to Mosley's office to go over the case. Mosley wanted to make sure again that what they were telling him—what they would say at the trial—was the truth. He and Price listened to the witnesses' stories over and over. They checked the stories against each other and against every statement the witnesses had made since Cordero first decided to cooperate. There were no flaws.

A few days after the sentencing, Zaher was in Mosley's office, about to go out for his first restaurant meal in nineteen months.

"Where do you want to eat?" one of the guards asked him (detectives, plainclothesmen, and federal marshals constantly accompanied the witnesses, to prevent their escape and to protect them from assassination).

"How about Salerno's?" he said, suggesting an Italian restaurant he had been to when he worked for Franzese.

"Salerno's!" Price said. "That's great. And Sonny walks in. 'Hi there, Blackie.' Beautiful."

Zaher laughed nervously. "Maybe you're right."

They decided on another place. It was raining out, and Zaher reached for one of several raincoats hanging by the door.

"Not that one, Blackie," a detective said. "Take one of the others."

"What's wrong with you?" Mosley said to the detective

when Zaher and his guards had left. "The guy's helping lock up Sonny and you won't even let him wear your coat?"

"It's the only one I've got," he said. "I don't want it back with blood and bullet holes all over it."

Smith was brought to Mosley's office and made it clear that he had no doubts about the Mafia's determination to kill him. At the bank-robbery trial he had gone on in some length about his fear of the Mafia's vengeance. He had testified, with the jury absent, that he and the other witnesses were "soldiers" in the Franzese "family," and that that meant "we do the dirty work—like robbing banks." He said he had once heard Franzese tell Parks, "When I tell you to do something, you do it. If I tell you to pipe someone, you pipe them. If I tell you to kill someone, you kill them." Sonny, Smith said, had even sent a threat to them in jail through his girl friend. She visited him and said she had been ordered to tell him that "the other guys"—the other witnesses—had signed statements against Mafia defendants in a federal case, and that Sonny "realized that I was in a bad position and that if I was going to jump on the bandwagon against [those defendants], that would be all right, but if I went any further [and implicated Franzese] to stop and think of the consequences."

He was asked what he thought was meant by "the consequences."

"To have me snuffed," he said.

When Mosley had finished questioning Smith, he was taken to a restaurant for something to eat. He explained what methods he thought Sonny's men could use to find him.

"Say the trial's over," he said. "I do a little time and then I'm out, right? And I go away some place. I'm not going to stay around here. So I go away. They can still find me. They can hire legitimate private investigators to look for me. The same way you would hire them to look for a lost relative. Or they can pay off a probation officer to get my address. They'll tell him, look, it's nothing, all we want is his address for something. So he takes a couple of grand just for the address and if he reads in the paper I'm dead, he can think, well, all I did was give his address. Or through my mother. My mother is a legitimate woman. She don't know nothing about Sonny or anything like that. They could send a guy to her house dressed like a priest, and he says someone has left him some money for me and he's trying to find me, or something like that, and she might figure it's legitimate and tell him. There's all kinds of ways. If they want to find you and want it bad enough, they're gonna find you."

They were in a restaurant called Luigi's, about two blocks from the court house, and it was a rare occasion indeed for the habitually imprisoned Smith. He sat at the bar with his hat on—he wore it constantly, even to the bathroom—and ordered rounds of "seven-and-seven" as if he were host at a party. He wore sunglasses—which he never took off either —and Franzese himself had seen to it that the lenses were prescription-ground. In the bank-robbery team, Smith in his role as vault man had on one occasion neatly hurdled the bank counter, but instead of scooping up the big stuff, he had grabbed only one-dollar bills. That was the first his confederates knew he had bad eyes. When they handed Franzese his share of the few dollars they had stolen, he threw it on the floor and exploded in obscenities. Other members of the gang escorted Smith to an optometrist and stood by while the lenses were replaced.

Smith's take from one of the bank jobs had been $10,000 ("ten big ones") and he had gone through it completely in one week. Now he ordered himself another seven-and-seven, waved an arm to include the guards around him, and told the bartender, "And a round for all these gentlemen." He noticed a boy and girl at the far end of the bar, and gestured expansively toward them. "And see what that young couple at the end of the bar will have."

Mosley smiled. "Now we know how he went through ten big ones in a week."

Smith got up and—disproving the old joke about himself—dropped a dime into the jukebox and read the tunes. After five minutes carefully examining all the titles on the list, he made his selection and played a song called "Laugh It Off."

Parks, unlike Smith, was a man far too intelligent and cunning to let a visit to a restaurant become the high point of his visits to Mosley's office. Often he settled for a sandwich brought in from a delicatessen, and spent his time studying his grand-jury testimony and the statements he had made to detectives.

A thoroughly insolent man (he referred to District Attorney Thomas Mackell, Mosley's gray-haired boss, as "the silver fox," and concluded a December letter to a U.S. attorney with "Many happy convictions for the new year"), he was jealous of the success of other men he felt had less intelligence than himself. Cordero once remarked to Mosley that Parks thought he had triumphed over one of the defense lawyers at the bank-robbery trial because the lawyer's high-pressure cross examination failed to rattle him. "Well, that's Richie," Mosley had said. "He thinks he could get into a witness chair and destroy every trial man from Cicero to Clarence Darrow, simultaneously."

Mosley had another problem with Parks, aside from his personality: was he himself an accomplice to the murder?

Parks had been told to deliver a car somewhere, and when he arrived with it, he saw part of the crime. Did this delivery of the car—even though he did not know what it would be used for—make him part of the murder? The question was a legal one, and extremely critical. In New York State courts, the testimony of an accomplice must be supported by other independent evidence tending to connect the defendant with the crime. The defendant cannot be convicted on the uncorroborated testimony of an accomplice. This rule does not hold in federal courts, and the prosecutor at the federal trials had not had to cope with it. But Mosley would. He was certain the defense would try to make Parks an accomplice, and then argue that the corroboration offered was insufficient.

As Mosley's preparation for the Franzese trial continued, investigation proceeded simultaneously in the Alice Crimmins case. The two cases could hardly have seemed further apart: one involving a young woman with casual sexual morals but no past criminal record; the other, the cold-blooded execution of a Mafia gangster. Yet a possible connection did appear. Mosley had John Cordero in his office and was questioning him about some old FBI reports. He came to a statement an FBI agent had made that Cordero claimed knowledge of the Crimmins case.

Crimmins detectives Jerry Byrnes and Jerry Piering were outside Mosley's office, and Mosley went out and showed them the report. They said they knew about it and that it had been investigated without result some time ago. But since Cordero was in the office now anyway they'd like to bring it up again. The three of them went back into Mosley's office.

"John," Mosley started, "what's this you told the FBI that you knew something about the Crimmins case?"

"Yeah." Cordero looked at Byrnes and Piering. "I told you about that a long time ago. Remember when you asked me about that, and I told you?"

"I do, John," Byrnes said, "but let's go over it a little more. What was it now, a shakedown or something?"

"That's right," Cordero said. "I'm in a car with two of Sonny's men and we're parked by this bar and I seen another car pull up across from us with this girl, I don't know her name, and two other guys. One of the men in my car with me says wait a minute and goes over and talks to the girl. Now, I don't know what it's all about, I figure they've got something going, you know, but I don't know what it is. And he comes back and says to the other guy in the car, 'It's all set.' Now at the time there had been some talk with some of Sonny's guys that they were going to shake someone down over the Crimmins thing, and I figured maybe this had something to do with that. Because they had asked me already if I wanted in on it and I had said yes. And then after a while—after I saw these people in this car, that I just told you—I was told to forget the whole thing. Not that it was off, but just to forget it. So I forgot it. I figured anyway all they wanted me for was to be the jerk who picked up the money, who had to show his face and get the money. Or some job like that. I figured unless they needed some dirty work done, someone piped or shot, what do they need me for?"

His description of the girl he had seen in the car matched one of Alice's girl friends. Cordero had also mentioned hearing the name of a bartender, and a bartender by that name worked in a bar Alice and the other girl went to often. Had Alice's girl friend decided to blackmail one of Alice's rich married boy friends, then taken her plan to the bartender, who passed it on to Sonny's men? Was John Cordero told to "forget it" because the victim had enough Mafia connections to block the shakedown? The answers already had been sought—the bartender interviewed, Alice's girl friend questioned—without results. But that had been months ago, and now the detectives would try again.

"I remember there was a lot of heat on in Queens then," Cordero continued. "Because of the Crimmins thing. There was detectives all over the place. I was sitting in a luncheonette with another guy, planning a bank robbery, and two detectives were right next to us, in the next booth, talking about Crimmins. They saw us, and they like kept giving us the eye, so we left."

"Were you heeled?" Piering asked.

"Sure I was. I had a .38 in my belt."

"You told us this before," Piering said. "I think you said one of the detectives was a small guy?"

"Yeah. That's right. One was a huge guy and one was very small."

"A small guy like me?" Piering asked, not smiling.

"Was it you?" Cordero asked.

"Yeah."

Byrnes laughed. "Beautiful. Two guys planning a bank robbery next to you, and they walk out."

Piering smiled thinly. Cordero kept a straight face.

Cordero was pathologically jealous of his wife Eleanor and of his ability to care for her. Any remark questioning their relationship met with instant fury. One day he was sitting in Mosley's office reading material connected with the case when he suddenly jumped from his chair, swore, and began to tear up the document in his hands. Detectives quieted him. The damaged paper was an early statement Eleanor had made about her life with The Hawk. Mosley, whose patience with the witnesses was growing thin, exploded.

"What the hell are you doing?" he shouted at Cordero. "Don't get it in your head you can come in here and start tearing up statements!"

He turned to the guards. "Take him back." He walked out of the office. When he was gone Cordero sat sullenly. The guards put on their coats.

"I'm not a witness anymore," Cordero announced angrily. "He just lost a witness. He can't talk to me like that."

It was lunchtime and Mosley walked up the street to Luigi's. A detective came over and told him what Cordero had said.

"Won't testify?" Mosley said. "He'll testify. If he doesn't he knows I'll call the federal judge. Or his wife." He smiled. "He'll testify damned fast when she's through with him. I never had anything like this before. Tearing up an exhibit. He might as well have hit me in the face."

Smith, Parks, and Zaher were in the office that day, too, and they all were brought to Luigi's for lunch.

"Listen," Mosley said to them, "one thing has to be straight. There isn't going to be any more of this. I don't care about the federal prosecutor, what he did or didn't do. You're in my ball game now. I'm playing straight with you, and I expect you to play straight with me. I don't need this case. I'm not going to get fired if I lose it. You understand? I'm going to play it straight down the middle with you. But I don't need any more of that stuff there with Cordero. It's my ball game, and we're going to play it my way."

They nodded silently. Even Parks appeared subdued.

Cordero soon forgot his anger at Mosley, but reports arrived from the jail that he and Smith and Parks were making trouble there. The witnesses claimed that inmates, not prison guards, were handling their food, and that they were afraid of being poisoned. They had complained to the warden about a guard who let an inmate deliver their food, and now, they said, the guard was trying to get back at them. In a moment of anger Smith had told one of the guards, a little too explicitly, what he thought of him. As punishment he had been locked up by himself, away from the others.

All the witnesses complained that their rations had been cut, toilet paper withheld, that razor blades were a hundred shaves old, and that guards went through the cells at night banging keys. Each group of cells had a television set rented by the DA's office. The sets were plugged into sockets beyond reach outside the bars. Cordero said he and Smith had been watching a baseball game on one of the sets, and when it was in the ninth inning with the score tied, two out and a man on third, a guard walked by and kicked out the plug.

Cordero was brought in to see Mosley and said that he thought it was bad for Smith to be taken from the jail to the DA's office. He said he thought the trips depressed Smith, that he had been in jail so long the trips only reminded him of what the outside was like. A plainclothesman who had guarded Smith supported this suggestion.

"When I took him to lunch yesterday," the plainclothesman said, "he got upset because I was married. He said he wanted single men guarding him because they would keep him out longer in the afternoon. The married ones were in too big a hurry to get home. When I said I had to take him back, he dropped his drink on the floor. After a while he really gets carried away. He gets where he's annoyed that you're there, like he's thinking, 'Hey, buddy, stop following me around.'"

Cordero said the guards were persecuting him and the other witnesses and that all of them were fed up. He wanted to know why Mosley didn't get the state to put up a little money and keep them in a hotel. "Or we could even stay right here," he said, looking around the office. "All we really need is just three cots and a TV."

A few days after Cordero's visit, the warden called Mosley and said he had had enough of the witnesses and was going to kick them out. They were making too much trouble. He said Mosley would have to find some other jail for them. They were federal prisoners, the warden said, and he was only keeping them to do the government a favor.

Mosley knew it would be almost impossible to find another jail where the witnesses would be available to him and at the same time safe from assassination. He listened to the warden's complaints and then said, "Well, you can kick them out, and then you're even with them and you got back at them, but my trial gets shot down. They've got to be available to me, and they've got to be alive."

He hung up and turned to Price.

"That's ridiculous," he said. "He's got three prisoners and he can't control them in a jail like that?"

The warden cooled off and kept the witnesses, but a few days later Mosley got word that there had been more trouble and that now the witnesses were all locked up in solitary in separate cells and had gone on a hunger strike. Again they claimed that inmates were delivering their food.

Eleanor Cordero, who had more influence over John than Mosley and the federal government combined, came into the office, and Mosley explained the problem to her. "If they don't start eating," he said, "the warden's going to get rid of them."

"If *John* doesn't start eating," she yelled, "*I'll* get rid of him."

"If he loses any more weight," Price contributed, "he'll be able to walk out by himself."

"I don't know what ulterior motives they might have for this," Mosley said. "They've got nothing to do out there but think. They may be trying to force things to the point where I'd have to put them in a hotel."

Eleanor said something about John getting poisoned by another prisoner.

"Look," Mosley said, "I've got four witnesses and with any one of them I've got a case, and if two get killed in prison then I go into court with that and I'm a winner. They're not going to poison all four. They're not going to poison anyone."

A couple of days later the witnesses were eating again, but they were still in trouble. Parks was brought in. He had a thick, black, two-day growth of beard, and he was full of fury.

"We're all locked up separately, alone," he said angrily to Price. "We've got short rations and they won't let us shave. If we're not out of that jail in two days, we're going to grab a guard and put a sheet around his neck and hold him as a hostage."

Mosley spoke to Parks, promised to do what he could, and Parks quieted down.

As the great witness war continued, another problem eased quietly toward crisis. To win a conviction in a Mafia murder case, a prosecutor must be assisted by a miracle or two, and even to get the defendants to trial can be a minor victory. In the case of the defendant John Matera, Franzese's driver and bodyguard, the road to trial was fought with particular bitterness.

Some time after Matera's participation in The Hawk killing—he helped hold The Hawk down while another man stabbed him—Matera went to Florida and tried to stick up a hotel. He was arrested, tried, and, in view of his superlative criminal record, sentenced to life imprisonment. His attorney was preparing an appeal, and Matera had little desire to return to New York for still another trial—certainly not one for first-degree murder. A life sentence in Florida offered the hope of parole after only eight years. In New York a life sentence was not parolable for twenty-seven and two-thirds years.

Matera's lawyer, a man named Louis Vernell, had a reputation as the top hood lawyer in Miami—and he looked it. Lean and wiry, Vernell was an anxious, quick-gestured little man with well-greased black wavy hair and a nervous habit of toying with the curls at his left temple. He evidently had orders to fight Matera's extradition with every gimmick and dollar at his disposal, and that promised quite a fight.

Mosley went to Miami to try to get Matera. He took with him Joe Price and Walter Anderson, whose job it would be to escort Matera back to New York if all of Vernell's legal barriers could be overcome.

Mosley faced two battles. He must first convince the Florida authorities—the State Attorney's Office—to agree to lend Matera to New York for trial. He then would have to go into court and convince a judge that Matera could be legally removed to New York. For that he would have to prove the three classic conditions of extradition: that Matera was actually in New York at the time the act charged in the indictment was committed, that the act charged was in fact a crime in the state of New York, and that Matera was actually the man named in the indictment.

That would not be difficult. The real enemy was time. Matera could be extradited, but could he be extradited in time to be in Queens County court June 5, the trial date?

"You have to remember," Mosley told Price and Anderson, "that this guy's got about nine million rights. He's a prisoner in custody, and he's got rights on top of rights."

Mosley arrived in Miami May 26, a Friday. Vernell intended to move for a new trial for Matera on the hotel-robbery charge. He was scheduled to make the motion June 13, eight days after Mosley's trial was supposed to begin. Normally it is not necesssary for the defendant to be in court when his attorney argues for a new trial, but Vernell was insisting that he needed Matera there. Obviously, if Matera was in court in Miami the thirteenth, he could not be in New York. Mosley's first job was to talk the judge into changing the June 13 date.

On Monday, May 29, Mosley went before a Miami judge and argued to have Vernell's motion for a new trial rescheduled. As the problem was discussed, the judge appeared ready to reschedule the motion for June 2 or 3, giving Mosley two or three days to get Matera out of Florida and into New York. Vernell jumped to his feet and in a flurry of rapid-fire phrases argued violently against the early date: "Your honor, the motion for new trial is expected to be quite lengthy. . . . To say that I could conceivably do this in this period of time . . . would place the defendant in a prejudicial position. . . . I'm sure the court would want to indulge him in every possible way . . . to see that his rights are protected. . . . The rights of the defendant should be protected. . . ."

The judge relented but set another date equally displeasing to Vernell. He said he would hear the motion August 23, giving Mosley plenty of time to try Matera in New York and then return him to Florida. Mosley promised to get him back to Florida regardless of the verdict in New York.

Mosley's victory in getting the date changed lasted only hours. An assistant state attorney, who had at first agreed to let Mosley have Matera, reappeared before the judge—without Mosley—and abruptly changed his position. He had thought things over, he said, and had discussed the matter with one of his office's extradition experts. He now thought it unwise to let Matera leave Florida before the motion for a new trial was heard. The judge quickly reset the June 13 date.

Matera would not technically begin serving his Florida sentence until the motion for a new trial had been heard, and the Florida authorities were afraid that if they let go of him before he started his sentence, they might never see him again. New York might keep him. Or in juggling him around between states, some obscure legal technicality might be violated, giving him further grounds for appeal.

While Mosley and assistant state attorneys probed the dense underbrush of legal technicalities, Price took a walk over to the jail and had a chat with Matera himself. He returned to the State Attorney's Office with interesting news.

"We're in there talking, throwing curves at each other," Price told Mosley, "and he asks what are his odds of beating this case—60-40, 50-50, 40-60? He's jolted. He's not worried about this bit here—eight years—he's worried about up there. Then he says to me, 'Do you want another witness?' And later when I start to leave he comes after me, 'Look, can't we have some coffee or something?' Maybe he wants to come over, Jimmy. Maybe on a long train ride back to New York?"

Mosley said that if Matera would plead guilty and testify

for the state he would give him second-degree man-slaughter instead of murder one. But he doubted if he would take it. "You see, once he pleads guilty he loses all hope. Now he can tell himself that with the way things are going these days in appeals courts he might get reversals on his convictions. But if he takes a guilty plea to something, that's it."

"Something else," Price said. "He told me he had heard that we came down Friday to get him. How did he know that? Vernell hasn't seen him. Who told him?"

"Interesting how these guys always know everything," Mosley said.

An assistant state attorney advised Mosley that it would help matters considerably if he could get an extradition warrant from the governor of Florida. This could take weeks under normal conditions, but if Mosley went to the state capitol in Tallahassee himself he might be able to get one faster, possibly in a day. The attorney called the capitol, then reported to Mosley that if he was there Wednesday morning he might be able to have the warrant that day and be back in Miami in time to have Matera by the end of the week.

Mosley and Price flew to Tallahassee at seven-thirty Wednesday morning. The governor's assistant for legal matters was an energetic young man named Gerald Mager. Mosley explained the case, pointing out that Matera had been seen pinning the murdered man to the ground while he was stabbed.

"It's an extraordinary case," Mosley said, trying to win as much extra effort from Mager as he could. "It's a gangland killing with witnesses. As a matter of fact it's the first gangland killing that's come to trial in New York in twenty years. And if we don't have Matera in New York by the fifth—or by the twelfth, if I can get a week's postpone-ment—he will never be tried for this murder. It's as simple as that."

Mager's concern was with getting Matera back to Florida after the New York trial. He decided that before the governor could issue an extradition warrant for Matera, he would need an agreement from New York's Governor Rockefeller to return Matera to Florida. The promise would have to be in writing, signed. He finally agreed to accept a telegram, with the assurance that a formal document would follow.

Mosley called the legal assistant in Rockefeller's office in Albany. It was still early in the day and he hoped to have the telegram and the warrant by that evening. Rockefeller's assistant was unimpressed by the need for speed. "I'll see about it and call you back around three-thirty," he said to Mosley on the phone.

Mosley looked angry and frustrated.

"Oh, come on," he said. "Not until then? How long can it take?"

The assistant reluctantly agreed to check immediately and call back.

"All right, I'll sit right here," Mosley said. He hung up and waited by the phone.

After thirty minutes, Mosley again called Albany. The assistant had gone to lunch. His secretary said he would be back about two-thirty.

Mosley waited.

At three-fifteen he again called Rockefeller's office. The assistant had not returned. Mosley was disgusted. "I could understand if they had to make a *decision*," he said. "But this is routine. All they have to do is send a telegram."

Mosley was standing by the desk of Mager's extradition

clerk, an efficient, get-things-done type of girl named Ruthie Dickson. She lifted a telegram that had just been put on her desk. "Maybe this is it," she said, and began to read aloud: "Am advised that extradition request will be made upon you by the state of New York re John Matera. . . ." It went on to request a formal governor's hearing on the extradition, and was signed by Louis Vernell.

"Beautiful," said Price. Mosley looked angry. A governor's hearing would mean a delay of days or weeks.

"They're pulling out all the stops," Mosley said. Maybe Matera had dropped something to Vernell similar to his remark to Price about "Do you want another witness?" Maybe they had decided that if he was thinking along those lines, they had better do everything possible to keep him away from anyone who might talk to him and offer a chance or a reason for changing sides.

"You know," Miss Dickson said, "there is precedent for not granting a hearing. The governor almost always does grant it, but he isn't required to."

To encourage Miss Dickson's willingness to help him get Matera, Mosley reached in his briefcase and pulled out a photograph of The Hawk's trussed and bloated body.

"This is the deceased," he said, holding up the picture a few feet in front of her. She winced but took the picture and examined it with interest. He showed her Matera's yellow sheet, his criminal record. "This is no Joe Jerk who killed his wife, you know," he said.

Mager returned from his lunch, and Miss Dickson showed him Vernell's telegram. She pointed out that the governor did not absolutely have to grant the hearing. She and Mosley both knew that the governor was likely to do whatever Mager suggested.

Mager agreed that perhaps the governor could deny

Vernell's request. "When Rockefeller's man calls back," he said to Mosley, "tell him to add to the telegram—in addition to everything about agreeing to return Matera to Florida—that the trial is scheduled for the fifth and that it is imperative that Matera be there on that date."

At three-thirty Rockefeller's assistant finally called from Albany. He promised to have the telegram out within thirty minutes. Mager saw the governor and got his agreement to deny the hearing and to issue the warrant when the telegram arrived. Miss Dickson was having the warrant drawn up. It was 4 P.M. The office closed at five. Mosley and Price had reservations on a 6 P.M. plane for Miami.

By five-thirty the telegram had not arrived. Miss Dickson gave Mosley the warrant anyway, on his promise not to serve it until he heard from her the next morning that the telegram was there.

Back in Miami the next afternoon, Mosley went into court again. "I have been to the state capitol," he said to the judge, the same one he had appeared before Monday. "I have a governor's warrant. I am expecting motions to be made by defense counsel. He has already asked for a governor's hearing, which has been denied."

Mosley asked that if the date for Vernell's motion for a new trial could not be postponed until after the murder trial, could it not be brought forward a few days. Then if Mosley could get his murder case put off a week, until the twelfth, he might have a chance of getting Matera.

"I don't mind losing murder cases," Mosley said to the judge, "but I would like at least a chance to try this one. If I cannot start, Matera will never be tried for this crime of murder in the first degree. That should not be."

The judge shifted on the bench. Reporters, as well as many attorneys, were in the room and he was reluctant to have it look as if he had had anything to do with Matera beating a murder trial.

"Let me ask you this, sir," he said to Mosley. "I am not expecting you to tell me your case, but what is the problem, June 13 being actually less than two weeks away? What is the problem if you don't try the case next week? You are losing the opportunity to try him at all?"

"It is very possible," Mosley answered, "that a severance [a separate trial for Matera] will be granted, and this is not the type of case where I can try four defendants and then one defendant. In any case, it is alleged that he held the deceased down while another man stabbed him about eighteen times after the deceased had been shot in the head. He was then thrown into Jamaica Bay. He floated up some three weeks later. It is very impractical to try four and then at a later time to try one, especially in view of the fact that my witnesses are in jail."

Mosley's recitation of a few of the more brutal aspects of the case had seized the attention of the courtroom.

"At least," said the judge, "you don't have a problem with the witnesses."

Price smiled.

"Oh, yes, I do. I do," Mosley said with feeling. "I have a problem keeping them. One of them is a material witness. The others are federal prisoners, and they pose a great problem to me. One of the defendants is a young lad in his twenties who has been continually making motions for a speedy trial or for a severance. So while I have Mr. Matera, who never wants to go to trial, I have another defendant who is quite anxious."

"What you are saying," the judge said, "is that the trial judge would be apt to grant a severance and force you to trial on the other four if you are not there [with Matera]?"

"That is correct," Mosley said. "Plus if I don't start next week I feel certain I will have to go over until the fall term, which will cause great problems with these witnesses. They have been given a type of sentence where a federal judge can take into consideration their forthrightness in a state court, so to speak, and they are quite anxious. I have already received a telegram from Governor Rockefeller, which is in the state capitol at Tallahassee, in which he has agreed that after the end of my proceedings in Queens County, no matter what the outcome, the prisoner will be rushed here at the state of New York's expense. I would ask, your honor, if you could possibly advance the date. Because if it is not advanced, I know that he will file a habeas corpus on the thirteenth and then delay. In other words, it will be drawn out as long as possible."

"When is the trial scheduled to begin?"

"The fifth, but I can foresee and handle a week's adjournment."

The judge thought for a moment. "One P.M., June 9. That is the best I can do."

"Thank you very much, your honor," Mosley said.

The next day Mosley went before a judge in circuit court to set the earliest possible date for the habeas corpus hearing, at which Vernell would argue that Matera could not legally be removed to New York. Mosley hoped that if he won that hearing, a request for an appeal would not be granted, and he could take Matera.

Vernell was in court, too, all smiles and good spirits. He spotted some local detectives in the hall. "Hi there," he called to them, "nice to see you guys some place besides in my rear-view mirror." They nodded but did not smile.

Vernell listened while the judge set the habeas corpus hearing for 4 P.M., June 9, three hours after his motion for a new trial. Outside court, he said hello to Mosley and smiled broadly. "You do get around," he said, referring to the trip to Tallahassee.

"I am going to get him if it takes me a hundred years," Mosley said.

"That's about how long it will take," Vernell said smiling, and then added sarcastically, "What's wrong, Mr. Mosley, don't you like it down here?"

"Oh, I'd like it a lot if it weren't for a certain consideration—the certain consideration being the administration of justice."

On June 5 another assistant DA appeared in the Queens court for Mosley, explained the absence, and received a one-week postponement.

On Wednesday, two days before Vernell's new trial motion and the habeas corpus hearing, Mosley got a call from an assistant in New York. Charlie Zaher, the assistant said, had decided he had had enough of civil jail. He was complaining that a prisoner with mob connections had arrived and that he was not safe. He wanted out and had sent a letter and a telegram to a judge requesting a hearing. Mosley said to try to keep the lid on, that he would be back soon.

At 1 P.M. on the ninth, Vernell made his argument for a new trial. It was immediately denied.

At 4 P.M. Mosley and Price showed up at the chambers of circuit-court judge James King for the habeas corpus hearing. Price, an optimist, had handcuffs with him. A Miami detective asked Mosley what would happen if Vernell came up with a witness who said he had been drinking with Matera in Miami the day of the murder.

"That'd be hard for them," Mosley said, "because I've got a lot of ammunition. I've got grand-jury minutes that put him in New York. Price can testify to information that puts him in New York. And he's got a record a mile long. They're going to put up some bum who says he was with him? I almost wish they would. Then I'd make him stick with that alibi at the trial, and by then we'd have it shot down good."

At the hearing, Vernell ignored the three standard requirements for extradition and instead argued that Matera should not be extradited for the simple reason that he had never fled from New York in the first place, that he was not a fugitive from justice. It was true, he argued, that Matera had left New York after the murder. But following his arrest in Miami he had been returned to New York for a federal trial, then taken back to Miami. His last trip to Miami had been made under custody, as a prisoner, and he had not fled illegally.

The judge listened to that argument, immediately rejected it, and discharged the petition for habeas corpus.

Vernell instantly replied that he would appeal the judge's ruling—and asked the judge not to let Matera out of Florida until the appeal was heard.

"We will direct the sheriff of this county," the judge said, "to hold the prisoner here pending the outcome of the appeal."

That put an end to Mosley's fight.

The look on Mosley's face when he walked out of the judge's chambers told Price he would not need the handcuffs. "Win the battle, lose the war," Mosley said, angry and disgusted. "We won the habeas corpus, but we still don't have the prisoner."

It was Friday, June 9. The trial was on for Monday. Mosley had been in Florida two weeks. Zaher was sure to get his hearing within a few days. Vernell's appeal could drag on for no one knew how long.

Mosley would have to go back without Matera. He would try to keep in touch by phone with the Florida State Attorney's Office, but they had their own problems and could not be expected to fight his war for him. He knew he would never see Matera in court.

When the trial date arrived, Franzese's lawyer pleaded that he was involved with other business and asked for still another delay. The judge consented and set the new date for July 6.

The witnesses continued with their pressure tactics. Cordero, Parks, and Smith said Sonny had sent word to them in jail that he would give them each $20,000 if they dumped the case. Though Zaher was reporting no bribe offers from civil jail, he was not without demands. A court hearing on his request to be released from jail—to have his bail lowered from $10,000 to an amount he could raise—was scheduled for the Monday after Mosley's return from Miami.

Before the hearing, Zaher was brought to Mosley's office. He was angry at his inability to get out of jail, and Mosley was angry that he was trying.

"What's your problem?" Mosley asked curtly.

"I don't have a problem," Zaher answered arrogantly, trying not very successfully to keep a grip on his temper.

"That's good," Mosley said, shuffling some papers on his desk.

"Just the hearing," Zaher added. "What are you going to do about the hearing?"

"What are *you* going to do about it," Mosley said hotly. "You wanted it."

"What's your protest?" Zaher said.

"What's *your* protest?" Mosley said.

"Why you don't want to let me out. That's my protest."

"I don't want to let you out," Mosley said loudly and slowly, as if to a small, not very bright child, "because I'm afraid you'll get killed."

"But you don't care what happens after the trial. I can't stay in jail the rest of my life, you know."

"I'm doing everything I can to get this case to trial and get it over with," Mosley said.

"So what are you going to tell the judge? Why can't I get out?"

"One, I don't want to let you out because of security. You might get killed. Two, because you're a junkie and I don't want you sticking a needle in your arm. Three, because of your criminal record. I don't want you sticking up another bank. And four, because you might flee and we'd never be able to find you. That's why."

Zaher was furious. "I'm not staying there till the sixth," he shouted. "I'll escape. I don't *like* jail, you know. You seem to have the impression I like jail. And if I do have to stay there until the sixth, then I'm not testifying."

"Oh, really?"

"If I'm on the street, I'll testify. But not if I'm in jail. I've been in for twenty months and I'm getting out now."

But he did not get out—at least not for a while. Bail was maintained, and he went back to civil jail.

Willie Rupoli, The Hawk's brother, came to Mosley's office and once again went over what he would tell the jury about identifying the body.

"You got a good case on Sonny?" he asked Mosley. "He couldn't of been there. The guy makes the contract is never there. He could of been waiting a few blocks away some place, but he wasn't there. It'd be hard getting a good case on Sonny."

"Yeah," Mosley said. "Well, Sonny has a big mouth."

To block the defense's contention that Parks, Cordero, Smith, and Zaher made up their stories to win light sentences for themselves, Mosley badly needed a fifth witness.

"The big problem is credibility," he said. "How do I keep the jury from thinking that these four guys cooked this whole story up in jail to buy time? If I had one legitimate citizen who saw them in the Aqueduct Motel that night of the sit-down—but how many legitimate people even went into that place?"

A legitimate citizen he did not have, but there was a thin, nervous gunman named John Rapacki. A few weeks after the murder, one of the defendants, Red Crabbe, had told Rapacki that he had helped to kill The Hawk. He had pointed to a picture of The Hawk in a newspaper and said, "We had to take care of him for the boss."

Now, three years later, Rapacki was in prison serving nine to ten years for assault and robbery. He came forward and agreed to repeat on the witness stand what Crabbe had told him. The actual words of the admission were not important—they added little to Mosley's case—but the man who had heard them was vital to Mosley's strategy. For John Rapacki did not know any of the other witnesses, had never even spoken to them, and could not possibly have contrived with any of them to invent a case against Franzese. Mosley intended to put Cordero, Parks, Zaher, and Smith on the stand, and let the defense scream that their entire stories were lies, concocted jointly to gain leniency. He would then—as his last witness—offer Rapacki, who would repeat Crabbe's admission and then go on to reveal that the other witnesses were total strangers to him.

"And there really isn't that much I can do to help Rapacki," Mosley said. "He's already doing time, and his cooperation can't get his sentence reduced. The main reason he's helping is probably just the hope that if I write a letter to his parole board and tell them he cooperated, they might parole him a little earlier than they would otherwise."

In prison Rapacki had studied law continuously and without assistance had won a reduction of his sentence on a technical point. He was an intensely serious, suspicious man, and harbored strong hatred and deep respect for Sonny and his men. In Mosley's office he spoke of their violence as casually as other men discuss the weather. He said he had liked working with Matera and Crabbe because they were "real stand-up guys. If you were on a job and they had to hit someone, they hit him. They didn't panic. If they had to shoot a cop, they shot him."

On July 6 Franzese's lawyer claimed ill health and managed still another delay for the defense. This time the judge put the trial down for September.

Nine days after the postponement, Zaher made good his threat—he and a companion escaped from civil jail. They filed through a light lock on a prison door, lifted $71 from the jail commissary, and fled down a fire escape. Zaher, who was getting $3 a day from Queens County as a material witness, left a characteristic note: "Get the money from Mr. Mosley in Queens."

For five days police searched quietly for Zaher, hoping to avoid news stories that would alert the Mafia to his freedom. When it became necessary to issue an alarm, the New

York *Daily News* quickly picked it up and headlined, "Police Racing Mafia for Escaped Informer."

Zaher hove back into view the following month when two radio-car patrolmen grabbed him and his escape companion near a Queens bank. They found a gun in Zaher's waistband, a stocking mask in his pocket, and an Avis car rented in his name idling up the block.

Zaher said he had spent his forty days of freedom with girl friends in Florida. He said he had bought the gun for self-protection. The stocking, he said, was to control his hair, which he had had done in an elaborate hippie hairdo at a cost of $50. It was not the bank he was going to rob, but a bookmaker who made deposits there. The police locked him up.

In September, Franzese's lawyer was involved in another case, and the trial was again postponed, this time until October 28. On that day the lawyer startled everyone by agreeing to begin—positively—on November 2, the following Thursday.

Before Zaher could be returned to one of the high-security cells at the Nassau County jail, he lived a brief life of terror in the Queens House of Detention. Some Mafia hoods were locked up with him, and one of them was Red Crabbe. Zaher told Mosley there were rumors among the prisoners that Franzese had offered an open contract of $50,000 to anyone who murdered him.

"I'm in there," Zaher said, trembling, "and I hear them yelling from the cells, 'If you can't make bail, hit Zaher and get fifty grand!' Even if it's not true, they don't know that. They'll kill me anyway."

The Tuesday before the trial starts, Zaher (who later that day will move back to the Nassau County jail) and the other three witnesses are brought together in Mosley's office. Zaher walks in last, and when he comes through the door, Parks smiles and says, "Hi, Blackie. I hear I can get fifty big ones if I kill you."

Zaher smiles, a little proud to have that price on his head, but still very frightened. He says that another prisoner represented by Franzese's lawyer told him that there was in fact a $50,000 price on his head, and that he himself could collect $250,000 if he agreed to sabotage the case.

"Did he say how long they'd give you to spend it?" Cordero asks.

"Crabbe found me in there," Zaher goes on, "and told me I'd get the $250,000 and everything would be all right, everything would be rectified."

Cordero laughs contemptuously. "He doesn't even know what rectified means."

Zaher is sitting on a table across from Mosley's desk, and with the other witnesses, plus Price and two guards, the office is jammed.

"So you just told him you'd think it over, right?" Parks says.

"Right," Zaher says. "And then he sees me going out this morning with all my belongings and it's like he's thinking, 'Hey, where are you taking him? He's with us!'"

"What else did he tell you?" Parks asks.

"He said they were going to push us hard, that each one of us would be on the stand for two weeks. He said they thought they had a 75-25 chance of beating the case."

"Yeah," Cordero says, "he's got to be optimistic. When you're going up for your natural life, you've got to be optimistic or you'll hang yourself in your cell."

"Crabbe told me, 'Do the right thing, and we'll get you so-and-so for a lawyer. Remember, you've got a wife and two kids, and if you have to do time, Sonny'll take care of them.' He said, 'How long do you think you'll last on the street anyway? The others will all be dead within a year.' He said if I agreed to go along with them, they'd give me $50,000 right away, before I testified, but like if I reneged on them they'd get my wife and kids. He said he didn't blame me, that I had to go along with the others, but now I should stop."

All four sit silent, thinking. Price and Mosley exchange glances.

Cordero leans forward, elbows on knees, and suddenly shakes his head in anger. "I'll let Sonny know," he says, "that if he hurts my family, I'll get him. He has a family too. He can bleed like everyone else."

"He says we're all dead," Zaher says, not trying to cover his fear. "He says they'll get each one of us."

"They may be surprised when it doesn't happen," Cordero says.

Zaher shakes his head doubtfully. "I can't go along with that. I'm pessimistic. They'll spend any amount of money. They'll hunt for us. They'll hunt, and they'll hunt, and they'll hunt."

The trial begins. Franzese's co-defendants—Florio, Crabbe, and a young baby-faced hoodlum named Thomas Matteo— sit with their lawyers at tables arranged in a semicircle on the left of the courtroom. (Matera is absent; Florida still refuses to let him out of the state.) At the center of the semicircle is another table, and there with his lawyer sits Franzese. The position is unfortunate for him, and the first mistake his lawyer has made. For there, surrounded by the others, he looks like what he is: a king at the center of his court. He is clearly the boss, and that is a dangerous piece of information to give the jury.

The jurors, when they are selected, will sit to the far right of the courtroom, facing the defendants, staring into the eyes of Franzese. Between them will be the judge's bench and in front of it, slightly to the right, a single table occupied by Mosley.

The courtroom is jammed with some two hundred citizens, almost all of them men, who have been summoned there as prospective jurors. The court clerk spins a drum, opens a panel in the side, and pulls out a slip of paper. He reads the name on the paper, and in the back of the courtroom an old man collects his coat and a book he has been reading, pushes past the others sitting by him on the pewlike seats, and hurries nervously down the aisle. A court officer directs him into the witness chair and administers the oath.

Mosley begins his questions.

Because probing a prospective juror's mind, trying to uncover the prejudices that lie hidden there, is too great a task for the few minutes available, defense attorneys and prosecutors fall back on systems composed variously of experience, intuition, and guesswork. For the prosecutor, the ideal juror is first of all a man (less sentimental than a woman, less reluctant to have a hand in punishment); he is getting on into middle age (too mature and experienced to be hoodwinked, more responsible than a youngster); his dress and appearance are ordinary, conservative, lacking mannerisms that suggest homosexuality or other maladjustments (a neurotic man might be too easily influenced or given to whim); his job suggests responsibility and steadiness, and he has held it a number of years; he is married and has children. At times the selection can get racial:

Negroes and Jews, because of a history of oppression, may be too lenient, less willing to punish. And in a Mafia case, Italians might be connected with the mob, or fearful of its vengeance.

The selection of jurors is critical—often the most critical portion of a trial. "What's a shame," Mosley says, "is that the case can be won or lost the first two days and you don't know it. A prospective juror comes up and it's 'What's your name?' 'McCarthy.' 'What do you do?' 'Engineer.' 'For whom?' 'Telephone Company.' 'How long?' 'Twenty years.' 'Married?' 'Yes.' 'Children?' 'Yes.' And he's a solid, upstanding citizen, and you accept him, and he's a juror. Little do you know that he had a run-in with a cop once and he wouldn't believe your witnesses the longest day he ever lived.

"I had a case once," Mosley continued, "and it was the most solid case I had ever had. There were no problems, no holes, it was solid. And the jury came back in, 'Not guilty.' I couldn't believe it. I went back into the jury room to talk to them and I could tell from the faces who the leader had been. Everyone looked very quiet and meek. Except the foreman, and he was strong, positive. I told him I had had weak cases before and lost them, but this one was solid, this one I shouldn't have lost. I asked him what went wrong. And he said he was just *positive* the guy was innocent. I told him I had a confession from the defendant that I couldn't use because of a technicality. I told him the defendant had actually confessed. His face dropped down to his knees. But the defendant walked."

Any prospective juror can be excluded from the jury "for cause" if he indicates an obvious inability to judge the case responsibly and impartially. If spending all day in court creates such problems at work that he can't keep his mind on the trial, he is excused. If he says he thinks everyone who comes to trial is guilty, he is excused. If he says he thinks all DAs are crooked and he wouldn't believe any of their witnesses, he is excused.

If there is no clear cause for dismissal, the prospective juror can still be excused on the arbitrary challenge of either the prosecutor or the defense. Normally, each side has twenty of these "peremptory" challenges, and they use them sparingly to exclude prospective jurors they consider dangerous to their cause. In this particular trial, the defense has asked that the number of peremptory challenges be increased to thirty. The judge has agreed.

As the drum is spun, and each prospective juror takes the stand and answers questions, it becomes clear that the screening process is going to take many days. Mosley's questions are generally routine and brief—occupation, years at the job, marital status—but the defense attorneys are more inquisitive.

They use the questions to condition the jurors. Of the many prospective jurors in the courtroom, twelve will eventually decide the case. No one knows which twelve, but whoever they are, they are in the courtroom listening. The defense's main argument will be that the prosecution witnesses are too evil and wicked to be believed, that they invented their stories to win light sentences for themselves. And so as each prospective juror takes the stand, the same questions come from the defense, each time loud enough to carry through the courtroom to the ears of the twelve people who will finally decide the case.

The attack is led by Maurice Edelbaum, attorney for Franzese. He is a short, fat man, 61 years old, with curly gray balding hair, rumpled suit, and horn-rimmed glasses. His voice is squeaking, grating, high-pitched; he has an ego immeasurably vast, and an arrogance his opponents find difficult to tolerate. In thirty-eight years of trial work he has defended whole dynasties of top Mafia executives, and played a major role in defending the Mafia hierarchy corralled in the 1957 Apalachin raid. In 1960 he himself took a guilty plea—to income-tax evasion—and the New York State Supreme Court suspended him from practice six months for failing to "observe and advise his client to observe the statute law" and for neglecting "to strive at all times to uphold the honor and to maintain the dignity of the profession and to improve not only the law but the administration of justice."

Now he goes to work again. "The people will call witnesses," he yells at a prospective juror, "who are *criminals,* bank robbers, drug addicts, who have not stopped at anything in their lives to get what they wanted. And they will testify here because they have made a deal to get years taken off their sentences. These are men who have gone into banks with *loaded guns,* and taken money that did not belong to them."

Loaded guns. The words come again and again. Edelbaum screams them, whispers them, spits them out. Mosley is not allowed to point out that the man who sent the witnesses into banks with loaded guns is Mr. Edelbaum's client, the same Sonny Franzese.

Over and over Edelbaum hammers equally at "the deal." The witnesses, he shouts, went into banks with loaded guns and when they were caught they made *a deal* with the prosecutor for light sentences. "Would you take *a good hard look* at that testimony? You would, wouldn't you? *Wouldn't you?*"

The defense uses the jury selection process, too, to drive into the jurors' minds the trial ground rules. The jurors must have read nothing about the defendants, heard nothing about them. They must not feel that the indictment of these defendants, that their presence in court, hints even slightly of their guilt. The defense is required to do nothing to prove innocence. The defendants need not speak. The defense lawyers need not speak. It is entirely up to the prosecutor to prove guilt. The defendant *is* innocent, until and unless the prosecutor can prove him guilty beyond a reasonable doubt.

A reasonable doubt means any doubt, any doubt at all for which you can give a reason. Not a capricious doubt, but a doubt with a reason. One doubt for which you can state an honest reason, and the defendant remains innocent.

"And I tell you—" Edelbaum is shouting at a prospective juror, but his words are meant for those twelve people in the courtroom who will finally be selected—"that before this trial is over, you will find a *thousand reasonable doubts.* You wouldn't convict a *mongrel dog* on the testimony you will hear in this courtroom!"

In picking jurors, Mosley relies heavily on his own personal, intuitive feeling about the candidate. "Usually, if I can't relate to the man personally, if I feel I don't understand him, I challenge," he says. A Negro man takes the stand as a prospective juror and readily admits that he was arrested in 1923 for possession of policy slips. Some prosecutors might be put off by the man's criminal record. Mosley is not. He accepts him.

"It was a long time ago," Mosley explains, "and if he can get up there today and volunteer that he was once arrested, then he's got a respect for the law."

A department-store shipping clerk looks and talks a little too dumb, but mentions that he is uncertain about serving on the jury because it will put a burden on the other man who helps him with his job. Mosley accepts him. "You can tell that he is honestly worried about that other guy not being able to handle the job. He has a feeling of responsibility, and even if he isn't the brightest guy around, my bet is that he has a good hunk of common sense."

Another prospective juror has a couple of bad points, but he appears honest and has a tough job as a manual laborer. Mosley decides to accept him. "He works hard for his living. And these hoods? They never did a day's work in their lives. He's not too stupid to see that."

Towards the end of the selection process, when most of the jurors have been picked, the judge calls a short recess, and Mosley, detectives, and attorneys stand in the courthouse hall discussing the case.

"You can see how it's going to go," Mosley says. "There are two trials here. There's the People of the State of New York versus these defendants, and there's these defendants versus the witnesses. By the time Edelbaum's finished, he'll have the jurors wanting to free the defendants and lock up the witnesses. You'll want to jump up and say, 'The witnesses aren't on trial, the defendants are.' "

Someone says something about the technique and theory of picking a jury.

"The prosecutor's strategy always has to be, 'When in doubt, challenge,' " Mosley says. "Because I need twelve men who can agree unanimously that the defendants are guilty. But the defense only needs one. If they can get *one* guy on that jury who, because he's a nut, or afraid, or for any reason at all, just refuses to cast a guilty vote, then it's a hung jury and they're the winners. They'll have to go to trial again, but meanwhile the delays are going to hurt my case. So they're looking for just one guy."

The task is made more difficult because Mosley must

challenge first. He must use his challenges to get rid of prospective jurors who appear unstable, for fear that if he does not, the defense won't either. Even if an unstable man appears to be *against* the defense, they may take him anyway on the chance he will change his mind and turn out to be that one irrational voice that will give them a hung jury.

"You have to watch out for the double fake," Mosley says, "especially when you're down to just a couple of challenges left. If they want a certain juror and they can tell I'm undecided about him, they'll try to appear as if they don't want him. Then I don't challenge, thinking they will, and zap—'acceptable to the defense.'"

Both sides know very clearly the kind of man the other side is looking for, and use this knowledge to try to embarrass each other. A young Italian is called to the stand and Mosley asks a few standard questions, announces "No challenge for cause"—meaning simply that there is no obvious, compelling reason why the man should not serve—and sits down to await the defense questions. Meanwhile, Edelbaum has passed word down the line that all lawyers are to ask no questions. One after another, the defense lawyers stand and repeat, "No challenge for cause." Mosley, with no time to check if the man has a criminal record or Mafia connections, has no choice but to challenge. Spectators, including prospective jurors, think to themselves: "A nice-looking young man. Why doesn't the prosecutor like him? The defense was perfectly satisfied, didn't even ask a question."

But both sides can play that game. A middle-aged, conservative-looking man takes the stand. The clerk announces his name—Irish—and occupation—utilities-company foreman. Mosley stands and without questions says,

"Acceptable to the people." He sits down. Now the onus of rejection is on the defense.

By the sixth day of jury-picking, Mosley has used eighteen peremptory challenges, the defense nineteen. Nine jurors have been accepted, sworn, and are seated in the box. Mosley is about to begin questioning the next prospective juror when the defense attorneys say they wish to point out that the prosecutor has only two challenges remaining. Mosley replies that he has used eighteen, they nineteen. With thirty challenges per side, he has twelve left, they eleven. Sorry, says the defense, there must have been some misunderstanding. When they had suggested that the customary number of challenges be increased from twenty to thirty, they meant for them alone, not for the prosecution.

It is the first low blow of the trial, and it has landed clean and crippling. The first mention that the defense intended to ask for extra challenges had come to Mosley from one of the defense lawyers. He told the lawyer then that he had no objections, providing, of course, that the increase was for both sides. "Of course," the attorney assured him. Certainly no prosecutor would agree to an increase only for the other side.

Mosley, the defense attorneys, and the judge retire to the judge's chamber to discuss the problem. The judge is Albert Bosch, a tall, heavy, red-faced man with eyeglasses, graying hair, and a reputation for being defense-oriented. Many judges today bend over backwards to favor the defense, reasoning that if the trial ends in conviction, there will be little or no grounds for appeal. By doing so, however, they may greatly handicap the prosecution and reduce the chances of conviction. And often it may appear that the judge is working with an awareness of the embarrassment that can come with reversal in the appellate courts. Acquittals can never be reversed. If during the trial some error damages the defense, a multitude of legal remedies lie ready to reverse the wrong. But should some error injure the prosecution, it will stand without correction. Appeal is for the defendant. For the people there is no remedy.

On the point of challenges, Bosch sides with the defense and rules that Mosley did indeed have only two challenges remaining—to the defense's eleven. Mosley is shocked and incredulous. Price tries to encourage him. "Don't worry, Jim," he says. "The Lord will provide."

With only two challenges left, Mosley knows he will have to save them for emergencies—for prospective jurors who are clearly prejudiced against the people. Marginal cases will have to be ignored. He will have to depend on luck, and hope that the clerk's spinning drum does not turn up any kooks or tough-looking Italians.

To take as much advantage of his situation as possible, Mosley now stops asking any but the most essential questions. Man after man takes the stand, and Mosley rises, puts no questions, and announces, "Acceptable to the people." The least he can do is make it apparent to the prospective jurors that for some reason he has been put at a disadvantage and that rejection of jurors is now entirely in the hands of the defense.

After two days, the twelve jurors had been picked, and Mosley had been lucky. There were a couple of men he was uncertain about, but no one really dangerous.

Two alternate jurors had to be selected—to serve if any of the first twelve became sick—and for that process Mosley and the defense each had two challenges. The defense lawyers quickly used both of their challenges and were in the position of having to take anyone who came along. Luck did not serve them as it had Mosley. The drum spun, and a prospective juror came forward. The clerk announced the man's name and gave his occupation as "retired."

"What did you do before you were retired?" Mosley asked.

"I was a police lieutenant."

Price leaned to the man next to him and whispered, "What did I say? The Lord has provided."

For almost an hour the defense attorneys interrogated the man, trying to get him to say that he could not be impartial, trying to get the judge to excuse him for cause. One after another they rose and took their turn. Would he believe a policeman more than anyone else just because he had been a policeman? Would he give the advantage of a doubt to the prosecution because he had been a policeman? Would he refuse to take into account the background of the people's witnesses, just because they were testifying for the people?

The man was unshakable. He insisted that he would judge the case fairly and without bias. Finally, the defense sat down. Mosley rose, "Acceptable to the people."

The next day, the day testimony was to begin, word was passed to the judge that a copy of the New York *Daily News* had been seen in the jury room. The paper contained a story about the jury selection and pointed out that Franzese had already been convicted of bank robbery. If a juror had read the story, then he knew of Franzese's past and would presumably be unable to hear the case impartially. The judge called the jurors one by one into his chambers and questioned them about the story. Four admitted having read it. The judge declared a mistrial.

A week spent selecting jurors had been wasted. One

hundred and fifty citizens had been interrogated, at a cost to the state estimated at $5,000. Now the entire process would begin again. Said Mosley, "It's getting so the more notorious a guy is, the less chance he has of ever coming to trial."

The judge called newspaper reporters who were covering the trial into his chambers and asked that they request their papers not to print news that could prejudice the jurors. A *New York Times* story about Sonny Franzese had triggered a mistrial at the beginning of the bank-robbery trial, and now the *Daily News* story had done the same thing here. The reporters agreed to pass the request to their editors.

The next day the lawyers again gathered in the courtroom to start picking a new jury. In defiance of the judge's request, *The New York Times* that morning had printed a story about the case, mentioning Franzese's background. The jurors would have to be even more carefully scrutinized, to make sure they were ignorant not only of the *Daily News* story but of this recent *Times* story as well.

The day began with another blow for Mosley. The reservoir of prospective jurors had shrunk to only a few men, not enough to provide all the people who would be questioned that day. To replenish the supply, court officers brought a panel of prospective jurors over from civil court. These prospective jurors had been in civil court because they had expressed reluctance to serve in criminal cases.

"You know what that means," Mosley said. "It means they haven't got the guts to convict. They didn't want to sit on criminal cases in the first place, because they didn't want the responsibility of taking a hand in putting people in prison. And now here they are. That's wrong. We need a strong jury, and we won't get it from these people."

For the second jury-picking, both sides would have

twenty peremptory challenges. And, correcting their original error, the defense lawyers had seen to it that their tables were now placed in a straight row. Florio was nearest the jury, Franzese furthest away. To see Franzese, the jury now would have to look past nine other men.

On the final day of jury selection, the day before Mosley's first witness would finally take the stand, another disaster threatened. John Cordero's 15-year-old stepdaughter disappeared from home.

From the start it appeared that the disappearance had no connection with the trial. Yet Cordero had been threatened, his family had been threatened, and now just thirty-six hours before the witnesses would start to testify—the coincidence was frightening.

Eleanor said that at about ten-thirty Sunday night—testimony was to begin Tuesday morning—the girl left home to visit friends. Before she went out, Eleanor argued with her about how long she could stay out. Then Eleanor waited up. She never came home. Eleanor called the girl's friends. None had seen her. In the morning, she called Joe Price, then came into Mosley's office. Price, Mosley, and Eleanor discussed the problem. If she had run away because of her argument with Eleanor, then she was probably safe somewhere and would soon return. But if she had been kidnapped, a police alarm should be issued immediately. The alarm, however, would have to include her last name—which was not Cordero—and her address, pieces of information that had been guarded with great care. No one could be sure the alarm would not find its way to a newspaper reporter. Page-one headlines that the stepdaughter of a key prosecution witness had vanished on the eve of trial would be almost certain to precipitate another mistrial. And the damage done to the girl—the public exposure, the involvement in the case—would be severe.

John was brought to the office. He agreed that possibly she was staying with a friend. Rather than risk exposure of her name and address, he suggested waiting out the day and night and seeing if she did not show up by the next morning. If she did not, then the police would have to issue an alarm and go all out to locate her.

"She picked one helluva time to run away," Eleanor said, and started re-calling her daughter's friends. Then she went out on foot, walking the neighborhood. At eight-thirty that night she found her daughter, wandering in a park. She had been with a friend.

Tuesday morning, and the judge looks down from the bench and says, "Mr. Mosley, you may open to the jury."

Mosley stands, moves out from behind his table, and takes a couple of steps to the jury box. He faces the jurors, tries to assess them: all men, none too young, four pairs of eyeglasses, one mustache, one bow tie; a white-haired German bartender; another white-haired man, very thin, with slits for eyes; a distinguished gray-headed fellow with a Scottish accent. The judicial net has been cast into a sea of man-on-the-street mediocrity and returned what Clarence Darrow once described as "twelve men of average ignorance." They stare at Mosley, eager for some hint of what the case is all about. They are attentive but impassive, subdued by the hammering harangues of the defense lawyers. And over and over, every time the court has recessed for five minutes or a weekend, the judge, as is required of him, has warned them to read nothing, listen to nothing, talk to no one, seek no knowledge, accept no knowledge, preserve ignorance—for on their ignorance does justice depend. They are men groping in the dark. The trial will be a process not of discovery and enlightenment but of deception and concealment. Of the thirty or so people directly involved in the trial, the twelve men with the greatest responsibility—the jurors—will end up knowing the least about the case.

Mosley and the defense lawyers finish their opening statements to the jury, and the judge calls a five-minute recess. The courtroom empties into the hallway. Walter Anderson comes into the nearly empty courtroom wheeling a hand truck. He stops at Mosley's table and unloads two cardboard boxes and two concrete blocks tangled with rope and yellow nylon cord and chain. He slides the blocks and boxes under the table.

Outside in the hallway a crowd of young attorneys and reporters form around Edelbaum. He wisecracks with them, tells them he expects no problems with the case. Every time he speaks, they laugh.

The recess ends and Mosley calls his first witness, a police photographer who introduces pictures of The Hawk's body. Then Mosley puts on the stand a patrolman who fished the body from the water.

"Will you describe what was with the body?" Mosley asks the cop.

"The body—what was with it was a nylon cord, yellow nylon cord tied around his wrists. And the body, when I first observed it, was in a position in the water like this." He bends over in the witness chair. "These chains and ropes were attached to the two concrete blocks."

Mosley is standing in front of the prosecution table. Now he stoops, reaches under the table, and pulls out a pair of concrete blocks. As he drags them from under the table the scraping noise fills the courtroom. Jurors stand and crane their necks to look.

The patrolman comes off the witness stand and bends over the blocks. He nods his head. "Those are the blocks," he says.

"Mr. Rupoli!" The clerk calls the words loudly enough to carry to the back of the courtroom. A short jowly man in his fifties rises, slips past the others in his row, and walks slowly to the front of the courtroom. All his life he has been a petty criminal on the outskirts of the mob, and is now a bookie. The men on trial are the bosses, and they have murdered his brother. He wants everyone to know that he is not frightened, not of the defendants, and not of the court.

He walks through the gap in the waist-high wooden railing at the front of the court and approaches the witness chair. He settles himself into the chair with great delibera-tion, taking his time. He might be in a hurry, but he is not hurrying.

Mosley waits until the witness is settled, and after a few formal preliminaries, asks, "Mr. Rupoli, are you the brother of the deceased in this case, Ernest Rupolo?"

"I am." The defendants stare at him, but he keeps his eyes fixed on Mosley.

"Now, on August the 4th, 1964, did you have occasion to see your brother?"

"I did."

"Tell us about that."

"Well, he was with his friend, someone by the name of Roy Roy. He came to my house about eleven-thirty, after I closed my place of business. He changed his clothes. I gave him a pair of my pants and shirt. It was a warm night, and he left with his friend on his way, and that was the last I saw of my brother."

"Did your brother have any injuries that you know of?"

"Yes. He was shot in 1932."

"Where was he shot?"

"He was shot somewheres in New York and—"

Spectators chuckle. The judge smiles.

"What part of his body?" Mosley says.

"His head."

"And what about the bullet?"

"The bullet was still in his head."

"And what about his eyes?"

"His eye was out."

"Was that as a result of the shooting?"

"That's right."

Mosley reaches into a cardboard box by his table and raises from it a pair of torn, crumpled, and faded pants. Keeping them at arm's length, and slightly averting his face to avoid the odor, he carries them to the witness chair.

"I show you a pair of pants, and ask you if you have seen those pants before."

The witness stiffens. "Yes. I saw them before." His voice is strong. He still has not looked at the defendants.

"Are they your pants?"

"Yes. They are my pants."

Mosley drops the pants back into the box. He nods toward the defense tables. "You may inquire," he says and sits down.

As Mosley questions his first witnesses, Zaher waits nervously in a lounge above the courtroom. He is thin and pale, and his hair is long—the jail barber, himself an inmate, has refused to cut the hair of a stool pigeon. A stairway leads directly from the lounge to the courtroom, reducing the chances of attack. At one end of the lounge a large electric clock is fixed to the wall, and above it hangs a speaker connected to a microphone on the clerk's desk in the courtroom.

For a time Zaher tries to play cards with his guards, then he gets up and paces.

Suddenly the speaker blares: "Zaher! Down!"

Zaher hastily stubs out a cigarette. Two guards rise, open the door of the dimly lighted stairway, and walk down with him. At the bottom, they open a door, and Zaher finds himself all at once in the bright lights of the courtroom, directly in front of Sonny Franzese. He hesitates an instant, then strides quickly and defiantly past Franzese, Matteo, Crabbe, Florio. He climbs into the witness chair and crosses his legs.

The defendants are to his right. He looks to his left, at the jury.

"How old are you, Mr. Zaher?" Mosley begins.

"Twenty-five."

"And are you presently awaiting sentence after having pleaded guilty to the felony possession of a pistol?"

"Yes, sir."

The defense will make known all Zaher's crimes anyway, and Mosley hopes to soften the effect by doing it himself. He brings out Zaher's police record, also that Zaher has pleaded guilty to bank robbery and received a suspended sentence.

"Do you know the defendants in this case?" Mosley asks.

"Yes, sir."

"Would you point them out, please?"

For the first time, Zaher now turns his head and looks at

the defense tables. The defendants stare back. Zaher points. "Mr. Florio, Mr. Crabbe, Mr. Matteo, Mr. Franzese."

Then, with questions pushed through an avalanche of defense objections, Mosley draws from Zaher a story that started on a Sunday in August 1964. Zaher had loaned his car to Richie Parks. Zaher told the jurors that Parks returned the car to him three days later and that the day after he got his car back he had a visit from Tommy Matteo. He said Matteo told him that his car had been involved in "a hit" and that "if I was you, I would get rid of it."

"What did you understand him to mean by the word 'hit'?" Mosley asks.

"A murder."

"A what?" Mosley wants to make sure every juror gets it.

"A murder."

"Now, do you recall a day sometime in July 1965, when you were at the Kew Motor Inn?"

"Yes, sir."

"And whom did you see there, if anyone?"

"When I pulled into the parking lot, Mr. Cordero and Mrs. Cordero were in the parking lot, and I pulled up alongside of them and they were arguing—"

Mr. Cordero and Mrs. Cordero. The names mean nothing to the jurors. Nor will the story they are about to hear. It will be told in fragments and confusion, and defense lawyers will fight to avoid clarification.

"—they were arguing, and just before I turned off the motor of the car, I heard Mrs. Cordero yell, 'Here comes—'"

"I object to what he heard," Edelbaum shouts. Any conversations between anyone but the witness and the men on trial is hearsay and inadmissible.

"Don't tell us anything you heard, any conversation," the judge warns Zaher.

"What happened after she yelled?" Mosley asks.

"Mr. Cordero took out his gun and started firing at Mr. Florio. I went out of my car, and I grabbed John. I tried to get the gun from him. But it was no good, and he went back into the Kew after Mr. Florio."

Zaher says he drove Cordero and his wife home and spent the night with them. He explains that the next night he and Cordero were ordered to a Mafia "sit-down" presided over by Franzese. The meeting, on the second floor of the Aqueduct Motel, was also attended by Red Crabbe, Whitey Florio, and John Matera.

"You spoke with Franzese?" Mosley asks Zaher.

"Yes, sir."

"Will you give us that conversation?"

"Mr. Franzese said he ordered The Hawk's hit."

That is it. The answer comes quickly, tacked right on to the end of Mosley's question. It is the answer Zaher has been waiting almost two years to give—the answer he might be killed for, the answer that could save him fifteen years in prison.

Through a heavy fire of defense objections, arguments, demands for mistrial, Zaher continues with his story.

"I told them what happened when I pulled into the Kew."

"Who spoke then?"

"Then Mr. Cordero says, 'What's this all about anyway? Isn't my word any good?' He says, 'Who cares about The Hawk? He was nothing but a rat. This whole thing is ridiculous.' "

Zaher's nervousness has caught up with him. He is very excited, talking very fast.

"Then what happened?" Mosley asks.

"Then Mr. Franzese jumped up. He says, 'This is ridiculous? Do you think I'd be wasting my time here if I thought it was ridiculous? I ordered The Hawk's hit and every man in this room had a hand in it. How do I know she didn't put him up to it? How do I know you won't be coming after me next? Did she ever ask any questions about it?' "

The jurors look bewildered. What are these people talking about? Who is this woman who might have put someone up to something? What caused the shooting in the first place?

Zaher continues: "Mr. Crabbe says, 'I say we kill her.' Mr. Matera said, 'Sonny, take it easy.' Then Mr. Cordero says, 'No, she never asked any questions about you or anybody else, not even Whitey. She never liked Whitey, and behind a few drinks she got carried away.' Then Mr. Crabbe says, 'Well, I'm for killing her.' He says, 'We got to put protection on ourselves.' Mr. Cordero says, 'No, you're not.' Then Mr. Crabbe says, 'I have more to say about this than you and a lot more to worry about. I killed The Hawk and dropped him in the drink, so don't tell me what's best for me,' and then Mr. Florio, he says—"

The moment Zaher begins to quote Florio, Florio's attorney is on his feet with an objection. Having failed to block Zaher's testimony by any other means, the defense is now about to try a dodge that will bring great amusement to Zaher and the other witnesses. Zaher, who in his brief life has been accused of everything from drug addiction to rape and robbery, is now to be accused of being a cop.

If the defense can prove that Zaher was a cop, then his testimony will be excluded by a rule requiring prosecutors to advise the defense in advance when a police agent is going to reveal admissions.

The judge listens for thirty minutes while Zaher—with the jury absent—is questioned about his police affiliations.

He then rules that in his opinion Zaher was not an officer of the law, and orders the jury brought back in.

"Will you tell us what the defendant Florio said to you?" Mosley asks.

"Well, Mr. Florio walked over to Mr. Cordero and extended his arm for a handshake and told Mr. Cordero that 'I know how you feel about this, but I had to go to Sonny about it. It seemed very serious. You see, I set The Hawk up for the kill and I had to go to Sonny about it.'"

That is the end of it. Zaher has said all he has to say. Now it is time for the defense to go to work on him, to try to convince the jury that he is simply too evil to be believed.

When Mosley finishes questioning Zaher, he turns over to the defense lawyers copies of every scrap of paper—every police report, every letter, every note—that concerns the witness. The law requires him to do this. The defense lawyers are given time to pore through these documents in search of ammunition they can fire back at the witness. Any slight variation in a witness's story over a period of years can be hauled out and made to sound like a total turn-around. Every request the witness made can be presented as a demand for a payoff. And in this trial the defense lawyers are allowed to read from the documents out of context—they may read aloud every sentence damaging to the witnesses and skip over every sentence damaging to the defendants. The jurors may not see the letters; they may only hear what is read to them.

While the lawyers study the letters, Mosley discusses the trial. He is counting on a little luck, hoping the witnesses will find a few chances to land blows of their own. On cross-examination, the witnesses are allowed to answer responsively to any question put to them by the defense. If the defense slips up and asks an imprudent question, the witness can fire back the answer without fear of causing a mistrial. The witnesses are eager to slip in clues about their fear, the threats against them, and the background of the defendants. And sometimes defense lawyers make mistakes, as Philip Vitello, Florio's lawyer, is about to do now.

Vitello first brings out a few facts about Zaher's escape from jail and then questions him about the pistol found in his pocket when he was recaptured.

"Tell us why you bought the gun," he asks.

Vitello wants Zaher to answer that he bought the gun to rob a bank. But that is not the answer in Zaher's mind. "Why I bought the gun?" he asks innocently.

There is no answer from Vitello, so Zaher hits him with it. "My life was in great danger in New York City."

Vitello has not understood. He thinks Zaher said his "wife" was in danger. Zaher had been grabbed with the gun in a restaurant near a bank, and Vitello thinks he will make Zaher look ridiculous by showing that it was the bank that held his interest, not his wife. He asks, "Where was your wife?"

"Home."

"And you had the gun on you in the *restaurant?*"

"That's right."

"And you bought the gun to protect your *wife?*"

Zaher lets him have it again. "I didn't say nothing about protecting my wife. To protect *myself!*"

Vitello retreats from that encounter and touches on Zaher's role as a wheel man in two bank robberies. This time he comes within an inch of letting the cat out of the bag. He has managed to place Zaher behind the wheel of a stolen car used in one of the robberies, and now pretends a look of shock.

"You mean that car was used in a *bank robbery?*"

"It certainly was," Zaher answers.

"What bank robbery?"

"I believe it was the Queens Central Savings."

"You helped *rob* that bank?"

"Yes, sir."

"Who helped you?"

The words "Sonny Franzese" are forming on Zaher's lips when Edelbaum leaps into the breach. "I object to all questions like this, your honor," he shouts.

Vitello looks stunned, objected to by one of his own confederates.

"Objection sustained," the judge says.

When the trial recesses for the night, someone mentions Vitello and his reckless questions.

"He's an idiot," Zaher says.

Mosley laughs. "Don't knock him. He's my secret weapon."

The next morning Zaher is in Mosley's office at nine-thirty reading newspaper clippings of his testimony the day before. Guards take him up to the witness lounge and play pinochle with him until the trial starts.

Zaher looks at the clock. "Twenty more minutes and then I'm back in that hot seat."

"Calm down, Charlie," one of the guards says. "You'll wear yourself out."

"I wish I'd taken the fifteen years," Zaher says. "This is murder."

Mosley's aloneness in the courtroom grows sadly apparent that morning. Not only is he by himself at the prosecution table, with the defense arrayed in a ten-man phalanx stretching almost the width of the courtroom, but the spectators too are almost to a man on the side of the defense. Members of the defendants' families and hoods who work for Franzese whisper insults and ridicule and hoot laughter at Mosley's objections. And the judge, by his manner and rulings, makes it clear that he intends to give every benefit of every doubt to the defense.

Then the defense tries to isolate Mosley even more by excluding Price from the courtroom. Price's step-by-step knowledge of the three-year police investigation is invaluable to Mosley, and the defense decides to get rid of him. All witnesses have been excluded from the courtroom and forbidden from reading daily trial transcripts, so the defense now claims that they might call Price as a witness. The judge accepts their story and tosses Price out.

With aloneness comes frustration and anger. Again and again, Mosley is overruled when he objects to the "I told him . . ." sort of hearsay the defense has successfully objected to earlier. Finally, when a defense lawyer asks Zaher, "Didn't Cordero tell you that he told the police . . . ?" Mosley becomes angry.

"I object to this, your honor. This is the *rankest* hearsay!"

"No," says the judge.

Mosley looks incredulous. "Did somebody tell him that he told someone else?"

"Overruled," the judge says, and then smiling adds, "You have an exception." An exception is granted to the defense, for the purposes of their later appeal, when they feel they have been incorrectly ruled against. Since prosecutors can never appeal a verdict, they are never granted exceptions. The judge is having a joke.

"And you *know* one of the conditions that your lawyer made was that if you *cooperated,* when your sentence came up in the federal court the District Attorney's Office would send a representative to talk to the judge on the day of sentence to appeal for leniency for you, is that right?"

Edelbaum is cross-examining Zaher, nose to nose, screaming into his face.

"Yes, sir." Zaher appears unrattled.

"And on the day that you were sentenced, Mr. Mosley *was* there, was he not?"

"Yes, sir."

Edelbaum turns, and nodding as if he has just made an enormously significant point (the jurors in their confusion might grasp at any hint as to what is significant and what is not) he stalks away from Zaher. Then he stops, turns, and shuffles back to Zaher's face.

"And Mr. Mackell, the District Attorney *himself*, was there, *isn't that right?*"

"Yes, sir."

"Well, you *got* a suspended sentence, didn't you?"

"Yes, sir."

"For *two* bank robberies! RIGHT?"

The sound of shock in Edelbaum's voice, the look of outrage on his face. There is no way Mosley can tell the jurors that the man Edelbaum so righteously defends bossed the very bank robberies Zaher is talking about.

"Yes, sir."

"For two *bank robberies*, where your companions walked in with *loaded guns*, into two banks! RIIIIIGHT?"

"Yes, sir."

When it is over, guards handcuff Zaher and drive him back to jail. Mosley goes down to his office. He is exhausted and discouraged. "I have never tried a case this heavy," he says. "I've never tried a case where *I* was on trial. I tried one in Manhattan once where a guy was sentenced to the chair, but *never* one like this. I've never objected and had people in the courtroom actually laugh. It's very disturbing."

John Cordero, the next witness, is brought to Mosley's office the next morning. He changes into a blue silk suit his wife Eleanor left for him in Mosley's closet.

"All right, John," Mosley says to him as he dresses, "remember. Just tell everything just the way it was."

Cordero nods. He is terribly nervous, and his voice is hoarse. He asks if someone can get him a pack of throat lozenges.

"Did you talk to Zaher last night?" Mosley asks. "They may ask you that, what he said to you."

"I've got a good answer for that they'll be sorry to hear. I asked Charlie how he felt and he says he's scared to death he's gonna get killed."

Cordero telephones Eleanor from Mosley's phone. She does not answer. When he has dressed, the guards take him up to the witness lounge. The guards sit in a corner talking quietly. Cordero goes into a phone booth in the lounge and calls his wife again. She does not answer. He paces. The only sounds are his footsteps and the low whispering of the guards.

Then his name explodes from the wall speaker, and suddenly he is on the stand, answering Mosley's questions.

"I pled about three different times for different banks." A package of Sucret's lozenges is on the railing in front of him, next to a white paper cup filled with water.

"How many banks did you stick up altogether?" Mosley asks.

"Seven banks." Spectators gasp and whisper, less for the number of banks than for the casual, matter-of-fact way Cordero drops the number. He says the banks were in New York, Massachusetts, Colorado, Salt Lake City. "I think that's about it." Then he tells about the shooting in the parking lot of the Kew Motor Inn, and the next day's sit-down. His version adds a few facts to Zaher's, but still not enough to give the bewildered jurors a clear picture of what happened. "I says [to the men at the sit-down] I wasn't trying to kill Whitey, I was trying to protect my wife. I wasn't interested in anything to do with The Hawk, he was nothing but a stool pigeon."

Franzese's wife has been in court every day of the trial. Now as Cordero testifies she puts her right hand to the side of her head, extending her forefinger along her temple. When Cordero glances toward her, she moves her palm out slightly as though a gun were pointing at her head. Cordero gets the message. He takes a sip of water and another Sucret. His voice sounds like wet gravel.

Cordero tells the jury that after the sit-down he had decided to move, and Florio came over with a truck to help him.

"We were in the bedroom," Cordero says. "We were making up boxes and everything to put stuff in. And I had some rope, I wanted to tie it up, and I was trying, you know, to break it up. So Whitey says, 'Can I take care of that for you?' He pulled out a knife and he flipped it, made it shoot out, and he started cutting the rope.

"So I asked him, I said, 'Is that what you used on The Hawk?' And he went, 'Shhh, don't talk like that in the house. There's other people here.' So I said, 'Nobody hears nothing. Did you use that on The Hawk?'

"So he just smiled. He said, 'Let's cut the box, pack the stuff, not talk about this thing.' So I let that go. And then I asked him, 'Seriously, Whitey, how did you get involved in this thing, you know, The Hawk?' So he said, 'Well, I don't want to talk about it. Forget about it.'"

"And then I pursued the matter, and finally he told me, he says he had a deal with The Hawk, some kind of a deal they got down together on to make some money together, and Sonny got wind of this deal they had. And Sonny told him, 'Don't have anything to do with this guy, The Hawk.' "

Edelbaum erupts. He demands a new and separate trial for Franzese, arguing that the words just attributed to him have so prejudiced the jury that Franzese cannot possibly get a fair trial from this point onward.

Other lawyers jump in with their own motions. They insist—outside the hearing of the jury—that if Cordero is about to quote Florio quoting Franzese, then Franzese's name should be concealed from the jury. Let the quotes stay in, they say, but don't reveal who said them. The defense argues that Florio should not be made a vehicle for admissions from another defendant.

Mosley fights desperately against this stand, for he knows the conversation Cordero is about to relate. The first time Cordero repeated this conversation to police, he reached the point he is at now—the point where Edelbaum interrupted—and then continued: "He had this deal going with The Hawk, and Sonny told him to call the deal off. When he told The Hawk the deal was off, The Hawk blew his top and threatened to kill him. So he went to Sonny and told Sonny that The Hawk threatened to kill him. Sonny said, 'Don't worry about it. I had enough of that guy. You're going to set him up for me.' And Whitey balked about that. He didn't want to get involved. And Sonny said, 'You want him dead, too, so you set him up for me.' Then he told me he had this kid Roy Roy drive him out to a motel or hotel and he says, 'I told him we were going to make some money together to get him out there.' "

To leave Sonny's name out of that would conceal the fact that he ordered the murder. The judge listens to all argu-

ments, then rules that Cordero, when he repeats the conversation to the jury, must omit all names but Florio's.

"All right," Mosley says when they are back with the jury,
"do you remember where you left off?"

"Yes, sir, I do."

"Okay, go on from there."

Cordero pulls himself together, trying to remember the
judge's instructions. "I am not supposed to mention any
names now, right?"

"I object to that, your honor," Lyon, Crabbe's lawyer,
says. He wants the names left out, but he does not want the
jury to know that Cordero has been *told* to leave them out.
"I object to his asking for instructions."

"It's hard to explain the conversation . . ." Cordero persists, guessing that if he has upset a defense lawyer he must
be doing something right.

"Will you please explain to him he is not to talk to me,"
Lyon says to the judge. "I am not carrying on a conversation with him."

Cordero continues. "I was talking to Mr. Florio at my
apartment, and he had mentioned that he had a deal with
The Hawk." He pauses. "Someone . . ." Another pause.
". . . told him to call the deal off. He didn't tell The Hawk
this. He just ignored The Hawk. The Hawk come down to
his place, his bar, and asked him, said, 'I waited all night
for you.' The Hawk blew his top. They argued about it. The
Hawk threatened to kill him. He went back and told
somebody else this."

"Who went back?"

"Whitey. He went back and told somebody else this, and
they told him, 'I had enough trouble with this guy. He's
been bookmaking, he's been taking hits on numbers, he
hasn't been paying off on them.' He said, 'We had enough

of him.' He said, 'You set him up and don't worry about it.'
Whitey said he didn't want to set the guy up because it
would show a connection between him and this guy, but
they told him, 'Don't worry about it. Set him up.' He said,
'Well, I got this kid Roy Roy to help me on one end and I
got this guy Offie to help me on the other end.' That was
it."

When Mosley finishes his questions, the judge recesses
the trial to give defense lawyers time to search through
Mosley's file on Cordero.

Mosley and Cordero go back up to the witness room.
Cordero's wife Eleanor is there waiting. "How was it? How
did it go?" she asks, very excited.

"You should of seen Franzese and them when I said The
Hawk was nothing but a stool pigeon and got what he
deserved. Like they're thinking I'm a stool pigeon, too,
right? So where do I get off saying that?"

Eleanor laughs. Cordero is sitting in his shirtsleeves with
Eleanor next to him. The guards and Mosley stand around
listening to him, watching his reactions. He is like a little
boy who has just come off stage from the school play.

"You should have heard them in the court when I said
seven bank robberies."

"Seven bank robberies!" Eleanor says. "My baby!" She
throws her arms around him. "But they must think we're
millionaires!"

When they are back in court, Vitello probes into Cordero's criminal record, from his first imprisonment at fifteen,
through hospitalization for drug addiction, further arrest
for possession of narcotics, for forgery, gun possession,
robbery. He makes the mistake of asking Cordero about his
education.

Cordero answers proudly that he studied in prison and

within the past year received a high-school diploma. Vitello drops that, and goes back to the criminal record. Then he introduces a letter from Cordero to the DA's office outlining demands—financial help for his wife, visits with his wife—which he said would have to be met before he would testify.

Lyon takes over and his questions reveal that Cordero has lied to the authorities in the past.

"You were pretty good at putting together a bunch of lies, weren't you?" he shouts.

"Yes, sir, I was."

"You make a practice of trying to fool the authorities?"

"Yes, sir, I did." Cordero tosses out a piece of bait, and Lyon grabs it.

"You *did*, or you *do?*"

"I did."

"Now you've stopped?"

"Yes, sir, I did."

"When did you reform?"

"When? When I realized I was through with this type of a life about a year ago, over a year ago."

"Over a year ago you decided to reform?"

"Yes, I decided. That's why I went and got a high-school diploma and tried to better myself."

Lyon quickly changes the subject.

Eleanor often joked that "someday I'm gonna get dynamited right out of my car." But both she and John knew it was not really a joke. Since her first contact with The Hawk, she had been living a reckless life, saying the wrong things to the wrong people, picking up dangerous pieces of the wrong conversations. There was reason to believe that even now as Cordero spoke from the witness chair, a contract was out on Eleanor. Her address was one of the DA office's most tightly guarded secrets.

"Is your wife here?" Lyon asks Cordero now.

Eleanor is, in fact, upstairs in the witness room.

"You can call her," Cordero says, stalling. Sonny's hoods are in the courtroom listening.

"Is your wife *here?*" Lyon demands.

"Where here? What are you talking about?"

"In the court house."

"I don't know." It is true. She could have left since he spoke with her.

"Do you know *where* she is?"

Cordero is insulted. "Yes. I know where my wife is."

"Don't you know whether she is in the courtroom or not?"

Mosley thinks Cordero might be weakening, and he does not want him tipping the hoods to her whereabouts. "I object, your honor. This is quite immaterial."

"No. Overruled."

"Don't you know?" Lyon presses.

"She was in the court house."

"When?"

"This morning."

"Is she in the court house *now?*"

"I don't know."

Lyon continues to ask about Eleanor, and finally puts a question which, though it seems mild and offhand at the asking, will resurface with explosive force at the trial's end. He asks Cordero if he knows who Eleanor went out with after The Hawk was killed.

"Yes," Cordero answers readily, "a fellow that lived in Long Island, a Polish fellow." He says he does not remember the man's name but can find out if Lyon wishes.

Through all the questioning, Cordero ignores the sarcasm

and abuse, answers the questions, and tries to give the impression of a man who, though he has been a liar, a drug addict, a bank robber, is telling the truth when he says he heard Franzese admit to murder.

When FBI agents first arrested Cordero for bank robbery, they found $10,000 in the house he and Eleanor had rented. Cordero now says The Hawk had long ago given Eleanor the money for their child. At this, Lyon stops shouting and the courtroom falls silent. He walks up close to Cordero, face-to-face, and letting the whispered words echo through the silence, he says, "Isn't it a fact that this $10,000 that was found in her house came to your wife Eleanor as the result of the murder of her husband, Ernest Rupolo?"

Cordero smiles. "Are you kidding?"

"No. I am not kidding."

"You must be."

"Isn't it a fact?"

"No. You know it's not."

"You say I know it's not?"

"Yes. You know."

"Isn't it a fact, sir, that your friends, Parks and Zaher, who wanted a promise that they wouldn't be prosecuted for the Rupolo murder, are the men who committed the murder for your wife?"

"How do I know?" Cordero says sarcastically.

Lyon sits down. "I have no further questions."

Now Mosley knows. From the start it has been clear that it will not be enough for the defense merely to yell that the prosecution witnesses are unbelievable. The defense will have to come up with its own version of the murder of The Hawk. This is it: Eleanor paid Zaher and Richie Parks to kill The Hawk. That will be the defense story—or so it appears.

"The fact that you had raised your hand to almighty God and swore to tell the truth meant *nothing* to you at that time, did it?" Edelbaum has just started on Cordero, and already he is screaming. He is referring to a lie Cordero once told a grand jury about his drug-taking.

"I object," Mosley says. "This is not proper. . . ."

"Overruled."

"It's a summation," Mosley persists.

"Overruled. Overruled."

"Did it?"

"Well, I didn't think of it like that."

Edelbaum has his hands in the pockets of his rumpled suit, and now he shuffles up to Cordero, puts his finger in his face, and screams, "But you thought of it like that to try and fool the grand jury, didn't you? *Didn't you?*"

Mosley stands. "Now, your honor, I object to Mr. Edelbaum approaching the witness—"

Edelbaum tries to interrupt. "I said—"

"—and shaking his finger at him and raising his voice."

"Don't badger the witness," the judge says.

"Yes, your honor. Sorry. What was your answer, sir?"

"I forgot the question."

Edelbaum shoots questions at Cordero, and Cordero struggles to ignore the noise and theatrics and follow the questions and not get confused. When he gives an incorrect answer to a misleading question and then later figures things out and tries to explain, he is shouted down by Edelbaum and cautioned by the judge to explain nothing, "just answer yes or no."

The defense wants to prove Cordero a liar, and Cordero himself makes no bones about it. He has done just about everything bad a man can do. Lying isn't half of it. He does not want to convince the jury that he has not lied in his life, only that he is not lying now. So when the defense tries to make him a liar, he responds with astonishing and sometimes humorous candor. Edelbaum points out that when FBI agents found the $10,000, Cordero without much of a reason lied to them and said it was not his wife's money.

"Right?" yells Edelbaum.

"Right," says Cordero.

"There was no *reason* to lie to the FBI—"

"Plenty of reason. I always lie to the FBI."

Edelbaum has not expected to see such candor in a liar. And he would not have wanted the jury to see it. "I mean . . . You always . . . You *always* lie to the FBI?"

"Oh, yes," says Cordero breezily, delighted at having the upper hand for once. "I have a lot to hide."

"You have a lot to hide?" Edelbaum is floundering.

"I had a lot to hide from the FBI."

"I see." Edelbaum composes himself and goes on. A few more questions and again he is screaming at Cordero, waving his finger, pounding on tables.

Finally Cordero rebels. "Will you stop yelling at me?" he says. "I can hear you pretty well. You are yelling and giving me a headache."

"You want a recess?" Edelbaum screams.

Cordero turns to the judge. "Your honor, the man is yelling. I can't even understand him any more."

"All right," the judge says sternly to Cordero. "Don't start arguing now. Just answer the questions."

As Edelbaum continues to shout and pound and storm around the room, it becomes distressingly obvious that he has taken over the court. He has turned it into a stage and is playing to two audiences—the jury, and the claque of young attorneys and hoodlums who laugh at his jokes, shake their heads with righteous distress at every setback. He has made Cordero the defendant, and does not hesitate to attack Mosley as well. When Mosley asks about a document Edelbaum is reading aloud from, Edelbaum shouts, "Here! Look at it yourself!" and throws the paper at Mosley.

When the defense has finished with Cordero, guards take him back to the witness room. Eleanor is there. He throws her coat on her and tells her to get out of the court house fast. Then he is handcuffed and driven back to jail.

Mosley asks Price what he thinks about not using Smith. Smith does not add much to the other testimony, and if Mosley calls him the defense will have another chance to hammer away at what rotten people the prosecution witnesses are. Finally Mosley decides to leave him out.

Price asks how Cordero did.

"I thought he was very strong," Mosley says. "He might be a liar, but he heard what he heard. I think he came across very well. They didn't rattle him."

"So you've got a conviction," Price says.

"Oh, I don't know about that. There might be seven guys on the jury who wouldn't believe these witnesses on a stack of Bibles."

Because Mosley badly needs one legitimate citizen who can corroborate his crime-stained witnesses, he calls a man who has no direct knowledge of the case but at least heard of the shooting in the parking lot of the Kew Motor Inn. Bob Greene, a crime reporter for *Newsday*, a Long Island paper, interviewed Florio in 1965—and Florio foolishly admitted that the shooting took place. If Bob Greene's testimony convinces the jurors that the shooting really happened, then they might be more willing to buy the testimony about admissions made at the sit-down.

"Tell us the conversation you had with the defendant Florio relative to Ernest 'The Hawk' Rupolo," Mosley tells Greene when he takes the stand.

"I asked Mr. Florio about reports that we had received that he was present at the John Doe Room of the Kew Motor Inn at a time when Mr. Cordero had taken a shot at him. He said that he had been in the John Doe Room, which is a bar, that Mr. Cordero had come in with the wife of Ernie 'The Hawk' Rupolo, that the wife of Ernie 'The Hawk' Rupolo had started to make disparaging comments across the bar to Mr. Florio, that she had accused him of having some part in the murder of her husband, that she used—this is his reply—that she used very bad language, that she was pretty much obnoxious, and that he said he felt Mr. Cordero was embarrassed by her behavior, and Mr. Cordero eventually talked her into leaving the premises, that he then went out to get into his car, that Mr. Cordero had turned around and fired a shot at him."

Now at last the jurors have a comprehensible account of why John Cordero threw shots at Florio in the parking lot, and why Franzese ordered the sit-down.

Mosley moves on to the next step. He has Medical Examiner Milton Helpern describe in detail the damage done to The Hawk by six bullets, twenty-five stab thrusts, and three weeks' submersion in Jamaica Bay.

"When I saw the body," Helpern tells the jurors, "the brain was quite decomposed and actually was liquefied and ran out through the bullet perforations. It was quite mushy, but that did not interfere with the tracking of these bullets."

A woman rises and leaves the courtroom. Franzese toys absently with the end of his tie.

"A body which becomes distended with gas will become very buoyant, and even though a heavy anchor is attached to it the buoyancy of the body can eventually float the anchor. We have had cases with the body floating even with heavier anchors than this."

A defense lawyer stands a court officer in front of the witness chair and asks Helpern to indicate on the officer's head where the bullets went in.

The judge smiles. "Without using a gun," he says. The defense lawyers laugh.

Helpern rises and fingers the top of the officer's head. "If we had a fellow without so much hair . . . ," he says. He explains how he can tell which scalp holes were made by entering bullets and which by departing bullets. A bullet going in, he says, makes a punched-in hole. Leaving, it makes a beveled hole—the same thing you get "if you fire a bullet through a piece of plate glass."

The next day, it is Richie Parks's turn to take the stand. Mosley walks into the witness lounge in the morning. Parks is there with his guards. He is very cool and businesslike. "All right," he says briskly to Mosley, making sure he knows what is coming, "so we'll start with '64 and then we'll jump to the sit-down and then the Tiki. Right? All very simple."

Parks had arrived from jail wearing a green corduroy sport coat and no tie. "Oh, come on, Richie," a detective says, "haven't you even got a tie?" The detective walks out to another office and comes back with a tie.

Someone asks Parks how he feels about testifying against Franzese. "Well," he says, "indifferent really. Except that it's embarrassing, subjecting myself to these defense lawyers. It's degrading. But as to testifying, I'm indifferent. If it was reversed they wouldn't stop to bury me."

The loud-speaker shouts and Parks goes down. Word is

out that he is the key witness, the eyewitness, and the courtroom is nearly full.

Mosley asks him about his having pleaded guilty to robbing seven banks. He asks him if he knows the defendants and to point them out. Then he says, "Mr. Parks, some time in 1964 did you have occasion to talk with the defendant Florio?"

Through a steady fire of objections, Parks begins his story. "Well, at that time, about 6 P.M. that day, I received a call from Matteo and he told me, Mr. Matteo told me, that Florio had something for me to do, some work for me to do, go down and see him at this bar, the Rainbow Bar. So I went down and I seen Florio down there. He was down there with Crabbe at the bar. He told me he wanted me to go to Manhattan and steal a car.

"He says, 'Get a late-model car.' He says, 'Try and get a four-door car.' And he says, 'I want you to get the keys to the car.' He says, 'Your best bet it to get it off one of the parking lots in Manhattan.' He says, 'Have it here by tomorrow night at six o'clock.'

"So I says, 'All right,' and I left. Now, the next day, about—this would be Sunday—about three o'clock, I went over and seen Zaher at his house, Charles Zaher, and I took [his] car down to the Rainbow Bar, Whitey's bar, and Whitey was there. This is about seven o'clock or so Sunday night, the next night. So I parked the car outside and I told him, 'The car is outside.'

"So he says, 'All right, you got the keys?'

"I says yes. So I gave him the keys.

"He says, 'All right, wait at the bar. I'm going to go out by the car.' I says all right.

"So about a half hour later he comes back and says to me, 'Why don't you take a ride with me behind the Aqueduct

Race Track?' He says, 'I want to change the plates on this car. I want you to help me.' I says all right."

As Parks speaks, his eyes roam up and down the defense tables. The other witnesses have tried to avoid the defendants' stares, but Parks invites them.

Mosley stands relaxed, his hands clasped in front of him.

"So we got in the car and went around behind the Aqueduct Race Track. Back there we parked the car. He opened the trunk of the car and in the trunk he had a set of license plates there and some tools, and there was some cement blocks in the trunk of the car, pieces of rope and chain. And we changed the plates on the car, and the plates that were on it we put under the floor mat in the front seat. And then we went back and took the car back to the Rainbow and we parked it on the side street by the bar.

"He told me, he said, 'I want you here tomorrow night about nine o'clock,' he says, 'and I'll call you and tell you where to take the car.'

"So I says all right. I says, 'How about some money, though, for this?'

"So he says, 'See me tomorrow night.'

"Well, the following night, nine o'clock—that's Monday— I went down to the Rainbow, and Crabbe was there with Florio. A few minutes later, he said, 'Wait here. I'll give you a ring on the phone,' he says, 'and I'll tell you where to take the car.'

"So I says all right. So I said, 'How about some money?' So he says, 'See me tomorrow night.' He says, 'After you deliver the car.' I said all right.

"So I wait that night and I didn't get no ring. He didn't call me that night. The following day I seen him at the Rainbow, and I asked him what happened, and he says, 'Well, we want you to wait again tonight.' He says, 'It's definite. You'll get a call.' So he says, 'Wait for the call.' So I says all right. He says, 'The car is outside.' He says, 'The keys are under the floor mat.'

"So I waited and later on that night I did get a call. And I'd say that call was about approximately 2 A.M. So Florio, he called me and he says, 'I want you to take the car out to the Skyway Hotel.' He says, 'You know where it is.'

"I says all right. He says, 'Look,' he says, 'I want you to put the car in the rear parking lot.' He says, 'Leave the keys under the floor mat.' And he says, 'Try and back the car in in the back in the rear parking lot.' So I says all right. He says, 'Well, come down right now. Right now I want you.' I said, 'All right, I'm coming.'

"So I took the car and I went down there and I parked it in the rear and I went around to the front, the front of the building, to go inside there to call a cab. And I didn't see anybody inside. I didn't see none of the defendants. Nobody I knew.

"So I went back outside to the parking lot and I went around to the back, and as I got to the back, I could view the car I brought there. I seen a car pull up right next to the car I brought there, Zaher's car, and in the car was four men. So they got out of the car. They had backed in right next to the car that I had and they got out and it was John Matera, Tommy Matteo, Whitey Florio, and Red Crabbe.

"So Florio, he was driving. Florio was driving the car. He got out and he went over to the car, Zaher's car, and went into the car and he opened the door and he got the keys from under the floor mat and he went back to the trunk of the car and he opened up the trunk of Zaher's car.

"And Matera, he opened up the trunk of the car that they had come in. And when Matera opened it up, Matteo was standing right next to him and Crabbe was standing next to him, and Crabbe reached in the trunk and he grabbed out a blanket, and he handed it over to Florio, and Florio started spreading it out on the trunk of the car. And Matera reached in the trunk of the car, the car they came in, along with Matteo, and they pulled a body out of the trunk of the car. And it was The Hawk."

"Who is The Hawk?" Mosley asks.

"Ernie The Hawk. But at that view there I didn't know it was The Hawk at that view. So the body had a blanket half draped around him."

The judge looks over and catches Edelbaum's eye. Edelbaum comes to life. "I move to strike out that it was The Hawk," he says.

"Strike it. The jury will disregard it," the judge says.

The jurors are disregarding exactly nothing. They are forward in their chairs, spellbound with Parks's narrative. Parks, on the other hand, appears bored. He tells the story with a supreme lack of emotion, monotonously, as if he has told it many times before—as indeed he has. Franzese sits impassive and expressionless, his fingertips joined in front of him.

"The body had a blanket half draped around it. It was hanging over the body. And Matteo had the feet, the legs, and Matera had him under the arms. And as they took him out of the trunk—they hadn't even started to move him yet, they just took it out—the man's arms went out to the side."

Parks throws his arms out.

"They were carrying him. He made an outburst. He said—he screamed the words—'No! No!' And then he started to say something else like—it sounded like—'What . . . What the . . .' But I couldn't make that out. Just sounded like the word, 'What.' But I heard him scream out, 'No! No!'

"And when he did that, immediately Matera pushed him to the ground, dropped him right to the ground, and got right on his shoulders, put his hand right over his face. And Matteo went down and grabbed the legs and held him to the ground.

"And Crabbe, he was standing next to Florio at the trunk of Zaher's car when that happened, and he pulled out a gun. And he rushed over to him, and Whitey said, when he pulled out the gun, he said, 'He's still alive!'

"And Crabbe pulled out the gun, and then he went to go over to the body and he took a few steps, and Florio grabbed him by the arm and he says, 'Not with the gun.' And he had a knife, and he had his knife in his hand, and Crabbe grabbed the gun—grabbed the knife—out of Florio's hand. And he bent down like on one knee, and he stabbed the body about three or four times in the chest.

"And then all four of them each grabbed a limb. They all grabbed the body, put the blanket more or less on top of it, folded it over, the sides of the blanket on him, and then they all picked him up and they put him in the trunk of Zaher's car. And at that time, when they picked him up, his head went back and at that time really for the first time his face was visible to me and I recognized it to be Ernie The Hawk.

"And they all put him in the trunk of Zaher's car. And Florio, he got in the car that they came in. He drove off by himself. And Matera, Matteo, and Crabbe got in the car that—Zaher's car with the body in it, and they drove off. And I waited for the cars to get out of sight, the both of them, because I was at this time—I had during this, when I first seen them pull up, I crept up within a distance of about—well, two cars away, Zaher's car and another car, and I was behind that car observing this. The building sort of like has the corner right there where this other car I was behind, and I waited for the cars to pull out, Florio by himself and the others in Zaher's car. And I went back inside the motel and I called a cab and I went home."

Parks pauses briefly, catches his breath, and goes on.

"Well, that same day I went down to the Rainbow. I got a call from Whitey. It was about six, seven, something like that, that night, and he told me, he said, come down right away. So I went down there to the Rainbow, and Florio was there by himself and he said to me, 'Where did you get that car from?'

"I says, 'Why?' He says, 'Well, Red Crabbe recognizes that car as belonging to somebody in the neighborhood.'

"I says, 'Well, it don't make any difference.' I says, 'It don't make no difference.'

"He said, 'What do you mean it don't make any difference? Suppose we use that for anything? It can be traced right back to us.' He says, 'You did a wrong thing. I want you to take the car, the plates are on it, it's outside, and get that car back where you got it from, and then I want you to get back here and let me know everything is all right.'

"I said all right, and I went outside and I got in the car and I drove a few blocks and I stopped the car and opened the trunk and there wasn't nothing in the trunk. Nothing at all. So I took the car and I went over to Zaher's house and I gave Zaher back his car. Then I went back to the Rainbow, a couple of hours later, and Florio was there and he was there with Crabbe and he says to me, Florio says, 'Is everything all right, did you get the car back?'

"I said, 'Don't worry about it, nobody knows anything about the car, nobody knows I even had it.'

"So he says all right. So I says, 'How about some money?'

So he says, 'Look, I'm very busy tonight. See me tomorrow night or over the weekend.'

"I said, 'Yeah, but I'm kind of tapped out.' He said, 'Don't worry about it, see me over the weekend.' I said all right.

"Crabbe said to me, he says, 'I want you to drive me to Brooklyn.'

"So we went outside, me and Crabbe, and when we got outside, we were heading toward my car. Another car was pulled up and in that car was Matera. He was driving, and he was driving Sonny. And Crabbe got in the car and got in the back and Sonny said to me, he says, 'I heard about the car.' He says, 'You took that from the neighborhood. You were supposed to get that from Manhattan.'

"I says, I know. So he says, 'Look, you do what you're told from now on. If you're told to take a car from Manhattan, you take the car from Manhattan. If you're told to shoot somebody, you shoot them. If you're told to pipe somebody, you pipe them, you don't shoot them. You do what you're told.'

"So I says all right. I says, 'I made a mistake.' He says, 'Don't let it happen again.'

"So that was the end of my conversation with them that night."

Mosley asks Parks about the shooting at the Kew Motor Inn and the sit-down the next night. Then he asks him about a conversation at a bar called the Tiki.

"I was at the Tiki with Cordero, James Smith, and Red Crabbe, and we had a conversation and during that conversation Crabbe said that he wanted to kill someone just like he killed The Hawk." (The jury was not allowed to know that the "someone" was a prosecution witness in another case.) "He said he wanted to drop him in the drink.

He said he wanted the pleasure and satisfaction of doing it himself."

Mosley finishes with Parks, and the court recesses for the night. Mosley goes up to the witness room. Parks is telling a detective, "I think it's gonna be a hung jury. Some of the jurors were very attentive, but the others looked like they were trying to psychoanalyze me."

Guards put handcuffs on Parks for the trip back to jail. "Well, Richie," one of them asks, "how'd it go?"

"Oh, I could have done a lot better," Parks says casually. "But, you know, there wasn't nothing in it for me."

Parks is the key. If Edelbaum and the other defense lawyers are to destroy Mosley's case, they must destroy Parks. They start their cross-examination on a Wednesday afternoon and continue it through all of Thursday and into Friday. Parks's account of the stabbing sounded so vivid that no one expected the defense to take him over it again, hoping for contradictions. But Lyon does. He starts at the beginning and detail by detail leads Parks through it, even uncovering an extra fact Parks had forgotten to mention the first time around. After The Hawk was shoved into the trunk, Parks adds, Crabbe picked up a piece of cloth from the ground, said, "The patch," and tossed it into the trunk with the body. The Hawk had worn a patch over his right eye socket.

As Lyon goes on and on, never confusing Parks, never pushing Parks into a contradiction, drawing from him more and more detail, Edelbaum grows restless, finally begins whispering to the other attorneys.

In the middle of Lyon's questioning, the judge calls a five-minute recess, and in the crowded hallway Mosley whispers to Price, "This is fantastic. Lyon is conducting the best cross-examination for the prosecution I've ever heard."

Walter Anderson walks up. "I just conducted a Gallup poll of the spectators and they say this guy Parks is the best ever."

"Tell me honestly," Mosley says. "You listen to him up there, through Lyon's cross, and is there any doubt in your mind that he was there? That he saw what he saw?"

After the recess, Lyon continues—and so does Parks. Sometimes agreeing with Lyon, sometimes correcting him on a minor point of how a man moved, how a car was placed, he builds and buttresses a single solid impression: Richie Parks was there.

And then comes the letter, the disastrous letter Parks wrote to discredit himself.

"Did you ever accuse Cordero of trying to have his wife's daughter murdered?" Lyon asks. That is in the letter.

"Did you ever complain that Cordero was making up lies and getting you and the others to swear to it?" That is in the letter.

"Didn't you say about Cordero that 'He is insane but like a fox'?" That too.

"You said that Cordero got pills to weaken Zaher's mind, didn't you?" "Did you say that you took Cordero's wife to a motel and slept with her?" "Did you say you had your friend sleep with her?" "Did you say that that's why Cordero hates you?" Everything is in the letter.

Through it all Parks sits sullenly, answers matter-of-factly, and looks terribly bored. "Yes," he says. "I told a lot of lies in that letter."

Lyon wants to suggest again that Eleanor Cordero hired Parks to kill The Hawk. He brings out that a couple of weeks after the murder Parks put down $2,000 on a new Buick, that he refused to testify until he received immunity from prosecution for the murder, that in prison he said he was afraid John Cordero would poison him. Then, winding up his cross-examination, Lyon screams at Parks, "Isn't it a fact, Mr. Parks, that you made up this whole story about this switch in the Skyway Motel?"

"No."

"Isn't it a fact, sir, that you got $2,000 from Mrs. Cordero after Ernie The Hawk was killed?"

"No."

Edelbaum takes over. He faces Parks squarely, and shouts at him. Then he turns his back on Parks and begins to play to his claque in the audience.

"I don't know whether the witness can hear Mr. Edelbaum when Mr. Edelbaum's face is toward the audience," Mosley says to the judge, borrowing some of his opponent's sarcasm.

"Where would you like me to stand, Mr. Mosley?" Edelbaum says.

"Does he really want me to answer that?" Mosley shoots back.

Edelbaum picks up Parks's letter and reads a sentence from it. "Was *that* true?"

"No."

He reads another quotation. "Made *that* up out of your own head?"

"Right."

He picks out another sentence. "And you invented *that?*"

"Right."

Another quotation. "And *that* was a pure lie?"

"Right."

Another. "*That* was an unadulterated lie?"

"Right."

Another. "Did you invent *that?*"

"Right."

And on and on.

Parks remains cool. He answers Edelbaum in bored quiet monosyllables and, to demonstrate his unconcern, lets his eyes wander absently over the defendants, the jurors, and the spectators. But as Edelbaum hammers away at him, fast and loud, Parks grows more and more annoyed. He wants desperately to hit back—not so much to help Mosley but to destroy the fat, screaming little man who is playing with him, ridiculing him, tormenting him. He keeps control of himself and waits patiently. Then Edelbaum slips. He asks if one of Parks's reasons for writing the letter was "to gain an advantage from the U.S. attorney."

Parks leaps. "I wanted to discredit myself as a witness. *That's* why I wrote that letter!"

It is a weak blow, an underdog's blow—but it helps to stir the rumblings of the silent issue—the Mafia—to hint at the fear the witnesses feel.

In his office that evening Mosley talks with Price about the trial. He is sitting at the desk, and he puts his head down for a moment to rest. "If it wasn't for that damned letter," he says into the desk, "we'd have a conviction for sure. Why did he have to write that letter? It was a cakewalk up until today."

"How is Richie reacting to Edelbaum's screaming?" Price asks.

Mosley sits up, smiling. "Ice cold. But me, I'm sitting there tight as a drum."

Mosley, Price, and a couple of friends walk across the street to Luigi's. They sit at the bar and order beer. When Mosley has relaxed a little he starts to think about the moment in a few days when the jury will withdraw to consider its verdict.

"You can't imagine," he says, "you just can't *possibly*

imagine how emotional it is when the jury is out and you're in your office or you're in a restaurant, and you're waiting. And then you get a phone call. They're coming in. It's unbelievable, the emotion. You go into court and you sit down and the jury comes in, and it's 'Foreman and gentlemen of the jury, have you reached a verdict?' And the foreman says, 'Yes.' And the clerk says, 'How say you?' And then—boom! That's it. You can't imagine it. All the movies, all the television—you can't imagine it. And on this case, this will be the biggest verdict I've ever had."

He lifts his glass of beer. "It upsets me just to talk about it." He takes a swallow and puts the glass down. "There's only one other guy who's more concerned about the verdict than you are. But *he's* the bad guy. *He's* guilty. And when the verdict is guilty, the elation you feel isn't that great because the defendant *is* guilty, the verdict *should* be guilty. But when it's not guilty, you just die. Because you know he's guilty, and you didn't convince the jurors. He's going to walk out. You had the responsibility and you failed."

Parks's slap at Edelbaum had been feeble, but Mosley means to make the most of it. *I wanted to discredit myself as a witness.* He wants to focus on the words, blow them up, underline them, make the jurors know something is hidden there, something crucial, something they should try to find. If a defense lawyer himself touches on a line of questioning forbidden to the prosecutor (in this case, Parks's reason for writing the letter), the taboo falls from the subject and the prosecutor too is allowed to pursue it.

"When you wrote this letter," Mosley asks Parks on the

stand the next morning, "you knew, did you not, that the letter would fall into the hands of defense attorneys?"

Edelbaum objects. Sustained.

"Well, was it your purpose in writing that letter—?"

Objection. Sustained.

Evidently it will not be possible to do this the nice way. Mosley takes the bull by the horns. "You stated you did not wish to be a witness when you wrote that letter, is that correct?"

"That's right."

"Were you *afraid* of being a witness?"

Explosion. Edelbaum on his feet, screaming. "I object to that your honor!"

"Yes. Objection sustained."

Fears, threats, Mafia vengeance—the rumblings are getting audible. Mosley has another clue to throw to the jurors, and Edelbaum is poised to knock it down.

"Since you first cooperated with the government," Mosley asks, "have you for the most part been kept out of prison population?"

"I object to this, your honor!" Edelbaum shouts.

"The objection is sustained. There is no need to yell at me."

Lyon had first offered the defense theory that Eleanor, Parks, and Zaher killed The Hawk. Now William Kleinman, one of Matteo's lawyers, will drop a hint as to whom the defense might call as a witness. After questioning Parks for several minutes Kleinman turns on him sharply and orders: "Parks! Look at me! Do you know a man by the name of Frank Breen?"

Parks does.

A few minutes later the trial breaks for lunch, and Parks

says to Mosley, "So there's gonna be a story. They're gonna come up with a story."

Price says, "Breen. I've heard that name. Who is he?"

"He's a good friend of Matteo's," Parks says. "They used to do stickups together."

"Does he have a yellow sheet?"

"Got to."

Price makes a phone call.

Parks keeps talking. "That's all? They're just gonna call Breen? They've got to come up with more than that."

"Richie," Mosley says, "all we can do is wait and see."

They are back in court, and Mosley says, "The people call John Rapacki." Rapacki climbs into the chair and Mosley leads him through his criminal record, which started with an armed robbery when he was 16. When the questions get down to pay dirt, Edelbaum objects, Mosley digs in, and the judge moves the battle to his chambers.

Mosley tells the judge and defense lawyers that Rapacki will testify that Crabbe, speaking of The Hawk, once admitted, "We took care of him. The boss ordered it."

Edelbaum, for the millionth time, demands a mistrial. He says it will be obvious to the jurors who "the boss" is and that "we could not possibly get a fair and impartial trial if this evidence comes out against my client."

Vitello suggests a compromise. Why not let Rapacki tell the jury that Crabbe said "We took care of him" but leave out the part about "the boss" ordering it? Mosley argues that standing alone and fragmented, Crabbe's admission sounds made up and phony. "It just doesn't sound like it's conversation, your honor."

The judge sides with the defense and orders Mosley to tell Rapacki not to say anything about "the boss" ordering the hit.

Back in court, Mosley asks Rapacki about a meeting he had with Crabbe after the murder.

"I seen him at a diner called the Target Diner. He drove up in his car, and instead of parking like he would usually do, he pulled over to the side and told me to get in. I got in the car and he had a newspaper there and he said, 'They found The Hawk.' So I looked at it. I didn't know at first what he was talking about. Then I seen it said something about, 'Body Found,' something to that effect.

"He said, 'From now on, whenever you meet me or whenever I'm with you, I want you to have a story why we're meeting together, that I'm helping you to get a job. Because I expect the cops to pick me up, the bulls to pick me up.'

"I asked him why. He said, 'Because we had to take care of him.' He pointed to the picture."

"In the paper?"

"In the paper."

Rapacki admits on cross-examination that he was once handcuffed to Zaher on a ride from the court house to the jail. They discussed their sentence, he says, but not the upcoming trial. And in any case that brief meeting took place long after he first came forward with Crabbe's admission.

Rapacki has come over better than any of the others. He is nervous and intense, and in his face and tone displays the desperate, you-*must*-believe-me eagerness of a man who is telling the truth. When it is over, Rapacki is relieved but still very nervous. He is angry with Mosley for giving the defense his file. He thinks Mosley should have "lost" the file.

"That Mosley is too damned honest," Rapacki says hotly to Price. "Some day one of these guys will get him in an alley some place and he'll find out how honest and decent they'll be with him."

Rapacki is in handcuffs, ready to return to jail. Mosley thanks him for testifying. Rapacki says he is upset about his wife. He is afraid Sonny's men will kill her.

And he is afraid for himself, too. He says he had a dream the night before that when he got back to the jail after his testimony, the warden met him at the door. The warden took him inside to a big, thick wooden door with a rope handle. The warden pulled the door open and said, "Right in here." Rapacki walked through the door and the warden swung it shut. "Then," Rapacki says, "when I was locked inside I saw that it wasn't a room I had walked into. It was a coffin."

After Rapacki, the prosecution rests its case. Mosley spends the weekend reading through 1,015 pages of trial transcript, studying the testimony so far, and guessing what is to come. He knows for certain that the defendants will not take the stand themselves—if they do he will be permitted on cross-examination to lay open their criminal history. What will the defense come up with? Will they produce a witness to say he was with one of the defendants the night Parks said he saw them in the parking lot? What will Breen say? Have they fed him a story?

Before the jury comes in to begin hearing the defense's case, the judge hands to Mosley and defense lawyers copies of a letter he received from a prisoner at Attica State Prison. Burton Pugach, a lawyer serving fifteen years for hiring thugs to throw lye in his girl friend's face, claimed knowledge of The Hawk murder. That is not a surprise. He has already falsely claimed knowledge of at least one other murder. He is one of those prisoners—there are quite a number of them—who use information picked up from newspapers to try to convince judges and attorneys that they have evidence. If they succeed, they might win a trip into the city and a little attention, perhaps notoriety. And if they actually help a defendant beat a case, they can look forward to valuable favors and rewards.

Pugach is not the only convict working on The Hawk case. Lyon tells the judge he has heard from another prisoner named Raymond Williams and in fact intends to call him as a witness.

Whoever they call, Rapacki will be hard to fight. If the defense is to stick to its claim that the entire people's case is a frame-up, they will have to connect Rapacki with the plot.

For their first witness, the defense calls to the stand the warden of the Nassau County jail. The warden says that although Rapacki had been in the jail at the same time as the others, he had never had contact with them. On one occasion, however, Cordero and Rapacki had been visited at the same time by their wives. But even then, the prisoners had been isolated in separate cubicles.

The defense calls Breen. A dark, heavy-set young man, he testifies that he is the manager of a Manhattan restaurant, has a conviction for petty larceny, and was tossed out of the Army with a bad-conduct discharge. He says he knows Parks and once had seen him with a new Buick Riviera.

"I asked him where he got the money for the automobile. He said he had done a favor for a girl and she advanced him the money, gave him the money."

"Now, in November of 1964," Lyon asks, "did you go out with Richard Parks and two girls?"

"Yes, I did. We went for a few drinks and then went up to their apartment. A little later on two other fellows came over and we left. We left the apartment and went for a cup of coffee and Richie called the apartment back. He was looking to go back up again. He talked to the girls and they told him not to bother coming back and hung up.

"We went back to the apartment house and he tried to get into the downstairs vestibule door, which was locked. He rang the bell, which they didn't answer. At that time I had a vehicle for the laundry I was working for. I stepped into the vehicle to leave, and he had taken out a pistol and shot the windows out of their apartment house."

Mosley is taking quick notes on a pad of lined yellow paper.

"Did you have any conversation with Richard Parks about this incident?" Lyon asks.

"Yes. The following evening we were discussing the events of the night before and he said to me that they didn't—the girls didn't—know who they were messing around with. They would go the same way The Hawk went. A month later we got into an argument in the same bar and grill that we were in that evening in November, and he took a pistol out on me and told me if I didn't stop pushing him around I would wind up in the river like The Hawk."

"Did you have any other conversations about the $2,000?" That is a slip. In his questioning of Breen, Lyon has not mentioned the amount Parks put down for the car. But Breen knows what to say.

"Well, around January or the first part of 1965, he had asked me if I wanted to go with him to visit a girl friend of his, and the girl that advanced him the money for the car, and at the time I refused."

"Did he ever tell you who the girl was?"

"I know her name was Eleanor, that's all."

"Did he ever talk to you about a John from Brooklyn?" This is a change. Earlier Lyon accused Parks and Zaher of killing The Hawk. Now it appears he will make it Parks and John Rapacki. Why the switch?

"At the time of the November conversations in the bar, when he mentioned the fact about the girls' not knowing who they messed around with, he had said at that time that it was—this fellow John from Brooklyn and he had taken care of The Hawk. That was the conversation."

Mosley does not want any juror thinking that Breen is a disinterested citizen who just happens to be testifying out of a desire to do the right thing for law and order. He wants it clear that Breen knows the defendants. Parks said Breen and Matteo pulled stickups together.

"Do you know the defendant Thomas Matteo?" Mosley asks when his turn comes to cross-examine.

"Yes, I do."

This is a defense witness now, and Mosley's manner shifts sharply from the slow, hands-clasped calmness he used to keep his own witnesses unruffled and relaxed. This is the enemy, and his questions come fast and laced with contempt.

"How long do you know him?"

"Since around 1959, 1960."

"Did you also reside near him?"

"Yes. I was in the same area."

He asks Breen about his employment record—he had held a long list of jobs—and then says cuttingly, "And isn't it true that you were fired from some of those jobs for theft?"

Breen says that is not true.

He asks Breen about Parks's shooting out the windows of the girls' apartment. "You went to the police about that, didn't you?"

"No, I didn't."

Mosley pretends to look shocked. He knows the jurors would have gone to the police about it. "You didn't report that?"

"No, sir."

Mosley asks about the incident with the gun in the bar. "Did you go to the police about *that?*"

"No, I didn't."

"Did you tell them that a man had threatened you with a gun?"

"No, I didn't."

"Did you tell anyone else about this?"

"No."

"Was he still a *friend* of yours?"

"I just passed it off."

Mosley looks astonished. "You *passed that off?*"

"Yes, I did."

Parks has testified that he saw The Hawk stabbed *immediately after* he cried out and moved his arms. The defense wants to claim that when The Hawk was stabbed he was already dead of bullet wounds and could not have moved or spoken, as Parks says he did. Dr. Helpern, the medical examiner, has refused to support the defense argument, or even to speculate on when precisely The Hawk died, on which came first, the bullets or the stabs, and on whether or not the bullets would have left The Hawk incapable of speech or motion.

Now the defense calls an expert they think will contradict Helpern. Dr. Joseph Spellman, Philadelphia's chief medical examiner, takes the stand and says that one of the bullets, which came to rest in The Hawk's spinal canal, would have left the victim paralyzed from the shoulders down.

"He would be able to breathe—he might be able to

breathe—but he would not be able to voluntarily move his hands or his feet." He further delights the defense by telling the jurors that "In my opinion, the bullet wounds came before the stab wounds."

"Doctor," Lyon continues, "would you tell us whether a man with those bullet holes—bullet wounds—in his head and in his neck would be capable of intelligible speech?"

"In my opinion he would not."

In other words, it might appear that The Hawk was shot, paralyzed, and incapable of speech and movement before he was stabbed, and that anyone who says he was stabbed immediately after moving and crying out is a liar.

Mosley must counter that suggestion. He asks if The Hawk's arms might have been capable of *involuntary* motion.

"I feel there would have been a complete paralysis, so that no voluntary or involuntary movement of the arms would be possible."

"Suppose he was being moved?" Mosley persists.

"The arms would be completely limp, and of course moving—if they would be moved—as pressure were applied to them—"

"Excuse me?"

"If you grabbed him by the arm, the arm would go up."

As he says that, he raises one of his arms—exactly as Parks did when describing how The Hawk's arms had moved.

"The way you just indicated?" Mosley says.

"Yes. He would be completely flabby."

"Of course, if he was grabbed under *both* arms, both arms could move the same way. Is that correct?"

"Yes."

Spellman is not aware how critical his gesture was.

Mosley moves on to the next point. "Doctor, could not this deceased have received the first gunshot wound, then have been stabbed, and then shot some more, and then stabbed some more? You see, there were eighteen stab wounds. That's why I say that."

"I do not believe so."

"Couldn't he have received the gunshot wound through the chest, and then have been stabbed several times, or once or twice, and then shot and then stabbed again?"

Spellman wavers. "Some of these stab wounds," he says, considering, "are described as not extensive."

"Right."

"I think it is possible that he could have been stabbed with one of these relatively mild stab wounds before being shot."

"What about Pugach and Williams?" Price asks Mosley after the defense has rested. "They're not going to call them?"

"Pugach they decided to forget. He's a nut. Williams, they probably took one look at his sheet and that was that."

Price says something about the summations.

"Edelbaum said that if I thought he'd been loud up till now I should get ear plugs for his summation. Tomorrow, I really dread. I've gotta sit there all day and just listen and squirm. You cringe inside when these bastards sum up."

"I submit to you that on the evidence in this case . . ." Kleinman, speaking sixty-five minutes, is ending his summation on a familiar note " . . . evidence from such polluted sources, from the rotten, filthy creatures who came before you here, that you wouldn't convict a *dog* on it. And here you are asked to convict a young man [Tommy Matteo, his client] of murder in the first degree. Are you satisfied in your conscience, in your heart, in your minds to a moral certainty beyond a reasonable doubt? *Are you?* If you are, then convict. But if there is *one single reasonable doubt,* you must acquit."

Vitello goes at it for an hour. " . . . Between July 7, 1965, and September 30, 1965, Mr. John Cordero averaged one bank robbery every twelve days. *That's* Mr. Cordero. He, together with Parks, *all by themselves* are a national crime wave. . . ."

"It occurs to me . . ." Lyon is taking his turn now " . . . that perhaps if one of us had taken over a new business and had been told that a certain Charles Zaher said, 'We better get rid of one of our employees because he's stealing from the till,' and not only that, but Cordero agrees with him, and Parks says, 'I happened to look at that till and I sneaked all over the room, and I *watched* him,' and we all discussed whether to fire this fellow or not, and somebody said, 'Wait a minute. Do you know who Zaher is? Do you know who Cordero is? Do you know that Parks said that he slept with Cordero's wife?' And we turn around to whoever said don't keep this man, and wouldn't we say to whoever brought this accusation, 'Are you *kidding?* Are you really *kidding?* You want us to fire a man from a job because this *scum* got together and told a story about him?' "

Again Lyon accuses Parks of conspiring with Eleanor and John Rapacki to kill The Hawk. He says that Rapacki's wife and Eleanor helped Rapacki communicate with the other witnesses.

"Do you remember, I asked Cordero who Eleanor went out with before she went out with Cordero, and do you remember what he said? He said she went out with a Polish fellow who lived on Long Island. Was that John Rapacki?

We found a witness and that witness told you that Parks was boasting he got $2,000 from a woman and he wouldn't mention the name, and six months later he said that woman's name was Eleanor. He says, 'He pulled a gun on me' and he said something to the effect that, 'Don't fool with me, John and I killed The Hawk,' or whatever language I don't remember exactly. *There* is your case."

Edelbaum begins. He rises from the far end of the defense table and shuffles the width of the courtroom to the jury box. "It now becomes my privilege to talk to you, and before I start, I would be indeed ungrateful if I didn't say to the distinguished gentleman who sits on this bench . . ." a nod toward the judge " . . . that I thank him from the bottom of my heart for the fair and impartial way he has presided at this trial, for his many courtesies that he has extended to me because of my busy calendar, for his patience with me, because by nature I confess to be a volatile man.

"Now—where do we start?" His voice rises sharply, and for the rest of his summation it will not descend. "I must tell you that *never* in my life, in all the years I have practiced law—and I have tried a great many cases—have I ever slept the night before a summation. Last night was no different, because I feel a great responsibility. I have been very volatile in this trial. Maybe I have spoken too loud at times. But it arises from indignation that in 1967, in a country as *great* as ours, such a case should be *permitted* to be brought into an American courtroom—that a district attorney . . ." he waves his glasses at the jurors " . . . will ask you to convict these defendants on the testimony of these *creatures,* who testified in this courtroom."

Edelbaum now extends himself and vilifies not only the witnesses but Mosley as well. "Oh, I have an idea what *he . . ."* a nod at Mosley *" . . .* will do in summation! You will see rolled into this courtroom the concrete blocks, the clothing. Why? To *prejudice* you! Is there any *doubt* that this was an atrocious crime? Is there any *doubt* that it was a despicable crime? The question for you to decide is have the people proved beyond a reasonable doubt to a moral certainty that these defendants committed this crime. So don't be fooled by that parade of the concrete blocks—and I feel sorry for the court officer who has to drag those things into the courtroom. What does *that* add to this case? But it will be paraded in here! You can be *sure* of that!"

Franzese looks half asleep. Mosley makes a note.

Edelbaum sips from a glass of water. He has succeeded during the trial in suppressing and distorting quantities of significant evidence. He has kept the jurors' ignorance—so carefully assured when they were selected—almost totally intact. Yet he knows that the concrete blocks, the bullets, the stabs, Parks's brief outburst about his letter, suggest Mafia. He must force the jurors not to react to that suggestion.

"Each one of you," he says now, leaning close to the jurors, "made me a promise under oath. I am confident you are going to keep that promise. You promised me that when you decide this case, you will decide this case only on the evidence in this courtroom. If you do that, there can be only one verdict in this case—and that is, not guilty. I say to you the only other verdict would come from something in your *mind*—not adduced in this courtroom.

He returns to his attack on the witnesses—and on Mosley, whom he now casts as hardly less sinister.

"What is the evidence against my client, John Franzese? Two bank robbers, who made a *bargain,* who make my sense of justice *cringe,* that a *district attorney,* an elected public official, would *bargain* with the likes of a Cordero. And with all of that—*all of that*—what do they claim? That my client, in July of 1965, at the Aqueduct Motel, said, 'I ordered the hit of The Hawk.' Now, ask yourselves! Do people who commit the kind of crime that was committed here in the County of Queens with the killing of The Hawk, do they go out and reveal their complicity to two known drug addicts? It shocks your common sense! But no—we'll parade in the blocks. We'll have these pictures with the man trussed up. And we will get a conviction. Is *that* the way to try a case?"

He speaks of Cordero and Zaher. "Motive to *lie*—those two men! Just *picture* this. Men who go into banks with loaded guns, prepared to *kill* if necessary, otherwise why are the guns loaded? If those men would do *that* to get a paltry sum of money, ask yourself what would they do to save themselves twenty-five years in jail—men who have already been in prison and know what it's like. What would they *do*? Would they *lie*? Would they *perjure* themselves? Of *course* they would!"

He mentions Zaher, who when he was jailed as a material witness was paid the customary $3-a-day witness fee. "The district attorney requested that he get a suspended sentence so they could hold him as a material witness so he could be *paid!*" In every word and gesture he oozes righteous outrage. He condemns "the deal" made with the witnesses for their cooperation and suggests to the jurors that if they return a guilty verdict, they themselves will be as evil. "You're going to *endorse* the contract made—*the deal*—by a verdict of not guilty—and let these gunmen walk out? Have the parole board parole these *gunmen* on the people of Queens County?"

He pauses. Silence. He sips from a glass. His performance

officially is for the jurors, but he cherishes, too, the other audience: the rapt judge, the young attorneys who have come to study his technique. The jurors have not caught the act before, do not know that it *is* an act, and so they alone accept it as reality.

Edelbaum speaks of Zaher's escape from jail, and his re-arrest with a companion. "And the grand jury of this county, this district attorney, indicted them for the felony of conspiracy to commit robbery in the first degree, and indicted them for possession of a weapon as a felony. And on *both* felonies, he was subject as a second offender. And *another deal* is made—ANOTHER DEAL!—for that scum! And *who* made the deal? *Mister* Mosley. Mr. Mosley made the deal. Mr. Mosley stood up before a judge of this court and recommended that he be permitted to plead guilty to at-tempted possession of a gun. And did Mr. Mosley stop there? No! He *promised* this man, 'If you will testify in this case, I will call to the attention of the sentencing judge your cooper-ation.' And Mr. Zaher by this time knows what *that* means. He got a *taste* of it. He got a suspended sentence for *two armed bank holdups*. Motive to lie? Do you need a *better* motive to lie than that motive?"

If Zaher is bad, he is nothing next to Parks. "Did you ever in your life see a more cold, calculated killer than Parks? He sat back in that chair and you heard how the answers came out. I tell you at times as I stood there and I cross-examined him I was very happy he didn't have a loaded gun at *that* time in his hand. Because I wouldn't have liked to have that loaded gun in front of *me!*"

He tries desperately to argue that Rapacki did know Zaher, and did plot with him. " . . . He *knows* Zaher! He was brought down to the District Attorney's Office by the same detective from the Nassau County jail in the same car to the District Attorney's Office. And he had the temerity to *lie* on that witness stand on direct examination and say he didn't know Charlie Zaher. Do you know why they didn't want it to be known that they knew each other? Because they *all* contributed to the story. These *gangsters,* these would-be murderers, they *all* contributed to the story!"

For a finish, Edelbaum puts the jurors themselves on trial. "You know, the symbol of justice is blind with the scales. I say *all during this trial*—since the inception of this prosecution—the symbol of justice has been hanging her head, that in an American courtroom such a trial could take place. All I ask you, gentlemen of the jury, is by your verdict of not guilty to have the symbol of justice raise her head again. Don't give these would-be murderers a license to go out—as Mr. Zaher did—and make a beeline for the next bank with a loaded gun. I'm positive you will do justice in this case by finding the defendants not guilty. Thank you."

The trial is recessed for lunch. Young lawyers and leather-jacketed friends of the defendants surround Edelbaum on his way from the courtroom. They smother him in handshakes, back slaps, congratulations.

Mosley sits in his office, going over his summation with Price and Walter Anderson. Edelbaum has put him on the spot with the blocks. He decides to use them, to have them on the floor in front of the jury box, but not to mention them, to let them just sit there as quiet symbols of the hidden issue, the Mafia.

Someone offers him a roast-beef sandwich. He refuses it. More detectives come into the office, and he goes up to the empty witness room. He sits alone and studies notes that now fill eighteen pages.

Downstairs in Mosley's office Price says to Anderson,

"You know, it must be like having your first kid. Right? Just before it comes?"

At one-twenty the court reconvenes and Mosley walks in from the door leading to the witness room. He faces the jury, and begins softly.

"You have heard over five hours of excellent summation by attorneys for the defense. I do not intend to take anywhere near the length of time that their combined summations have taken. I am not possessed of the oratory, or the experience, that they are. As a matter of fact, after hearing these four eminent defense attorneys, I feel somewhat the way Carl Hubbel must have that day when he faced Ruth, Gehrig, Foxx, and Cronin."

He backs off from the jury box and stands with his hands clasped tightly behind him. His voice goes up. "Now, what kind of a crime are we dealing with here? You heard Mr. Lyon talk about the man with his hand in the till. *That* isn't the kind of crime we are dealing with here."

He holds up a picture of The Hawk's trussed and weighted body lying on the beach. "*This* is the kind of crime that we are dealing with here. A crime committed in secret, a crime that was never intended to be discovered. But it was bungled. It was bungled by the perpetrators. And it *was* discovered. And it *was* solved.

"Mr. Edelbaum made a point: 'Will you let these bank robbers walk the streets by convicting the defendants?' You are not *asked* to do that. You know what the deal was—the deal in quotes—between the United States attorney and these witnesses, and between the district attorney and these witnesses. Whether they go free or not, or when they go free, in no way—*in no way*—will be determined by your verdict. It would be *immoral* to make such a deal with people. 'Unless the defendants are convicted, you won't receive any consideration.' That would be immoral!

"What is the issue here? The issue is really, *did* these witnesses lie? *Not*, are they capable of lying? *Not*, did they lie in the past? *Not*, did they lie under oath in the past, as Mr. Cordero admits having done. *Not*, whether they have motives to lie. Of course they have motives to lie. The issue is—*did they lie?*

"You have heard—oh, really, two trials here. The trial by the people of the State of New York, and the trial of these witnesses as to whether or not they have lied in the past, as to whether or not what they wrote in certain letters to a United States attorney and to a district attorney was true or not. We are interested in the *first* trial—the trial of the people of the State of New York against *these* defendants."

He knows he must explain why Zaher and Parks refused to testify about The Hawk murder unless they were themselves granted immunity to prosecution for the murder.

"Let me ask you this. If you were Mr. Zaher, living in the strata of society that he lives in, and you knew that your car had been used in a hit, and you knew your background, wouldn't you ask the district attorney for immunity before you cooperated with him? Wouldn't you? Whether or not you're actually guilty of the homicide, wouldn't you ask for immunity? Doesn't your common sense tell you that you would? You would take no chances."

Mosley is taking no chances on the jurors' ignoring the witnesses' hints of fear and vengeance. The defense has struggled to keep the jurors from thinking about the Mafia and gang slayings. Mosley wants to emphasize that it was fear of Mafia vengeance that made the witnesses try to avoid testifying. "It was brought out that Mr. Zaher faked a suicide attempt—another attempt at delusion, another attempt to con the authorities, as the defense would say. *Why* did Mr. Zaher attempt suicide? He told you. He didn't want to be a witness!"

Kleinman throws the block. "Your honor, I object to that. There is no evidence in the case—"

"Mr. Foreman and gentlemen of the jury," the judge says, "remember it's *your* recollection of the evidence that prevails. What Mr. Mosley says is not evidence in the case, and his recollection is not binding on you any more than the recollection of any other person in this courtroom."

Mosley holds up a picture of The Hawk's bloated body. "There is evidence in *this* record as to what happens to squealers!"

Kleinman jumps back in. "I object to that in connection with the context of Mr. Mosley's argument to the jury. I submit it is improper. It brings in an element in this case of which there is no evidence, and I move for a mistrial."

"Denied. You have an exception."

"It was suggested to you," Mosley goes on, "that the district attorney asked for a suspended sentence [for Zaher] so that the district attorney could put him in the civil jail where he would get paid." Mosley cannot come out and say that Zaher was jailed to protect him from Mafia assassins, but he can try to hint at it. "Do you think for one minute that this was the reason why he was put in a civil jail? So that he could get paid?"

Kleinman sees what Mosley is trying to tell the jurors, and tries to stop him with an objection. The judge instructs the jury to disregard Mosley's last remark. Mosley continues, pressing the point. More objections. "I submit," Mosley shouts finally, trying to bulldoze his point through the interruptions, "you might also draw the inference, after listening to him and hearing about his background, that when he hits the street sometime in the future, it won't be for long!"

Objection. Motion for mistrial. Denied.

Mosley leaves Zaher and moves on to Cordero. "I think it's conceded that Mr. Cordero could not be an accomplice to the murder, since he was in prison at the time. Does he have a motive to lie? Of course he has a motive to lie. Did he lie? That's for you to decide. He admitted here that he lied under oath in the grand jury. You accept that. You'll believe him when he says that, won't you? Of course you will. He stated here that he always lied to the FBI. Why wouldn't he? He tells them the truth, he is obviously going to spend more time in prison. Certainly, he lies to the FBI. It would abuse your common sense if he ever stood on that stand and said, 'I always tell the FBI the truth when they pick me up.'

"You heard the letter that he wrote, in which he makes demands, some of which were acquiesced to. Well, who do people who commit crimes like this crime talk to? I submit they talk to people like Mr. Cordero. So how do we get Mr. Cordero to tell us—by us I mean the law-enforcement agencies—what he knows about a crime? It *has* to be a quid pro quo. I don't like it. I think it's terrible. But what are we going to do? How are we going to solve these kinds of crimes? Does it mean that because of *this* he is lying?

"Mr. Parks was cross-examined at length about a letter, a very, very vituperative letter, which Mr. Edelbaum would suggest to you destroys his credibility and his believability as a witness here. Mr. Parks stated that he wrote that letter full of lies *just for that purpose,* that he didn't want to be a witness for the government. That doesn't make him a liar here. There is no testimony he ever lied under oath at any of the government trials.

"If these witnesses were to have taken that stand and if they were to have said, 'We don't expect anything in return for our testimony. We don't expect a thing,' would you believe them? Would you really believe that people like this will testify without expecting some reward? Of course not! So you see, it's because they're in prison, and because they have records, that the defense puts you in a bind. They're lying because they have reason to lie. So the implication is that no prisoner could ever be trustworthy. Your common sense tells you that that is not so."

Rounding out his assessment of Zaher's version of the sit-down, Mosley says, "Now, this testimony, is there anything implausible about it? Isn't this the way that people who had committed a killing such as this—isn't this the way they would talk among their associates? A problem arises, a shooting, a drunken woman making an accusation. You've got to keep the thing quiet. Let's sit down. Let's talk about it. 'What's the big deal?' It's a big deal because the accusation happens to be true. These people were involved in the death of The Hawk. So it *is* a big thing, and they sit down and they do discuss it."

The defense has claimed that the whole case, the whole plot to frame Sonny, was initiated by Cordero. "Was *Cordero* the boss in this case?" Mosley shouts suddenly. And as he shouts, he spins around, away from the jurors, toward the defense tables. His arm goes straight and stiffens toward Franzese, sitting calmly at the other side of the room. "*There* is the boss! Right down there at the end of the table!"

Mosley turns back to the jurors. The hoods in the audience exchange worried glances.

"Now, you heard it said, 'Where is the corroboration here? All you heard testimony from was convicted criminals

that are bargaining, that are looking for a break.' I submit
that Mr. Rapacki, Mr. John Rapacki, is corroboration to this
whole picture. Mr. Rapacki testified that he spoke to detective Joseph Price in 1965, was brought down to a grand jury
in Queens in September of 1966. Then, in a futile attempt to
show collusion, the argument is advanced to you that
because of the fact that the Nassau County jail has visiting
hours at a certain time, the wives of Cordero and Rapacki
somehow got together and concocted Rapacki's story. I
submit to you—doesn't that abuse your common sense?
They weren't together until *after* the grand jury, number
one. They were never together in the jail, number two.
They weren't even physically in the same institution until
after the grand jury!

"Rapacki's asked on the stand, 'Do you know Charles
Zaher?' He says no, he doesn't know the man. He spent half
an hour with him being brought down to the District
Attorney's Office. Does he know him? Do you know someone if you share a taxi ride while going to an airport? That
isn't knowing someone in any sense of the word. And the
defense would have you believe that because of that he's a
liar."

Mosley begins his windup. "Now, where do you get the
answer? How do you solve this kind of crime? How many
times is this kind of crime ever solved? Eyewitnesses? Even
now we don't know where the man was shot. We don't
know where he was dumped into Jamaica Bay. How do you
ask about it? Do you just bury Ernie and shake it off as
another statistic? No one is going to talk about it to any
legitimate witness that I could produce here.

"This case comes right out of the sewer, right out of the
gutter. Where do the police have to go? Where does the

district attorney have to go—whether we want to or not? Right down into the sewer, right down into the gutter.

"But the police were lucky in this case through a combination of circumstances. Number one: the killers apparently didn't open him up enough because enough gas formed in him to raise up 135 pounds of cinder blocks and float it into Breezy Point. So the crime was discovered. Number two: apparently in their haste they left his identification on him. Number three: the individual had enough identifying characteristics—one eye, a bullet in his head, a mesh in his stomach—that he could be identified.

"Then the biggest stroke of luck of all. Over a year later, the widow gets a few drinks in her and accuses the defendant Florio of having something to do with his death. And this precipitates a shooting in which her boy friend fortunately—fortunately—fires shots at Florio. Florio panics. And the next day a meeting is held, and the whole situation is discussed. What about this widow? What about Eleanor? What about John Cordero firing shots? We are all very concerned about this because we all had a piece of it and we don't want anything to come out about it. So let's talk it over. Let's sit down and talk about it. And they come to an agreement, a meeting of the minds.

"Of course, now, the police know nothing about this, about this meeting. But it has happened. About the same time the police, still investigating the case, talk to Mr. Rapacki in August of 1965. The investigation continues.

"Now, here is the next piece of luck. These three bank robbers get caught, get arrested, and they're facing long prison terms. And they work the quid pro quo, with some misgivings as they testified to—a letter full of lies where one didn't want to testify, an attempted faked suicide because another one didn't want to testify. They're playing with dynamite here to save a few years in prison. They make their decision, and the district attorney and the police then have a decision to make. What do we do now? We have these bank robbers, and we have a brutal gangland assassination."

Lyon doesn't like the word "gangland." He objects. The judge sustains him.

"Well," Mosley goes on, "you have heard the testimony as to the deals that the police department and the United States attorney and the district attorney made with these people. You ask yourselves *why*. If such deals weren't made, would this kind of case ever—*ever*—be solved?"

Lyon objects again. The judge sustains him.

"Well, gentlemen, I submit to you that credible evidence *has* been brought before you. I don't vouch for the character of these witnesses. I think that's quite obvious. But the whole point is—did they lie *here* or not? I submit to you they have *not* lied here. There is *no evidence* that they have lied *here*."

Edelbaum is up. "I object to the opinion of the district attorney. He knows that's improper. He says, 'I submit they did not lie.' That's an opinion of his. That's for the jury to determine."

Mosley turns to the judge. "*He* has been yelling that they *are* lying, your honor. What is this?"

"Now, let *me* rule on the situation," the judge says. "Please don't make statements. The objection is overruled, with an exception."

Mosley is finished anyway. "I submit, gentlemen of the jury, that this case has been proved beyond a reasonable doubt by witnesses who told the truth here in this courtroom. And I submit in the name of the people of the State of New York that the people have proven the guilt of the defendants of the crime of murder in the first degree."

He sits down. There is no jubilation now. The defendants' friends and relatives file out slowly, silent and unsmiling.

Mosley goes down to his office. Rapacki is there, angry and scared. A Long Island newspaper has printed the address of his common-law wife. He begs to have police radio cars keep a special watch on her house. "She doesn't drive anymore," he says, "so at least they can't put a bomb in her car."

Mosley and Price try to calm him. Rapacki shakes his head with fear and frustration. "They've got to put Sonny away, Mr. Mosley. They've got to. I'm praying and praying that they put him away. I want him away."

Mosley finished his summation at two-fifty, and an hour later he, Price, Anderson, and some friends are in Luigi's having a beer. There is nothing more to do.

"Tomorrow," Mosley says, "we listen to the judge's charge, and then we come here and we wait. The whole thing boils down to the fact that it's a gangland killing and they either accept these witnesses or they don't. You could talk a million years and not change that. If you listen to the charge tomorrow you'll find out the burden in proving some one guilty. You'll hear all the conditions that have to be met before the jury can return a guilty verdict. You'll wonder how anyone is *ever* found guilty."

They discuss the trial and the summations that have just ended. "When I was in front of the jury," Mosley says, "I thought, they *can't* acquit. They just can't. How could twelve men reach a verdict of acquittal on this case? But now I don't know. I have a feeling they won't be convicted, an intuition."

When Mafia men are in trouble, help has a mysterious way of arriving in the nick of time. Now, the morning after Mosley's summation, it will come with only thirty-one minutes to spare, from a killer imprisoned in Sing Sing's death row. The judge has said that at 10 A.M. he will instruct the jury and lock it up to deliberate. At exactly 9:29—the time is stamped on the envelope—a letter arrives for the judge. He summons Mosley and defense lawyers to his chambers. After several minutes, Mosley comes out angry and shaken. He grabs Price by the arm and heads for his office.

"Some guy named Sher up in the death house," Mosley tells Price, "wrote a letter to the judge that he was locked up with Rapacki and Rapacki told him he had dealings with The Hawk, had trouble with The Hawk, and killed him. There's enough in the letter so you know he really knew Rapacki."

Price is stunned. "They had to come up with something, didn't they, Jimmy? So now we know. This is it."

Rapacki is in Mosley's office talking to his guards. His fear has driven him to the edge of his sanity.

Price and Mosley debate how much, if anything, they should tell Rapacki about Sher. The trick is to find out everything Rapacki knows about Sher without telling him anything about the letter. Mosley wants to know exactly what Rapacki told Sher in prison. He does not want Rapacki to panic and start trying to shift facts around to make things sound better.

"If this guy Sher takes the stand, I'm dead," Mosley says.

A detective comes down and says the judge is on the bench. Before he leaves to go up to court, Mosley makes up his mind about Rapacki. "All right," he tells Price. "Talk to him."

Price goes into Mosley's office and sits down and stares at Rapacki. Rapacki knows something is wrong. After ten seconds of hard, silent staring, Price gives up the one fact he must give up to get things started. He says simply, "Walter Sher."

"What?"

"Walter Sher."

"What about him?"

"What do you know about him?"

"Murder."

"What kind?"

"Jewelry-store holdup. He was in the death house. They brought him down to the jail I was in for something. Why?"

"I'm trying to find out. Were you friends?"

"No. I just talked to him. You talk to anyone in there."

"You didn't tell him anything?"

"What would I have to tell him? I just talked to him. Anyway, you know me, Joe. I don't tell nobody nothin'. I'm not an idiot. What is it?"

"I don't know." Price leaves the room and sends the guards back in.

Mosley comes down from court, where the judge has told the jury he is delaying his charge a day, and Price tells him Rapacki admits knowing Sher. Mosley decides to read Rapacki the letter. He walks into his office and sits down behind his desk. Price sits facing Rapacki, studying his reactions. Rapacki—very thin and even paler than usual—is forward in his chair, very nervous.

"I want to read you something, John," Mosley says calmly, and begins. "Honorable Judge Bosch: my name is

Walter Sher, prison number 132-921, and I am currently confined in the death house of this prison under sentence of death. I feel that I must write to you in order to make you aware of a gross miscarriage of justice. I will be as brief as possible in this letter, but I am also quite willing to testify to the following information. In 1965, on October 1, I was taken from this prison and transferred to the Nassau County jail. During this period of time I met and became friendly with another inmate named John Rapacki. Mr. Rapacki was extremely nervous and worried about his wife and about his case, and he used to ask me frequently for my opinion on various aspects of his case—"

Rapacki breaks in, angry and excited. "There's a frame coming up, right?"

Mosley reads on. "He attempted to find out the details of my case, and when I discouraged all his attempts at this, he then attempted to enlist my aid in an escape plan to which I also paid no attention. He told me he had cut his veins in an attempt at suicide so he would be sent to the hospital where he might perfect his escape—"

Rapacki pushes up his sleeve to show the scar where seventeen stitches closed a slash on his arm. "That was a *real* attempt," he shouts. "My wife wasn't visiting me and I tried to kill myself!"

"John," Price says gently, "we know. Just listen."

". . . However, this failed and they even shackled his ankles in chains when they brought him to the court. Mr. Rapacki said that all his money had gone to his lawyers in Suffolk and Nassau counties and that he would never have had to stick up that restaurant except for the fact that his partner, whom he called Hawk, had swindled him out of his share of the proceeds of a job that they had pulled together. He told me that he and Hawk stuck up a bank and got about $13,000. He let Hawk hold the cash because he, Rapacki, was being harassed by the Suffolk County police at the time. Later he needed some cash in order to pay his lawyer in Suffolk County and he asked Hawk. He was told that Hawk shylocked the money out in loans to some businessmen, and Hawk told him that their money was lent out at 25 percent interest. Mr. Rapacki continued to ask for his share of this money over a period of time, but to no avail. Finally, Hawk told him that the businessmen refused to pay and also that if he, Hawk, continued to bother him he would notify the police. Mr. Rapacki told me that he knew all along that his crime partner was beating him out of his share of the cash, but that he wanted to let him hang himself. He said he went along with all of it so that he could catch Hawk off his guard. He told me that he succeeded in doing this and that he, Rapacki, killed Hawk. I did not question him on this as I could not even understand why he told me this story. Later I concluded that he was just trying to impress me and I forgot the entire incident."

Rapacki cannot control himself. He is almost hysterical.

"Give me a lie-detector test! Give us both one! Let me alone with that punk for a minute! Now I know why they wanted immunity. Zaher told me in the car they had immunity because they were afraid Sonny would frame them. What a *jerk* I am! I'm getting *nothing* out of this, and now I'm being framed for murder!"

Price and Mosley calm Rapacki, and another detective comes in and leads him out of the office.

Walter Anderson comes in. "Price and I are going to Sing Sing," Mosley says quickly. "Call CIB and see if this guy is in the family [Franzese's gang]."

"It's being done," Anderson says.

Rapacki is sitting with a guard next to Mosley's secretary. He is still upset, talking about a frame. On his way out, Mosley tries to soothe him. "Look, John, it's ridiculous. I know that—but I've got to prove it."

In the car with Price, Mosley says, "You don't know what this guy Sher is doing. Maybe all he wants is a trip down to New York." Mosley knows Sher might have written the letter just to get a ride to New York, or because he hoped— or had been promised—that Franzese would reward him with some expensive legal talent (his appeal is currently in the hands of a court-assigned attorney), or simply because to have rescued Franzese from a murder conviction would make him a prison hero.

Because Rapacki's testimony was most damaging to Crabbe, it is Crabbe's lawyer, Herb Lyon, who will handle Sher. Mosley wants to beat him to the prison. The car heads up the New York State Thruway and holds 85 mph.

"Maybe I shouldn't see him at all," Mosley says. "If I do Lyon will say I was up here trying to get him to change his story." He thinks for a moment. "We'll have to check if he wrote any other letters like this on any other cases."

"When we get there," Price says, "we'll go over his whole package."

After an hour's drive, Price and Mosley pull up to the high gray prison walls. They walk through the iron door of the administration building, show credentials, and sign a register.

Lyon has not arrived yet.

Mosley goes to an office to check Sher's file. A guard takes Price to the death house.

After more than an hour, Price comes back to Mosley. "He says just what he said in the letter," Price tells Mosley. "He doesn't budge. He's a very careful, cunning guy. Before

I went in, the guard said to me, 'Look out for this one, he's very, very sharp. Watch yourself.' He's made up his mind what he's gonna do, and he's gonna do it."

They get back in the car and head for New York.

"Nothing's ever final," Mosley says after a few minutes' silence. "I thought I had a shot at it. I thought I had it. And now this eleventh hour—the only thing that was ever final was the electric chair, and they took that away."

"The long arm of the law isn't so long, is it, Jimmy? Who has more connections, the cops or Franzese?"

"We could talk to John forever and the condition he's in now he'd never admit he said anything to Sher. Probably Rapacki told him everything that's in that letter, except 'I killed The Hawk.' All Sher has to do is just add those four little words. So they'll just put Rapacki back on the stand, and they'll ask him if he knows Sher, and he'll say yes, and they'll ask him if he made the admission to Sher, and he'll say no, and then they'll put Sher on the stand. And I'm dead."

"Did you find anything in Sher's file?"

"He's a nut. He said before his trial that he heard voices, and people were trying to poison his food. His mother committed suicide. He was in Matteawan [State Hospital for the Criminally Insane] for seven months before his trial. But if I ask him about that he'll say he said those things because he didn't want to stand trial. You could put the psychiatrist on who said he was insane, but then they'd put on the guy who later said he *was* sane. He was officially *certified* sane, and that's more than you or I can say."

"This is a very vicious guy, Jim."

"But how do I show the jury that—the things going on in this guy's head? When he takes the stand, he's going to kill me. I know that. Last night I thought that at this time today it'd be over and I'd be either laughing or crying. And here I am in the same spot I was in yesterday—only worse."

"Jimmy, won't the jury figure it out? If Rapacki had done it, why didn't he ask for immunity?"

Mosley ignores the question. "How could they set someone up in death row? It's from left field. *Completely* from out in left field."

"Not all the scum's in prison, Jim. You heard Cordero and Parks right from the beginning. 'They've got to come up with something.' And then Parks, when they called Breen, and Parks says, 'That's all? That's all they're gonna do? Just Breen? There's got to be more than that.' And there was.

"When I walked into the judge's chambers this morning and I heard him say 'letter,' I knew it was going to be something like this. If it was a different kind of case, I wouldn't have thought anything. But in this one. . . ." Mosley is silent for a moment. "That's the most logical approach, isn't it? The logical approach is to have someone say one of my witnesses told him how he framed Sonny. Or that one of my witnesses said he killed The Hawk. Now all of a sudden you begin to understand Breen, to see how really powerful he was for them. He said Parks told him that he and a guy named John from Brooklyn killed The Hawk. Oh, boy, they hit me below the belt today."

They pull up in front of Mosley's home. "Maybe it'll all go away," Mosley says. "Maybe today didn't happen. We were not at Sing Sing. There is no letter."

Price smiles. "The grass'll look greener tomorrow."

"Yeah? I don't know how or why."

The next morning the judge grants defense demands to reopen the case for Sher's testimony. At 10 A.M. Mosley signs the necessary affidavit to withdraw Sher from Sing

Sing. Price, Anderson, and another detective leave for the prison to get him.

Rapacki is in Mosley's office, more than ever on the edge of hysteria. "Give me a sodium test!" he begs. "Ask me if I ever committed a murder, if I ever murdered The Hawk! I thought they'd kill me. But I never thought they'd do this. If Sonny hits the street he'll kill my wife. I know they'll kill her. They know I cut myself over her once so they know they can hurt me by killing her."

Mosley takes one of the guards aside. "Don't leave him alone in there," Mosley says. "Not even for a second. He tried to kill himself once, and I'm afraid he might try it again."

Rapacki goes on. His voice shakes. He is near tears. "They're going to kill me. They're going to poison me. They're going to poison me in prison."

"Calm down, John," a detective says. "Everything will be all right. You shouldn't get so upset."

"They're going to kill me. These people are more powerful than you—" he points— "and you and you! If Sonny beats this he's gonna figure no one can touch him."

Mosley tries to quiet him. He comes out of the office and says to Audrey, his secretary, "I don't know if I even ought to let him shave before he takes the stand."

Lunchtime comes and Price has not returned with Sher. Mosley paces in the hall outside his office and does not eat. He does not go in his office because he does not want to listen to Rapacki. Rapacki is telling the detectives, "I know my dream is going to come true. I believe my dream. I know this dream is going to come true."

At 2 P.M. Mosley looks out the window and sees Price's car pull into the parking lot. Sher gets out, handcuffed and in leg irons. He is a young, good-looking man, wearing a brown suit, white shirt, and striped tie. The wind blows his hair. His face is solemn. Surrounded by the three detectives, taking the short steps forced by leg irons, he walks to a back door of the court house.

Five minutes later the judge is on the bench, and the defense attorneys and Mosley are at their tables. The defendants file in. Franzese spots his wife in the third row, smiles and winks. The jury enters.

Lyon stands. "At this time, your honor, the defendant Crabbe respectfully requests permission to reopen the case for some short testimony, newly discovered."

"Application is granted."

"Thank you. At this time I will call John Rapacki to the stand."

Rapacki walks in. He sits in the witness chair, crosses his legs, clasps his hands around his knee. A court officer whispers to him that he is still sworn. Rapacki nods.

Lyon stands in front of the witness chair. "Mr. Rapacki, since the last time you testified, has anybody from law enforcement spoken to you about the trial of this case?"

"Yes."

"And do you know what you're being called back for?"

"Yes, I do."

Lyon looks at the judge. "And may I have Walter Sher brought into the courtroom?"

Then to Rapacki, "While you're waiting, will you tell us, please, who spoke to you?"

"Mr. James C. Mosley and Detective Price."

"And they were the ones who told you why you're being brought back?"

"They related something that was in a letter, to me. They

told me—they read this letter to me." His voice rises sharply and he lets go of his knee. "They asked me about it. I told them it was an outright lie and I could prove it!"

"Now, now," the judge says, "don't volunteer anything."

Rapacki looks apologetically at the judge, settles back in his chair, and takes another grip on his knee.

Walter Sher walks in from a side door and strides confidently to the judge's bench. Lyon says to Rapacki, "Do you know this man?"

Rapacki's eyes burn holes through Sher. "Yes. I do. I know this man."

"What is his name?"

"His name is Sher."

"What is his first name?"

"Walter Sher."

"Thank you." Lyon turns to the judge. "May we have him identified to the court?"

"Give your name," the judge says.

"My name is Walter Sher."

"Where are you now?"

"Sing Sing prison."

Lyon asks, "May we have where in the Sing Sing—where in Sing Sing prison are you?"

"Condemned cells in Sing Sing prison."

Spectators gasp.

"Okay, take him out," the judge says.

"Now, Mr. Rapacki," Lyon resumes in a low, icy voice that is super-calm, "isn't it a fact that you and Walter Sher were in the same tier in the Nassau County jail between October 1 and October 26, 19–?"

"I don't believe it is. I was in the hospital from September 22, approximately ten days. . . ."

There is some quibbling over precise dates, then Lyon asks, "So it is a fact that during the month of October you and Walter Sher were in cells in the same tier?"

"That's right."

"And on this tier, isn't it a fact that you were permitted to leave your cells and mingle on the tier?"

"That's right."

Lyon is walking up and down in front of Rapacki. "And during the time that you mingled on the tier when you were on the same tier, did you have conversations with Walter Sher?"

"Yes. Yes. I had conversations with everyone on that tier."

"Now, isn't it a fact that somewhere between October 2 and two or three weeks after that, you told Walter Sher that The Hawk in 1964 held $13,000 that belonged to you and him—?"

Rapacki shoots forward in the chair and opens his mouth to speak.

"Let me finish the question," Lyon says, and continues calmly, "—for safekeeping, because the police were harassing you at that time?"

"That's an outright lie!" Rapacki shouts. "And I can prove it!"

"May I—" Edelbaum says, and is interrupted by Vitello: "Move to strike out the second part."

"Yes," the judge says, "strike out the latter part. The jury will disregard it."

"Will you please answer yes or no to these questions," Lyon says. "If it is a fact, say it is a fact. If you contend it isn't, say it isn't. If you admit it is, say it is."

Instructions to the witness should be given by the judge, not the questioning attorney. Mosley objects. "Yes," says the judge, turning to Rapacki. "Just yes or no. That's all."

"Isn't it a fact," Lyon says, "that sometime between those same dates you told Walter Sher that The Hawk would not give you your share of the $13,000 when you asked?"

"No! That's a lie!"

"Isn't it a fact that you told Walter Sher between those same dates and at the same place that The Hawk explained to you that the money was out on the street because he was shylocking?"

"That's a complete lie! No!"

"Isn't it a fact that you told Walter Sher that The Hawk told you that he couldn't give you your part of the money until the 'vig' started to roll in?"

"That's a lie!"

"Isn't it a fact that you told Walter Sher that The Hawk finally told you that he couldn't get the vig or the money because he had loaned it to businessmen and they would beef to the police if he pressed it, so he told you the money is gone?"

"That's a lie! I never said any such thing!"

"And isn't it a fact that you then told Walter Sher that when The Hawk told you that you couldn't get your money back, you killed The Hawk?"

Rapacki screams his answer. "That's a lie! And I can prove that if you will give him a truth serum test, and give me one, too!"

"Mr. Rapacki," the judge says, "just take it easy. Strike the latter part. The jury disregard it."

Lyon hands Rapacki a letter. Rapacki glances at it. "This is a letter that was read to me already in Mr. Mosley's office," Rapacki says.

"This was read to you?"

"And I was asked about the truth or falsity of it. I told

him I would take a truth serum test and he'd find it's a complete fabrication!"

Vitello objects.

"Strike it out," the judge says. "The jury will disregard the latter remark."

"Did anybody tell you what to say in this court?" Lyon asks.

"Nobody told me a thing. I'm up here on my own. I have no lawyer, nobody."

Lyon finishes. Mosley gets up. He must show the jurors that prisoners often discuss personal affairs with each other, and—most important—he must get Rapacki to admit that he discussed his private life with Sher. He wants to be able to argue on summation that Sher just took everything Rapacki told him and added to it: "I killed The Hawk."

"Mr. Rapacki, you say that you were on a tier with this Walter Sher?"

"Yes. I was there with this person. He was locked in for some of the time he was there. I think his attitude was belligerent or something, and they locked him in."

"May we have that stricken?" Edelbaum says.

The judge turns again to Rapacki. "Mr. Rapacki," he says, a little irritated, "I admonished you to just answer the question yes or no."

Rapacki sits back in the chair, but his muscles do not relax. "I know, but I'm a little upset, your honor."

"I understand, but you cannot volunteer any information."

"All right."

"The latter remark will be stricken and the jury will disregard it."

Mosley continues. "Did you discuss things with him? Did you talk with him?"

"Yes. I talked to everyone on the gallery."

"Do you discuss each other's cases?"

"No—the law part of the case. Unless a man pleads guilty, then he tells, you know, the rest of the case, because he doesn't want to take a chance that someone will go and say it, and even then—"

"I object to this," Edelbaum says, "and move to strike it."

Again the judge faces Rapacki. "Mr. Rapacki—"

"All right." He tries to settle in the chair but cannot relax.

"It is a very simple thing to answer the questions," the judge says.

"Sometimes, yes," Rapacki says.

"And you discuss lawyers?" Mosley asks.

"Yes."

"Who has whom for a lawyer?"

"Yes."

"Do you discuss your—on occasion—your personal affairs with—"

"If it's not too intimate, yes."

"—with other prisoners. And did you, on occasion, discuss these things I've talked about with Sher?"

"I don't recall exactly. I'm not positive. I discussed these things about my wife with other people in there, yes, and on the twenty-second day of September, as a result of no visits, and all, then I wound up in the hospital."

Mosley takes a slow step toward the witness chair. Standing very calmly, trying with his own composure to settle Rapacki and give him confidence in the truth, he says, "All right. Now, do you know whether or not you ever discussed your connection with The Hawk with Mr. Sher at all?"

"No, I don't believe I ever did."

"At all?"

"I don't believe I did."

"Are you *positive* about that, or not?"

"Well, I am not positive, but I don't believe I did."

Mosley takes a couple of steps back, then in a stern, come-across-with-it-now voice he hopes will make the answer more impressive to the jurors asks, "Mr. Rapacki, did you have anything to do with the death of The Hawk?"

"No! I did not!"

"Do you have immunity for that crime?"

"No. I have no immunity for any type of crime."

"Did you ever ask for immunity?"

"No, I did not."

"That's objected to as irrelevant," Lyon shouts.

"I did *not* ask for immunity," Rapacki says, louder this time.

"I submit it's *very* relevant," Mosley says to the judge.

"Overruled, and you have an exception. Just take it easy."

"Did you ever ask for immunity in the death of The Hawk?" Mosley asks again.

"No! I never did!"

"Did you ever tell anyone that you were involved in the death of The Hawk?"

"No, I did not."

In August of 1965, two months before he met Sher, Rapacki sent word out of jail that he had knowledge of The Hawk murder. When Price visited him, he told Price the same story he repeated at this trial. Mosley wants to point out to the jury that Rapacki would not have been so stupid as to tell a detective that Crabbe admitted killing The Hawk, and then turn right around and tell another prisoner that he himself had done it. To make this argument to the jurors, Mosley needs to reveal to them that what Rapacki said in court was precisely what he told Price in August

1965–before he met Sher. Mosley's problem is that rules of evidence forbid buttressing a witness's testimony by revealing previous consistent statements. A witness's statements prior to his testimony can be used only if they are inconsistent with his testimony and tend to show that he is lying. They cannot be used when they are consistent and tend to show that he is telling the truth.

In this case, Rapacki's prior consistent statement is the only way to the truth, and Mosley tries to bring it out. "Do you recall talking with Detective Price in August of 1965?"

"Yes, I did. I talked to him."

"He came out to Nassau County and talked to you, is that correct?"

"That's right."

"And that's before you ever met Mr. Sher, is it not?"

"That's right."

"And didn't you tell—"

Edelbaum sees what is coming. "I object to—" he shouts.

"—Detective Price just what you testified to?" Mosley is shouting over Edelbaum.

"Yes!"

"Wait a minute!" Edelbaum screams.

"Just what you testified to?" Mosley is screaming, too.

"Yes! I told Detective Price *exactly* what I said here!" Rapacki is yelling louder than anyone.

"Mr. Rapacki," the judge says, "just take it easy."

"Your honor," Edelbaum yells, "I rose to make an objection. Mr. Mosley—"

Mosley has had about enough of Edelbaum. "We don't need the speech," he says sarcastically.

"He cut out the whole objection!" Edelbaum screams back.

"We don't need the speech!" Mosley repeats.

The judge comes to life. "Will you *please* stop it!"

"May we have the question and the answer stricken?" Edelbaum says. "What he told Detective Price."

If what Rapacki told Price is stricken, Mosley will not be allowed to refer to it on summation. "I submit it's proper," Mosley pleads.

"Your honor, I submit it's *not* proper," Edelbaum yells.

The judge interrupts. He is inclined to side with Mosley. "Well, it has to do with the question of the credibility of this witness, and that's what's at issue here. And if there are circumstances which would tend to verify, substantiate the statements of the witness, they can be admitted."

Edelbaum is not going to stand for that. "May we have a discussion on this, your honor? And I didn't hear the question. I'd like to hear the question." The battle has shaken Edelbaum's poise.

"Why did you object if you didn't hear the question?" the judge asks.

"Because of the way—I'll tell you why, your honor— because he started to ask a question of what Detective Price told him, which I believe was improper."

"He's a mind-reader, your honor," Mosley says dryly.

Edelbaum turns on Mosley, his stubby body trembling with rage. "You kept talking, you tried to get it before this jury before I objected. That's what I'm objecting to!"

"Are you finished?" the judge asks.

"I have to—" Mosley starts.

"Are you *finished*, gentlemen?"

"Yes, I am," Mosley says.

"May we have a discussion about this, your honor?" Edelbaum insists. He wants a chance to get offstage, into the judge's robing room, where he hopes the combined force and numbers of the defense attorneys can prevail.

"All right," the judge says, and he retires with Mosley and the defense lawyers to the robing room.

Edelbaum argues, Mosley argues, Vitello, Lyon, and the other lawyers argue. The discussion becomes a morass of legal technicalities. In the end the judge rules in favor of the defense.

Back in front of the jury, Mosley is totally discouraged. He tries another tack. "Mr. Rapacki, all the years that you have been in state's prison, have you ever admitted to *anyone* any crime to which you had not already pleaded guilty?"

"No."

"That is objected to," Edelbaum shouts.

The judge thinks. "I am going to sustain the objection."

"May we have the answer stricken?" Edelbaum insists.

"Yes," the judge says.

"Will your honor instruct the witness not to answer—" Edelbaum is back in control.

"Don't answer if there is an objection until I rule on the objection," the judge tells Rapacki.

"Have you ever had any other prisoner admit to you any crime to which he had not pleaded guilty?" Mosley asks.

"Same objection," Edelbaum shouts.

"Objection is sustained."

"That's all," Mosley says. He sits down, tired and distressed.

Lyon is up. "May we have Walter Sher?"

Sher, very businesslike, walks quickly to the stand. He carries a folder of papers under his arm.

"Mr. Sher," Lyon says, "you said before that you are in the condemned cells in Sing Sing prison?"

"Yes, sir." His voice is quiet and controlled.

"Is that what is commonly known as the death house?"

"Yes, it is."

"And have you been convicted of the crime of murder in the first degree?"

"Yes, sir."

"And you are presently awaiting the execution—the sentence of execution?"

"Yes, sir."

Again the spectators stir. They are fascinated. They have never before looked at a man sentenced to die. He is so calm about it, so reserved. The jurors' faces look as if they are carved from rock.

"Will you tell us, have you ever been convicted of any other crimes?"

"I have been convicted of grand larceny and possession of marijuana."

"Now, sir, did you write a letter to the judge of this court on December 10, 1967?"

"Yes, sir, I did."

Lyon moves to show Sher the letter. The letter is a statement of Sher's made prior to this testimony. Mosley reasons that if Rapacki's prior consistent statement to Price was inadmissible, then Sher's prior consistent statement to the judge, in the letter, should be inadmissible also.

"I object to this, your honor," Mosley says. "This is immaterial. This is a prior statement. I object to it."

"I am not introducing it," Lyon explains. "Is that the letter that you wrote?" he asks Sher.

"Yes, sir."

"Now, did you see me yesterday?"

"Yes, I did."

"Where was that?"

"In Sing Sing state prison." He answers with quickness and confidence.

"Now, before yesterday in the Sing Sing state prison—"

"I object, your honor," Mosley says.

"How does he know what I am going to say?" Lyon asks.

"Go on, say it," Mosley says with irritation.

"—did you ever see me before?"

"I object, your honor. That's immaterial."

The judge considers. "Well, overruled. Go ahead."

"Did you ever see me before yesterday?"

"No, sir, I didn't."

Sher also says he has never seen the other attorneys. He testifies that on October 1, 1965, he was transferred from the death house to the Nassau County jail and that while there he was on the same tier with John Rapacki.

"And between August 1—I'm sorry—between October 1, October 2, and the period about two weeks after October 2, did John Rapacki tell you—" he looks at the letter—"in words and substance—"

At the start of the trial Mosley was forced to thread his questions through defense objections—invariably sustained —that he was leading his witness. Now Lyon, constantly referring to the letter, leads *his* witness, and Mosley objects.

"Overruled."

"Your honor—" Mosley persists.

"Overruled. Go ahead."

Mosley cannot believe it. Not only is Lyon leading his witness, but he appears ready to read from a letter which is not in evidence and which constitutes a prior consistent statement.

Mosley stands up. "You're going to let him read from that, your honor."

"Overruled."

Mosley sits down, his face covered with disbelief.

"Did John Rapacki tell you, in words or substance—"

Lyon refers to the letter—"that The Hawk was holding $13,000 that belonged to The Hawk and John jointly?"

"Yes, sir, he did."

"During this same period, did John Rapacki tell you that he asked The Hawk for his share of the money?"

"Yes, sir, he did."

"And did John Rapacki tell you that The Hawk told him that the money was out on the street where The Hawk had shylocked it?"

"Yes, sir, he did."

"And did John tell you that The Hawk told John Rapacki that he would give him the money as it came in on the vig?"

"Yes, sir, he did."

"By the way, can you tell us what vig means?"

"From what I understand, it's accumulated interest on money lent out, as it comes in."

"Now, did John Rapacki tell you that The Hawk said, 'I can't get the money, and if I press these men, who are businessmen, they'll call the police, so the money is gone'?"

"Yes, sir, he did."

"And did John Rapacki tell you, in words or substance, that he killed The Hawk?"

"Yes, sir, he did."

"Did John Rapacki tell you, in words or substance, that he had been married previously to the woman he was living with?"

"Yes, sir, he did."

"And did John Rapacki tell you that he lived in Brooklyn at one time?"

"Yes, sir, he did."

"And did John Rapacki tell you that he faked a suicide attempt?"

"Yes, sir, he did."

"You may inquire." He sits down.

Mosley faces Sher, and speaking with hatred hanging from every word, he asks, "Mr. Sher, when is the last time you had a trip down to New York City?"

Sher pretends not to understand the question. "New York City, sir?"

"Right."

"Last time I was down in Nassau County jail. That was October 1, 1965."

"You get the papers up in Sing Sing, do you not?"

"Yes, sir, I do."

"And you've been reading these papers since you've been incarcerated up in Sing Sing, have you not?"

"Yes, sir, I have."

"As a matter of fact, you knew last September or October of 1966 that the defendant Franzese, together with the other defendants, were indicted for the crime of killing The Hawk, is that right?"

"I must have read it, sir."

"You *knew* that, didn't you?"

"Yes, sir."

"You didn't tell anyone *then* about this conversation you had with Rapacki, did you?"

"Did I tell anyone then?"

"Yes."

"I had told someone before that, sir." Sher wants Mosley to ask him whom he told. Mosley follows the first rule of good cross-examination: when a witness asks to be asked a question, don't ask it.

"No, no," Mosley says. "When you read that the defendants were indicted, these defendants here, for the crime of killing The Hawk, did you get in touch with any of the defendants or their attorneys?"

"No, sir."

"And you knew then that you had had a conversation with Rapacki relative—about The Hawk—is that right?"

"Yes, sir."

That point made, Mosley changes the subject. He wants to expose a half truth Sher has just told, and he wants to remove any sympathy the jurors might feel for Sher because he is supposedly on the verge of execution. "Did you state that you were presently awaiting execution? Didn't you state that in response to Mr. Lyon's question?"

"In response to his question, yes, sir, I did."

"Well, that's not a fact, is it?"

Sher knows what Mosley is driving at and tries to dodge. "Is that the fact that I'm presently awaiting execution?"

"Awaiting execution."

"The way you phrase the question, sir, I'd have to answer yes again. Yes, sir."

"Well, you know that your sentence will be commuted, don't you?"

"Yes, sir, I do."

"So you know you're not awaiting execution."

"My sentence—I'm still under the sentence of death, sir."

"Yes, but you have a letter from the governor—"

Sher holds up his sheaf of papers. "Yes, sir, I have it right here."

"So you're *not* awaiting execution."

"No, sir."

Mosley must let the jurors know the rewards that could have inspired Sher to make up his story. He has already brought out that Sher's letter won him his first ride to New York in more than two years. Now he touches on the time he must serve and the fact that his lawyer is court-appointed.

"You were asked if you knew counsel, if you knew Mr. Vitello, Mr. Lyon, Mr. Kleinman, and Mr. Edelbaum, and your answer was that you do not, is that correct?"

"That's correct, sir."

"Have you *heard* of any of them?"

Edelbaum objects. "How is that material, your honor?" He is objecting because he knows how it is material. A man facing life in prison, who reads in the paper that top-money attorneys are defending Mafia gangsters, might try to come up with some plan to get help from them on his own case.

"I'm going to sustain the objection," the judge says.

"You say your case is still on appeal?"

"Yes, sir."

If it is on appeal, if his conviction is not yet nailed down, he will not want to confess the murder for which he was convicted. Mosley hopes to discredit him by forcing him to take the fifth amendment.

"On April 5, 1962, in a jewelry store in Manhasset, New York, did you shoot and kill one Donald Hanson in the course of a robbery?"

"I respectfully refuse to answer on the grounds it may tend to incriminate me, sir."

Mosley asks three more questions about the murder, and each time Sher takes the fifth. Mosley moves into Sher's psychiatric record, and Sher admits that he received psychiatric treatment in the Army, spent seven months in Matteawan, and once accused prison authorities of trying to poison him.

When it is Lyon's turn again, he has Sher testify that he was discharged from Matteawan as sane. Then he asks Sher when he wrote the letter.

"I wrote the letter the tenth."

"I offer the letter in evidence," Lyon says.

Mosley looks as if someone has hit him over the head. If the letter is admitted into evidence, Lyon will be allowed to read it to the jurors, to use it to repeat and emphasize Sher's testimony. Rules of evidence clearly forbid this. Mosley is surprised that Lyon would attempt it.

"I object to it," Mosley cries. "I object to it."

The judge appears not to hear Mosley. "People's 83 for identification," he says coldly, "now defendant's L, Crabbe —in evidence."

Mosley is astonished. "You are overruling my objection?" he demands.

"Yes, I am."

A court officer hands the letter to Lyon.

"You want to read it to the jury, read it," the judge says.

"Thank you," Lyon says, and reads it.

Mosley listens, his face red with rage.

When Lyon finishes, Mosley again cross-examines Sher. He ends with a question shouted in anger. "You have been told in the last few days that if you're responsible for the acquittal of Mr. Franzese and these defendants, you will be a big man in the yard for the next twenty-six years—"

He can get no more out. Edelbaum jumps to his feet with the objection. The judge sustains him.

"Did anybody offer you anything to testify here?" Lyon asks.

"No, sir."

"Anything else?" the judge asks.

"No, your honor," Lyon answers.

Sher leaves the stand. Attorneys gather up their papers. Then Mosley makes a sudden decision.

"I have rebuttal," he says. The defense attorneys' heads shoot up. The judge looks startled.

"The people call Detective Price," Mosley says.

Price is opening a door to let Sher out when he hears his name. Surprised, he turns and finds a courtroom full of eyes staring at him. He walks to the witness chair and sits down.

The judge has allowed what appears to be a prior consistent statement of Sher's—the letter—into evidence. Now Mosley wants to see what he will do about a prior consistent statement of Rapacki's—the story Rapacki first told Price.

"Detective Price, in August of 1965 did you have a conversation with John Rapacki while Rapacki was in prison?"

"Yes or no," Edelbaum shouts.

"Yes," Price says.

"What was that conversation?"

"I object," Edelbaum shouts.

"Objection," Lyon shouts.

The judge squirms in his chair. After a few seconds he says, "The objection is sustained."

All of the trial's failures and frustrations, the insults and outrages, suddenly congeal and descend on Mosley in a lump of fury. Sher's letter is in evidence, but not the letters written by the prosecution witnesses, letters that could explain so much about their fears, why they lied in the letters, why they were terrified to testify. In a final, futile gesture of rebellion, Mosley now makes a desperate move he knows cannot succeed. If the judge wants to give the jury Sher's letter, let him give them all the letters—Parks's letters, Cordero's, Zaher's.

"Now," Mosley says, his voice tight with emotion, "I offer

in evidence at this time all the letters that have been marked for identification to the United States attorney and to the district attorney." If the judge admits the letters into evidence the jurors will be able to read them completely, including the parts prejudicial to the defendants.

Kleinman jumps out of his chair. "The district attorney seems to be abandoning the case, your honor! I object to it!"

"I am *not* abandoning the case!" Mosley screams across the courtroom at Kleinman. "How *dare* you say that?"

"Just a minute," the judge says. "I am still in control here." He looks at Kleinman. "That was highly unnecessary."

"How can he make an offer of a great big file?" Kleinman says.

"Mr. Kleinman, I said that was highly unnecessary."

"I am sorry if I offended your honor—" he jerks his head toward Mosley— "but not him."

"Your offering is denied," the judge says curtly to Mosley. "Now, do you rest or don't you?"

"Yes," Mosley says. "People rest."

Lyon begins his summation. "I don't know whether I'm going to be too coherent now," he says to the jurors. "As you probably guess by now, I am very tired. I think it has come out in the evidence that I was up in the death house yesterday, that I have been in various other places during the trial. It has been a long job, and I think, if you remember, we said that we really are not obliged to do this. We are not obliged to try to solve the case for you. And I don't say we have, although—and I hope this isn't followed, I am sure the case is going to end now—but I am beginning to think that maybe if we had a couple of more days, we *would* solve it."

Mosley objects. The judge smiles. "I might say, Mr. Lyon, if you want a couple more days, I will gladly give it to you."

"I don't know whether I have the strength, Judge. I don't know whether I have the strength. I will say this. I submit that a lot of evidence has now been brought before you that ties in everything that went before. You have heard now a man who had no motive. He is in the death house. You read his letter—you heard his letter—and this man says that Rapacki was the one who said to him he killed The Hawk. And Rapacki's first name is John, and if you remember, we had a witness here by the name of Breen who said that Parks told him that he, Parks, hit The Hawk with a John from Brooklyn. And if you remember, Cordero said that before he started to go out with Eleanor and after The Hawk died, she went with a Polish fellow from Long Island. Rapacki told this before we questioned him this time, told us the last time that he lived in Long Island. Does it hang together? Do we now have for the first time a motive, a motive for this crime?"

He goes on for a few more minutes, then finishes with a plea to the jurors to "give us what you have sworn to give us, and that is a fair shake."

Mosley stands. He has been making notes with a yellow pencil. Now he throws the pencil angrily onto the table. "Gentlemen," he says, struggling to control his anger, "*here* we are faced with it. *Here* it comes. After summations, just before a charge, and out of I don't know how many prisoners in New York state prisons and federal prisons, a letter comes down from a man—an admitted psychopath, according to psychiatrists—saying—"

"That is objected to," Lyon says.

"It is in evidence, your honor," Mosley says. The judge

sits silent. Mosley continues, his voice trembling with compressed rage. "A *psychopath* comes down and says he had a conversation with a witness, and just at the tail end he decided to write a letter. And he is going to be in prison for the rest of his life. And *you* think about how he will be treated in prison by the other prisoners when he is the guy that got off John Franzese and the other defendants."

"Your honor, I object to that," Edelbaum says.

"And I submit *that* is his motive to lie!" Mosley has heard a lot from the defense attorneys about motives to lie. Now the shoe is on the other foot.

"Just a moment," the judge says, trying to avoid another shouting match.

"I submit that is a motive to lie, your honor!" Mosley insists.

"Objection sustained. The jury will disregard it. Confine yourself to the evidence produced here today."

"Well, it was introduced here today, your honor, that he is a life prisoner. He is a good Samaritan? Did he come down—did he write—immediately when these men were indicted that he had an admission from Rapacki? Did he write then? When was his recollection refreshed? When he hears that Rapacki is a witness?"

The fury confined so close beneath the surface begins to erupt. Mosley is shouting. "I submit it's a tissue of lies, that man's testimony! Sure he was in prison with Rapacki! There's no doubt about that. But can you imagine John Rapacki talking to Detective Price in August of 1965 and *two months later* making an admission to a homicide to a psychopath? *Can you imagine that?* This Rapacki—who is a criminal, there's no question about it—he is going to make an *idle* admission to another criminal? I submit that abuses your common sense. It never happened. He mentioned to this man he was in some kind of illegal activity with The Hawk. *That* happened. But he never told this man that he killed The Hawk. Rapacki is not a nut! The other man is a nut!

"Then we have this elaborate machination. What kind of a scheme can you call it that Mr. Lyon invented—that first Eleanor wants her husband killed, first it's Eleanor and Richie Parks, and then it's Richie Parks and John, and now we find out it's John, because of a bank robbery, some imaginary bank robbery where Ernie The Hawk wouldn't give him his share! What schemes will they give you next? Give them until Monday, and they will have *another* scheme!"

"I object to that," Edelbaum says. "Who is he referring to?"

"Just take it easy, gentlemen. Strike the latter part. The jury will disregard it."

Mosley leans in close on the jurors. The case is slipping away. There are so many things he wants them to know, things he is not allowed to tell them, things he can only hint at. His face is agonized. "Think about it, gentlemen! Just *think* about it—this tail-end, last-minute piece of evidence." He stops talking, sighs, returns to the prosecution table.

"That's all, your honor," he says.

It is 4:45. The judge calls a short recess, then begins his charge to the jury, going over the testimony, explaining the law, repeating to them the concepts of reasonable doubt and presumption of innocence.

At 7:15 the jury is taken to dinner. After dinner, they will begin deliberating. They have been three weeks in court, have watched a case projected before them like a movie run too fast, with a lamp too dim and half the frames chopped out. Now they are told that if they have a reasonable doubt about the film's success in proving four men guilty, they must acquit the men.

Mosley goes down to his office and calls his wife. He tells her the jury will be out well into the night and that it will be late when he gets home. He hangs up, smiles wearily, and says to Price, "Helen says she's listening to the radio and some guy just got five years for protesting the draft, and Sonny is walking the streets—so what kind of a prosecutor am I?"

Mosley, Price, Anderson, and some friends go to Luigi's to eat and to wait for the verdict. Mosley orders a shrimp cocktail but does not eat it. He is distressed at having lost control of his temper in the second summation. "When I was screaming," he says, "I was stung. I was thinking, 'There's nothing I can do. I've got no way out.'"

Just as there are generally accepted ideas about what makes a good or bad juror, there are ideas about when it is good or bad to have a jury deliberating. A prosecutor does not want the jury out after a meal (full stomachs do not encourage guilty verdicts), before a holiday (nor do tidings of joy and good cheer), on a Friday (nor thoughts of happy weekends at home), or late at night ("All right, not guilty— let's go to bed").

Tonight everything seems stacked against Mosley. The jury has just finished dinner, it's Friday, and Christmas is only ten days away. A detective sums it up: "Who could go out, eat a big dinner, think about a weekend of skiing, the Christmas season, and then vote a man into prison for the rest of his natural life?"

The phone rings and Mosley jumps. It is not for him. Another ADA, who handles the office's press relations, says, "Take it easy, Jimmy. It's just another case."

"It's *not* just another case," Mosley says, annoyed. "*No*

case is just another case. It's a war. Your job is to convict someone who's guilty."

A defense attorney comes to the table, talks for a minute, and then says, "Well, anyway, we're all on the same side."

"Yeah?" Mosley says with sarcasm. "What side is that?"

The lawyer grins weakly. "Law and order, and all that."

"Really?"

The lawyer leaves.

Mosley sits quietly. Price, Anderson, and a couple of others are at the table too, but no one speaks.

"Maurice Edelbaum," Mosley says slowly. "Maurice Edelbaum. M.E. The great ME."

Price is worried about Rapacki. "To me," he says, "this is the biggest guy in the case. For once in his life he decided to trust a cop, and look what it got him. I'm worried about him tonight, Jimmy. I'm afraid he'll hang up in his cell. He told me, if they're framing me I'm gonna hang up."

Mosley says, "This is the one guy that made me think I had a shot at the case."

"Don't worry about him," Anderson says, trying to remove some of the gloom. "He'd come out tomorrow and stick this place up and kill us all."

"But he's going to do the next two and a half years in solitary confinement because of something he did for us," Mosley says. He goes to the phone and calls the jail. He comes back and tells Price, "They said they'd put a special watch on him tonight."

Mosley sits down and thinks for a minute. "That's a hell of a thing, isn't it? You've got a jury out on a murder-one case, and you have to call a jail to make sure your star witness doesn't hang himself."

One of the detectives who drove Sher back to Sing Sing comes in.

"How was he?" Price asks.

"He laughed all the way back," the detective says.

Price shakes his head. "Three years—days off, weekends —and then to come up with something like this, this Sher. Rapacki was our icing on the cake, and Sher was theirs."

Mosley leaves the table and paces up and down in the empty restaurant.

At 12:30 the phone rings. Mosley grabs it.

"They have a verdict," he says.

They walk back and Mosley takes his seat in the front of the courtroom.

The jury comes in. A clerk rises from his desk by the judge's bench and says, "Gentlemen of the jury, have you agreed upon a verdict?"

The foreman, a short, chubby man with glasses, stands.

"Yes, we have," he says. He is shy and embarrassed.

The clerk speaks in a fast ritual monotone. "Jurors, please rise. Defendants, please rise. Jurors, look upon the defendants. Defendants, look upon the jurors. What say you? What is your verdict?"

The foreman reaches into his inside jacket pocket and comes out with a piece of paper. He reads from it. "We, the jury, find the defendant Florio, not guilty—"

A man in a yellow suède jacket jumps to his feet and laughs and yells. Court officers silence him.

The foreman goes on, reading fast. "—Crabbe, not guilty. Matteo, not guilty. Franzese, not guilty."

More cries of delight, hushed by court officers.

The clerk says, "Harken to your verdict as the court records it. You say you find Joseph Florio, William Red Crabbe, Thomas Matteo, John Franzese, not guilty. So say you all?"

"We do."

"Be seated, please."

The judge looks at Mosley. "You want the jury polled?"

"No." He is slouched in his chair. He waits for the judge's final words, words that end the trial, words he's heard a hundred times before.

". . . I want to take the opportunity to thank both the district attorney and the attorneys for the defendants for the courtesy extended to the court. I realize it has been a tremendous burden that you have borne on your shoulders in espousing your particular case on behalf of the people, Mr. Mosley, and on behalf of the defendants, Mr. Vitello, Mr. Santoro, Mr. Lyon, Mr. Landsman, Mr. Kleinman, and Mr. Edelbaum. Thank you very much."

J300483